WHAT IT MEANS TO BE WHOLE

What It Means To Be Whole

Andrea Andersen

Contents

Content Notes

This story has been reviewed by sensitivity readers. Meaning, though the author is not deaf or heard of hearing herself, persons who are deaf or hard of hearing have read this story and provided feedback on its authenticity, as well as appropriate verbiage to use regarding D/HH culture.

Similarly, this story has also been reviewed by readers with Generalized Anxiety Disorder. Along with the author's personal experiences with GAD, the hope is that the story discusses these topics with the respect and care that they deserve.

Trigger Warning

This book contains sensitive subjects, such as:

Foul Language
Explicit Sex
Religious Trauma
Cannabis use
Mental Illness

To those who are desperately looking for their other half, you are already whole.

1

I was standing at my full-length mirror tying my hair up into a ponytail when a bang sounded at my door and Courtney busted into my bedroom.

"Shit!" I jumped, not expecting that sort of entrance this early in the morning. It was 7:00am and we had to leave in about fifteen minutes to catch the bus to work.

"Sorry!" Courtney apologized, no remorse in her tone. "I just wanted to drop these off for you really quick before I forgot again." She made a show of holding up a handful of stickers for me to see before dramatically dropping them onto my bed.

"What are those?" I asked, turning back to the mirror to double check my appearance. I was wearing a plain white V-neck t-shirt, with one of my many pairs of black leggings. I always liked the way a white t-shirt made my skin look less transparent, and that my dark brown hair contrasted nicely against it. Another plus to this outfit was that it was loose and flexible, which was preferred for my work attire. More than half of my time at work was spent crawling around the floor trying to encourage babies and toddlers to communicate, so both flexibility and comfort were a must.

"I got a new vibrator yesterday, and it came with almost

a dozen stickers," Courtney explained, plopping down on the edge of my bed next to her collection. She pulled a hair tie off her wrist and wrapped her blonde hair into a messy bun. She wore similar clothes to mine, but she opted for a peach t-shirt that made her look nice and tan. A true California girl, even though she was originally from Oregon. I remembered complimenting her on her entire 'look' back in college, adding how pretty I thought her hair and face were. Her response was a polite amount of gratitude, along with the fact that her honey blonde hair and symmetrical face were what helped her get away with her "hideodorous" birthmark on her right hand. It looked like a semi-colon, or poop if you were immature and in middle school.

I told her that at least her ears still worked. She laughed, and we had been best friends ever since.

Courtney was beautiful, her brown eyes always had a mischievous glint in them. She was more athletic than I was, meaning she enjoyed going to the gym even if she didn't successfully convince me to tag along. She and my grandmother bonded over yoga when Courtney first moved in with us a couple of years ago.

"Really? What do they say?" I asked, curiosity about her delivery piqued.

"This one says 'clit it or quit it'!" She grinned up at me as she held them up one by one to read them, birthmark on display, "'Good vibes only' with a picture of a vibrator and pretty flowers around it, and 'Every princess deserves a magic wand'."

I snorted my laughter, slipped on my Birkenstocks (a gift from Courtney a few years ago), and walked over to join her.

I rifled through a few, "Are you keeping any for yourself?" I asked.

"Of course. I already added my favorite one to my water bottle." I didn't notice that she had brought it in with her, but she bent down to pick it up off the ground and turned it so I could see her newest addition.

In a plain black serif font, the word "vibrator" stood out like a sore thumb against her growing collection of colorful stickers. No capital letters or exclamation points. Or color. It was so un-Courtney-like.

"That's...underwhelming," I admitted, looking at all the colorful ones on the bed.

"That's the beauty of it! Think about the reactions people will have when they see the word 'vibrator' on my water bottle in public. They'll ask themselves, why does she have that? Does she really mean *that* kind of vibrator? What is the message?"

"What *is* the message?" I lifted a skeptical eyebrow at her with my question.

"That vibrator isn't a bad word, and that every woman should have one...or, that I know people will be offended by the sight of it, and I like to cause chaos," She explained with a shrug, checking her phone for the time and standing up from the bed, "We gotta head out soon."

"I'm just going to throw on some mascara real quick." I grabbed my makeup bag off my dresser and walked back to the mirror.

"Ugh, I wish I had your eye color," Courtney sighed dreamily as I looked at our reflection and started applying.

My eyes were hazel; sometimes green, sometimes more brown. It all depended on what I was wearing and how light reflected off them.

"I wish I had your pointy nose," I smirked at her, settling into the familiar game we played.

"I wish I had your dainty ankles."

"I wish I had your chin freckle."

"I wish I had your left eyebrow."

"I wish I had your shitty birthmark."

"I wish I had your shitty ears—" and then she covered her mouth with a laugh when I paused my makeup application to snicker at her. We started doing this almost eight years ago back when we were roommates in college. The running joke behind it was this; being envious of what you don't have is generally a waste of time. Women's bodies were all uniquely beautiful in their own way and should be praised.

If men were incapable of praising women's bodies the way we deserved, then we had to lift each other up instead.

I was a sheltered, traumatized, confused shell of a person when I first met Courtney Henderson. College was the first time I had ever been out from my parents' tight religious clutches, and she picked up on that about me right away. She got me out of the dorm, socialized me (against my will half the time), and introduced me to new ideas and lifestyles.

Ideas like: women were just as powerful and strong as men, and that we didn't actually need men in our personal lives if we didn't want them. Sundays are really just second Saturdays to the non-religious population. R-rated movies were usually the best kinds of movies. Taylor Swift was a feminist icon (and that feminism was actually a good thing), and so much more that I was too scared to question growing up.

Lifestyles like: going to karaoke bars, and actually having the occasional drink. Wearing a two-piece bikini bathing suit to the beach, and not worrying about whether or not I've been turned into some pornographic image in some man's mind. As Courtney so delicately put it, "It's not your responsibility to keep other people's thoughts pure for Jesus or whatever."

She also introduced me to the medicinal benefits of marijuana, something I wish I had gotten a hold of as early as my freshman year of high school.

"But if I ever catch you smoking anything, I'll slap your boobs so hard that they will swell too big for any of your bras or shirts to fit," she scolded me one day after adding cannabis oil to my nighttime tea. I'd had an exam the next day that I had been panicking over all week and sleep was escaping me, becoming replaced by anxiety. I had seen her use the oil on occasion and I decided to ask her about it. She never pressured me to experiment with cannabis but offered her honest opinion and any helpful information she had. When I asked if I could have some, she gave me the lowest dose she thought I needed. She was like that about any topic I brought up with her.

Cannabis.

Feminism.

Religion.

Politics.

Sex.

After living with Courtney for a year, and after I watched

her go on a handful of dates with boys from her classes, I asked her if she was a virgin. I was worried I would offend her since virginity was a woman's worth-defining concept where I came from.

"Oh, hell no, I got that over with as soon as I could," she waved her hand as if to shoo her virginity away. "But I don't sleep with everyone I date, either." She smiled at me, almost looking happy that I was broaching this subject with her. Like she had been waiting for me to finally open this one last can of worms.

As it turned out, she had noticed a couple of copies of some romance novels that I had checked out from the library. Books I was embarrassed by and usually tried to keep hidden. I was processing the fact that for my entire life, I had been groomed to stay this pure, delicate, feminine woman for a strong Godly man to marry and have children with. Even though I was kept in the dark about most things regarding actual sex.

I knew the basics. I had made it to a few health education classes in elementary and middle school before my parents learned what specifically was being covered and pulled me out for the sex ed portion of the material. It was embarrassing because I felt like a sinner for wanting to know the details of how babies were made, and why I sometimes felt the need to address that part of my body specifically.

So, when I stumbled across my first romance novel in college, I was hooked. Did I love reading a book with a guaranteed happily ever after? Yes. Did I love reading about all the individual and unique flaws the characters had? Of course. Did I love reading about how these people expressed their love for each other with their bodies? Abso-fucking-lutely. When Courtney discovered my romance novels, I was starting to come to terms with the fact that I would probably end up having casual sex with someone before I found a partner that I wanted to commit to marriage with. The only concern I had after reading a handful of romance novels was if every single man in the universe had a foot-long dick, or if that was common for romance authors to exaggerate.

I knew how big my tampons were.

Big enough.

Being skewered in half didn't seem that thrilling to me.

Courtney bought me my first little bullet vibrator because she was "a great friend" or so she told me. She had helped me come to terms with the need to express my own sexuality and didn't shame or judge me for being a functioning human with functioning body parts. Sometimes I wished I had grown up with her as my mom instead.

"I'll meet you downstairs," Courtney slapped my butt and skipped out of my bedroom, shutting the door behind her while I finished applying the rest of my mascara in the mirror.

I went through my daily affirmation routine in my head, thanking the universe for my health, brain, body, and life.

I hadn't spoken to my parents in person for years. We would send off the occasional text or email, and sometimes my mom would call me to "check in" and test the waters of where my faith was, but nothing else with real depth to it. It was hard, and I would still go through waves of anxiety and depression because of how my relationship with my parents had gone. However, that did not change the fact that I had no regrets about my life choices since leaving home.

I inhaled and exhaled through my nose, closing the hazel eyes that I shared with my grandmother and father. After a moment I reopened them and I grabbed my backpack on the way out of the door to catch the bus with Courtney.

2

"I got all day, little one," I grinned as I spoke to the two-year-old girl sitting in the corner of my office, where my bookshelves were. This was my third session with her, and I could see that her mother was already starting to get worried about her child's progress. To be honest, every parent I met with was worried about their child's progress. If they weren't, they wouldn't have been meeting with me in the first place.

"Here, honey, like this," the mother, whose name completely escaped me now, scooted over to her daughter who was doing her best to ignore the both of us by flipping through a cardboard storybook. The mother attempted to grab her daughter's hand and guide it over to the iPad that we were using as a potential assisted communication device, or AAC for short. This child was nonverbal but very vocal. She reminded us of this by releasing a sharp, high pitched squeal in protest when her mother tried to take her attention from the book.

The mother sighed and inched away from her daughter, giving her space.

All parents did this; stressed sooner than necessary. Kids would always have their own timelines, no matter how hard society tried to push them into a specific mold.

I gave the mother an encouraging smile and took my turn to scoot over to the little girl.

"Hey, Maddy," I cooed in a soft, friendly voice that she had no problem ignoring, "I see you're reading a book, oooh I see a cow!" I pointed to the image she was looking at and mooed at her again. That got her attention.

Maddy was probably the cutest client I had. As soon as her brown ringlets swooshed when she turned her head to look at me and locked onto my gaze with those chocolatey brown eyes, my heart would burst. I needed to focus because she was making direct eye contact with me. That was something she wasn't willing to do until now.

"Mooo," I made the cow sound again. She looked down at the image of the cow, and back to me, "Do you want me to do *more?*" I asked her, and then used the iPad to hit the button that made the sound of a woman saying, "more."

Maddy glanced at the iPad and looked back at me. So, I mooed again. I wanted to reward her for the eye contact she was giving me. When she looked at the picture of the cow in her book, and back to me, I reiterated what needed to happen.

"I see that you want me to do more, so we are going to ask for *more,*" I hit the more button on the iPad again, and we repeated this process a few times until she finally turned the page and got bored with the cow and the mooing.

"...She still isn't wanting to try the tablet," her mother commented when I adjusted my position on the ground. Most of my job involved me sitting on the floor of my office because kids generally responded better when the adults got on their level. Not all kids learned sitting at a table or desk.

"But she's making great eye contact, and she clearly understands what the iPad does. We are just working on her motivation, I think," I smiled at the mother, and she gave me a tentative one back. I noticed that she had a hint of dark circles under her eyes, and I wanted to hug her.

I didn't have kids of my own, but they sounded exhausting. I only worked with kids for eight hours a day tops, and during the week I hardly had the energy to do anything else after work besides order dinner and go to bed as early as possible. I tried to show as much empathy towards the parents as possible because being a parent to a high energy human was already exhausting—let alone a high energy human who was experiencing global delays.

"So, you think Maddy is making progress?" The mother clarified, sounding hopeful. I was sure she had heard this before, but in case she hadn't, I offered her the reminder.

"We do speech therapy a little differently here than other clinics," I started, scooting over so I was in Maddy's line of vision while she continued to flip through her storybook. This one had textures on it, and she was very focused on gently touching them, "Most speech therapy clinics will focus on sitting a child at a table and making them do a lot of guided, structured activities. This puts a lot of demands on young children and can make the experience unnecessarily stressful. Because the kids here at our facility are usually also in OT, PT, Infant Stimulation, or Group Therapy, we try not to overwhelm them too much since their plates are already full."

"Yeah, no kidding," the mother agreed. Maddy was also in Physical Therapy, Occupational Therapy, and Infant Stim. She and her mom came here four days a week, thirty minutes away from their home in south Orange County.

"So, with kids like Maddy specifically, we try to focus on more foundational communication skills before pushing verbal or signing. She's been meeting with Courtney for a while, and they have very successful sessions now, but I am a new therapist to her, so we must work on the foundation building again. Things like eye contact and repetition and modeling. Just because she's able to throw a few signs around with Courtney and communicate her needs effectively, does not mean that she will be willing to do so with me right away. It seems like it takes a while but based on what Courtney has told me about Maddy, she'll show up to Speech one day and it'll all click," I snapped my fingers for emphasis, "So don't be too discouraged. The fact that she engaged with me at all today is a huge step. Even if she wouldn't touch the iPad specifically."

The mother was nodding as I finished the very familiar reassurance speech that I gave to almost all the parents I met with.

Shoot, what is this woman's name? Audrey? Amanda?

"That's good, that's comforting to hear," Maddy's mom smiled at me as she checked her watch and realized the session was up, "Alright, Maddy, we are *all done.*" The mom signed, *all done* by raising her eyebrows and rotating her splayed hands forty-five degrees. I personally thought all parents should incorporate ASL into their child's language skills, especially if they weren't speaking yet. Hopefully, if Maddy started to get the hang of the iPad and Alternative Communication app, that would be a steppingstone for her to want to use her own words.

Maddy heard the words "all done" and perked right up, shoving her storybook away and shuffling to her feet so she could lift her arms for her mom to pick her up. She was happy and smiling and, even though it was because she was getting away from me, I was thrilled that she was smiling at all in my office.

"I'll see you next week!" I waved to them both after I opened the door to let them out. As they walked away the mother pulled her vibrating phone out of her pocket with one hand while holding Maddy on her hip with the other. She answered the call and brought the phone to her ear, "This is Ava…" she said into the phone as she made her way down the hall towards the building exit.

I snapped my fingers and leaned my head back, "Ava! That's her name."

"You forgot the mom's name again?" I heard Courtney's voice behind me and jumped.

Damn, it was easy to sneak up on me.

I held my hand over my quickly beating heart as I turned around and nodded my head, not trying to hide the fact that I sucked at remembering the parents' names. It was a challenge I would always face while working there.

She raised a blonde eyebrow at me. She wasn't wearing mascara that day, unlike me. Courtney normally chose to go without makeup for work.

"Of course I did. Her name is Ava by the way," I smirked

at Courtney as I went back into my office to double check my schedule. Due to one of my kiddos getting a cold and canceling last minute, I had some time to kill until my next appointment that day.

"I know, I've been meeting with her and Maddy for about a year," Courtney entered my office and almost closed the door, leaving it open a crack in case anyone else wanted to speak with me. She shook her head once, "You're distracting me."

"From what?"

"From why I came here."

"Oh. It's not just because you come here all the time due to the fact my office is superior to yours in every way?"

"Well, yeah, there's always that, but—shit, you're doing it again," Courtney pretended to scold me by wiggling her index finger, "I have half a mind to not warn you and to just surprise you."

"Warn me about what?" I sat down in my office chair, which was much more comfortable than the floor. I did a casual spin on it before turning to face Courtney again. She had a flirty gleam in her eye.

"The fresh meat!" Courtney whisper shouted and then smirked at me, proud of herself.

"The…what?"

"You're right, that sounds too hazy. I mean the new Physical Therapist Pat just hired. The *male* Physical Therapist she just hired." Courtney wiggled her eyebrows suggestively and peeked out of the window next to my cracked open door as if waiting for someone to randomly sneak up on our conversation.

"A guy, I'm surprised," I genuinely was. Our field was generally female dominated. Which was great, because we deserved to have just as many female dominated careers as there were male dominated ones. Not that I was against men working for our non-profit, but parents were generally more agreeable with their children receiving this kind of care from a woman. It was just the current dynamic of things until the world decided to pull its head out of its ass and become a better place.

"Yeah, he's super hot." Courtney lowered her voice even more, but she wasn't smirking or wiggling her eyebrows. She looked like she was dead serious.

"Court. This is our coworker."

"Beck. He's hot as balls."

"Court."

"Beck."

She was staring at me intently, with no silliness on her face or tone. She really wanted me to understand the level of attractiveness our new coworker was.

I sighed and rubbed the bridge of my nose with my fingers while releasing a giggle at my best friends' antics. This wasn't Courtney getting nervous at how attractive our new coworker was, this was her trying to explain to me that he was a visually attractive person.

This was part of an ongoing conversation, or investigation, on Courtney's part regarding my sexuality. I opened up to her about this a couple of months after college graduation. We were both working in Orange County but living in different cities and working at different jobs. So, we decided that we needed to have mandatory monthly (if not weekly) brunches where we could catch up and keep our friendship thriving. The brunches would sometimes last hours.

During one of our brunches in a small corner of the trendy restaurant Courtney had seen on social media, I told her that I realized during college that I didn't feel physical attraction like other people seemed to. I couldn't just look at someone and feel my heart rate increase, or my breathing stop, or whatever else was generally supposed to happen by looking at a stranger who was by-the-book good looking.

"But you enjoy sex?" Courtney asked, with no judgment at all in her voice. She sipped her mimosa and created a safe presence for me to list all my concerns, just like she always had.

"Sometimes." I splayed a hand flat in the air and wiggled it back and forth, "I haven't ever gotten off with random hook-ups, like at a party or something."

"Very few women in the history of ever have. And if they say they do, I'm inclined to think that they are lying. They must be," Courtney shrugged. "But with Spencer?" In reference to the only steady (but temporary) relationship I had during college.

"I think Spencer was different," I furrowed my brows. "We were friends first, then project partners, and then we made out one time… but I'm pretty sure I initiated our first kiss."

"Okay, but more specifically, you got off with him when you guys were…intimate?" It said a lot about how seriously Courtney was taking this conversation, because she used polite words instead of her usual slang, like "fucked."

"Not the first time, but he knew I didn't, and we quickly did work to remedy that. The longer I was with him though the more frequently I did get off with him." I smiled at one memory. After a month or so of dating, he had finally gotten me off with his fingers. I could still see his fist pumping the air in victory afterward, proud of his accomplishment and happy that I was satisfied.

He truly was a decent first boyfriend.

"...Have you ever considered the fact that you might be asexual? Or demisexual?" Courtney bluntly asked. I had paused and a blush stained my cheeks as I held the fork up to my mouth, mid bite. I set it down and pretended to get a better scoop of food.

"I enjoy having sex, so I don't think so," I mumbled, embarrassed.

"That's not what that means," Courtney replied. She then explained to me the watered-down version, that I might be someone who required an emotional connection to a person in order for me to be sexually attracted to them. Based on the very little evidence I had at the time, I considered it a possibility. That was also when I learned that there was a lot more depth to sexual orientation than I originally thought. Again, I grew up sheltered. I appreciated Courtney being someone I could continue to open up to so much. She and Gram were the only people in the universe I felt safe like that with.

I still didn't know if I would have put my sexuality in a box like demisexual or asexual because I didn't really think labels like that mattered, but I could count on one hand the number of times my body had triggered a visceral response just by looking at someone. Half of those times were during middle and high school, and I'm pretty sure puberty and sexual frustration had a lot going on there.

Courtney snapped her fingers in front of my face, still covered by my hands while I smiled at her. She was almost looming over me as I sat in my office chair.

"You have to see him," Courtney insisted, "for science."

"Well, if he works here, I'm sure I will."

"Yeah, but I need to be there the first time you see him."

"What? Why?"

Courtney groaned as if I was being super annoying, "For *science!*"

I laughed in response to that.

Then we both heard Pat (who was a very loud talker) coming down the hallway outside my office, "...And back here is the Speech wing. You probably won't spend a lot of time back here, but it's good to know where the rest of your coworkers' offices are."

Courtney clasped her hands together and raised her gaze to my office ceiling. "Praise be, the stars aligned," she then quickly opened my door as wide as possible before running back to my desk and leaning a hip against it in an attempt to look casual.

I pinched her thigh, and she grunted right as Pat's pale blonde bob came into view.

"Morning, ladies!" Pat was in her fifties and was the director of the facility. She was hands down the best boss I had ever had. She was professional and efficient, but also friendly and treated everyone like respectable human beings. For some reason that was a difficult feat for most jobs.

"Morning, Pat!" Courtney smiled as she rubbed the spot on her thigh that I pinched. I noticed someone waiting out in the hallway, someone much more masculine than Pat's petite middle-aged frame, and wearing a navy-blue long-sleeved shirt.

"I just wanted to stop by and introduce our newest team member," Pat started while stepping into my office and gesturing for the man standing there to enter, "This is Adam Hall—"

I honest to god could not have told you anything else Pat said after that. As soon as he stepped into my office, not really leaving the door frame that he filled, I was visually impressed.

The first thing I noticed was his hair, it was a specific shade of dark red that made me think the correct term for it was auburn, but I wasn't sure. It wasn't too short, yet it wasn't too long and unkept either. It was full and luscious, with a gentle wave to it that I admired instantly.

The next thing I noticed was how tall he was in the doorway. I was five seven, so I guessed he was closer to six feet if not taller. He leaned one shoulder against the door frame as he nodded his head to both Courtney and me, and as soon as his light brown eyes met mine my heart jumped into my throat. I tried to clear it, but I swallowed my spit wrong and started coughing.

"You okay?" Courtney asked, no real sympathy in her voice as she pounded her palm firmly on my back.

"Yeah—I—" I coughed again to make sure my throat was truly clear this time, using the crook of my elbow to cover my mouth, and found myself looking at the man again.

Maybe it was because of my coughing fit, but as soon as I looked back at him and realized I had his full attention (probably because I was gasping for air) I felt my heart rate pick up speed. It was unnerving. It felt close to an anxiety attack. Moisture started to coat my palms, so I began rubbing them on the thighs of my black yoga pants.

He had a couple of freckles that dotted the bridge of his nose, the only other characteristic of your stereotypical red-head. I generally pictured red-heads as children, because a lot of the time the red hair turned either brown or blonde with age. Not him. He was obviously a full-grown man. With high cheek bones, perfectly proportioned lips, and a jawline that made me wonder if I should somehow be doing more neck days at the gym.

Can you even exercise that part of your body?

I was incredibly nervous. I wanted to escape the entire situation, but instead, I let out a nervous giggle that I couldn't hold back and said, "Sorry, I'm Beck."

"Yeah, Pat introduced us already." I could hear the smile in Courtney's voice.

"Want me to grab you some water?" Pat asked, mother hen mode activated. She looked insanely small and frail standing next to him.

"No, no, I'm fine. Just swallowed my spit wrong." I lifted a shoulder as if it was totally normal to admit that I was a full-grown woman who couldn't handle the simple function of swallowing spit.

"Okay…Well, Adam here is going to be working with a lot of Julie's clients since she left, so you three should become well acquainted since you will be working on the same team."

Pat continued, her dark eyes flicking back to me occasionally to see if I suddenly couldn't breathe again.

"Of course, we're happy to fill you in on the cute kiddos." Courtney smiled, acting totally unaffected by Adam's presence.

Meanwhile, blood was rushing in my ears.

Oh my god, what is happening?

"That would be great." His face was relaxed but somewhat cold. He never smiled at us once during the entire interaction. He was clearly just going through the motions of mandatory introductions. He maybe even looked a little uncomfortable, which was justified because he had just walked into a room where a woman started coughing hysterically from one glance at him.

Pat smiled at all of us and clasped her hands together. "Well, I still have lots of people to introduce him to." Pat and Adam shifted their bodies as if they were going to leave the room, but Courtney stood up from my desk and held her hand out. "It was nice to meet you!"

I knew for a fucking fact that Courtney was only doing that to make it weird if he didn't also shake my hand.

"Likewise," Adam said as he stepped forward to give her hand one shake, then he turned to me and offered his hand.

"Oh—" I blinked rapidly as I felt like my voice was working faster than my brain, and my throat was dry. "I shouldn't—I just coughed everywhere, and...germs..." To make the moment even more weird, I tucked both of my hands under my armpits protectively. As if I was worried that he would somehow force me to shake his hand.

"Ah, good point." Even my shitty ears could tell that his voice was deep and masculine. With him being a couple of steps closer to me I found myself staring at his lowered hand a little longer than normal. I noticed a couple of freckles dotting the top of his hand too.

I then started to wonder if he had freckles on other parts of his body. My gaze traveled up his completely sleeved arm, with a hint of bicep flexing through. I noticed his wide shoulders, where I saw a couple of freckles peeking out near the collar of his shirt, and finally up to his face where I caught his gaze for a second before he turned to follow Pat out of my office. My eyes widened with embarrassment.

Shit, he saw me checking out his arm. Like a creep.

Based on how his brows lowered, I gathered that he was not pleased that I ogled his arm.

Fuck. What is happening to me?

It was silent in my office for a few minutes before I saw Courtney step forward and shut the door. She then turned around to face me, both of her lips tucked between her teeth in an obvious attempt to keep from laughing.

"Oh. My. God!" It was all I could manage. I lifted both of my hands, which until then had still been tucked under my armpits, and pressed my palms to my face. Thankfully they smelled like my freshly applied deodorant, not the sweat that I swore was covering most of my body. My face was so hot. I must have looked red. I probably blushed through that entire encounter.

"Beck, holy shit!" Courtney laughed quietly in case they were still close enough to hear. Or if anybody was close enough to hear. This was a super inappropriate conversation for the workplace.

"What is happening?" I asked.

"You know exactly what just happened," Courtney emphasized this by placing both of her hands on her hips and raising her eyebrows at me, like a teacher leading a student to the correct answer.

"How—what—"

"I know, girl. Trust me, I know," Courtney sighed and stared at a point behind me, probably thinking about his light brown eyes and freckles just like I saw myself doing in the foreseeable future.

"I don't—I—" I shook my head once, twice. Blinked a few times, and lowered my hands to my lap before turning my body in my chair to face Courtney fully, "I felt like I couldn't breathe."

"Well, you were literally choking for a moment there."

"Besides that! I looked at him and it was like my body panicked and decided we didn't need air anymore. God, my heart is racing." I placed my palm over the speeding organ.

"Okay, I'm going to be real honest, even I didn't react that embarrassingly when I first saw him. But, I've also been physically attracted to many men for as long as I can remember. So when I saw your face go bright red from the first second you took him in, I was filled with joy." Courtney laughed again, obviously finding this entire situation comical—at least one of us was enjoying it.

"What do I do?" I asked, panic starting to set in.

"What do you mean, 'what do you do'?" Courtney asked, she seemed both humored and genuinely confused.

"I can't work with him!" I hissed quietly at her, "I couldn't even say normal words! I hid my hands in my armpits like this!" I tucked my hands back in place under my arms.

"Yeah, I know. I was there."

"So, what do I do? I can't be on the same team and work with him. I just proved I can't talk to him like a normal person."

"Yeah, you can, and you will." Courtney smiled encouragingly at me, her brown eyes glimmering at my reaction to all of his. I stared at her with desperation, because I felt like I was suddenly pushed way out of my element. She just placed a hand on my shoulder and patted me encouragingly.

"Beck, most humans go through feeling attracted to their coworkers or business partners or other people they have to see every day. This isn't some wild new concept. You're just going to have to play catch up with the rest of us and learn to live with it." Courtney shrugged.

Learn to live with it.

I nodded. I could do that. I had been able to handle seeing Spencer in a professional setting regularly and I had been literally sleeping with him. I had only said maybe three words to Adam, so I told myself that I could get through this newly discovered physical attraction just fine.

...What if I were sleeping with Adam? Did he have more freckles on his back? Chest? Shoulders? What would that potentially freckled back look like if I was underneath him and he was gripping my comforter and—

"Hey, where did you go?" Courtney snapped her fingers in front of my gaze, which had zoned out. I felt my cheeks heat immediately, and I stared at Courtney wide eyed. She furrowed her brows at me in confusion, but then a second later understanding dawned.

"Oh no! No! No!" Courtney started shaking her finger at me, "You save those thoughts for when you're *not* at work!"

"I know! I know!" I squeezed my eyes closed and pressed the heels of my palms into them, willing the dirty images to go away.

Porn had never really done it for me.

I wasn't against porn, as long as everyone had truly consented and it was in a safe environment, but the content itself never really got me there. I would just be sitting there on my computer after typing in some key words Courtney suggested I use, watching these two people panting and screwing each other in the wildest of situations, and I would wonder to myself, *how do they know each other? How long had they loved each other? Did they love each other, or was this a random fuck? What's their story?*

So why the absolute fuck did I immediately picture that dirty image of my new coworker?

"...Or you could ask him out," I heard Courtney suggest. I dropped my hands and gave her my best 'what the fuck are you talking about' face.

"I don't think that's on the table," I clarified, in case my expression didn't say it enough.

"Usually it's not, because dating your coworkers is generally a no-no, but I'm pretty sure as long as you clear it with HR first, you're golden." Courtney snapped her fingers with emphasis as if it was all that easy.

"I—what—no. One step at a time…how did you handle it?" I asked on an exhale, folding my arms against my stomach in an attempt to force my body to relax. It was starting to get there once I redirected the attention off of me.

"How did I handle what? Being turned on in public?" Courtney asked.

"I am not turned on."

"You're turned on. All the way. On high."

"Fuck." I groaned. Thankfully, I was calming down, my skin was starting to feel cooler and my heart was beginning to slow down.

"Have you noticed how often you and I swear here? We work with kids. We need to be better at controlling our-selves." Courtney mused.

"Yeah, sure," I agreed, "Distract me, tell me about your first sexual awakening, or whatever it is we are going to call this in the future." I rubbed a hand down my entire face, in an attempt to wipe the humiliation away.

Courtney grinned at me as she clasped her hands together and bounced a couple of times on the backs of her heels, "Oh, sure! Let me paint you a picture. I was fourteen and I was watching the baseball scene from *Twilight* for the first time…"

3

"You both are fussing for no reason!" Gram pretended to scold as Courtney and I wandered around the kitchen gathering bowls and spoons. Courtney, who loved cooking, had made us matzo ball soup because Gram had a mild case of the sniffles. We all were confident it was allergies, since Gram was prone to them every season, but Gram was also "old as fuck" as Courtney liked to put it. So, we wanted to look after her, in case it was something worse than allergies.

"Oh hush, you love being spoiled," Courtney rolled her eyes as she patted Gram's shoulder before setting her bowl of soup down in front of her.

The three of us all lived together. I knew that was a weird setup, but the cost of living in Orange County, California was known for being crazily inflated. The weather was perfect, and the economy knew that. Everything was expensive, which made it near impossible to live on your own in your early to mid-twenties. After college, I moved in with Gram. I knew she was getting older and that I had a limited amount of time left to spend with her, so when I asked if I could move into her new townhome in Lake Forest, I was relieved when she squealed with joy at the idea, and hugged me tight.

A couple of years later Courtney's FOMO kicked in. Rent

kept increasing for her studio apartment at a rate she couldn't afford, so we welcomed her into the third bedroom of the townhouse with open arms.

The townhouse was a mixture of design themes, but it was mostly modern with houseplants scattered all over the place. Lots of spider and snake plants that could still live if you forgot to water them for a month straight. Gram was all about having plants that could thrive in this climate, specifically. She also loved the idea of houseplants creating clean air inside the home.

The furniture was colorful and bold, and so was the artwork and bookshelves. That balanced out all the white walls and grey tiles the house was built with. Just last year, Gram got sick of all the monochromatic colors built into her home and the three of us decided to paint the trim and doors a light, bright blue.

I didn't personally care for bright blue trim and doors, but it made Courtney and Gram incredibly happy. I just felt bad for the next potential owners of the house.

"Yeah, you're right. It's just polite if I protest a little first." Gram smirked as she scooted her chair closer. Gram may be old as fuck at age seventy-four, but she kept it tight. She was lean and relatively fit thanks to her lifelong obsession with yoga. Lately, she was into her daily hot girl walks, thanks to her involvement on social media. Her long grey hair was usually kept in a messy bun on top of her head, and her hazel eyes matched mine. I wished I had known her better before her hair turned mostly grey, but I could still pick out a few dark brown pieces that matched mine. I always felt more connected to Gram as my family than my actual parents, but that was for a myriad of reasons.

"What is this? Cilantro?" Gram asked before scooping a bite into her mouth.

"We didn't have any dill, and I wasn't willing to go back to the store for it. So I figured cilantro was a decent substitute." I explained while filling my own bowl and walking to the table to join Courtney and Gram.

"Huh, not bad." Gram nodded her head with approval, closing her eyes and humming at the taste.

"Thank you, thank you," Courtney pretended to bow to us and then shoved half a matzo ball in her mouth with her spoon. That didn't stop her from continuing to talk, though, "Susan, guess what happened to Beck today?"

I rolled my eyes and quickly shoved more soup in my mouth to avoid the conversation. Gram didn't respond; instead, she just lifted her eyebrows at me expectantly.

"Go on, tell your grandmother about your sexual awakening." Courtney encouraged before taking another bite. Gram spluttered on her soup a little, surprise showing in her eyes. Not from discomfort, but from joy and probably some curiosity.

"Sexual awakening?" Gram asked. She set her spoon down to give me her full attention, tucking her hands under her chin and setting her elbows on the table as if she was going to be there for a while.

I realized that it was weird to talk about this with your grandparent, but Gram was not your average grandparent. She was a trailblazer for her time and was at the front lines for almost every single social movement she could attend since being born in 1948. She had been alive for both the Korean and Vietnam wars, and when Alaska and Hawaii officially became US states. She was alive for the Civil Rights Act being signed, as well as the drama involving the ERA ratification in the 70s and 80s. She spent her 20s and 30s happily protesting for a woman's right to marry whoever she would like, as well as the right for a woman's healthcare to stay between her and her doctor. She was an OG feminist, and proud of it.

I was also proud of Gram, or Susan Scott before she became a grandmother. I loved to hear her stories. She had always been such a woke woman. Because of her beliefs, Gram was very open about sexuality and anything involving a woman's overall happiness and fulfillment.

That is also what drew the separation between her and her only child, my father, who was not as proud of Gram's political involvement as I was.

"Courtney is teasing me," I explained after Gram continued to stare at me with expectant eyes, "A new PT started at work today; a *man*." I feigned false shock for my Gram.

"No, no. That's not the important part of the story." Courtney waved her empty spoon at me to encourage me to continue, her face gleaming with excitement. Gram's eyes bounced between the two of us.

"Oh. Right. How could I forget? He's also very good looking." I smirked at Courtney.

"No. That's not right." Courtney shook her head, challenging.

"It's not?" Gram asked.

"No. He's *hot*. And Beck is hot for him, specifically,"

Courtney clarified, acting properly as she focused on her food, not making eye contact with either of us.

Gram's head snapped in my direction.

"Really?" Gram asked, a smile creeping onto her face. That's when I felt my face get red again, and not from the hot soup we were all eating.

"I think so, though it felt more like crippling anxiety than physical attraction," I frowned into my bowl, I didn't want to replay the horrifying two-minute interaction.

So, Courtney did it for me. She filled Gram in on the entire thing, adding in how hard I was blushing and the light layer of sweat that covered my forehead after Adam left.

"Oh, this is exciting!" Gram clapped her hands, having been filled in on my attraction dilemma years ago. There were literally no secrets between the three of us. This home was our safe space. There was a time while I was living here with her when Gram kept reminding me that it was totally acceptable to not be attracted to men and that if I wanted to date women or non-binary people then I could invite them over and she would make herself scarce.

"I mean, it's not a huge deal." I saw Gram's eyes start to glint with mischief, and I wanted to tone it down.

"You should have heard her, 'What do I do now?' As if the world was ending," Courtney laughed, taking her empty bowl and mine from the table to add them to the dishwasher.

"I'll admit I might have overreacted, but to be fair, I was taken completely off guard." When those words came out of my mouth Courtney snapped around and glared at me with her mouth open, blonde hair whirling around her face and shoulders.

"You were not! I *specifically* came to your office to warn you how pretty he was!" Courtney reminded me.

"Yeah, but you have 'warned me' about so many men I became desensitized to it!" It was true. For the last year or so Courtney had thought it was best to plant seeds in my head before I met a guy. For a time, she thought that her telling me the guy was attractive beforehand would somehow trick my brain and body into actually being attracted to him. When that didn't work after a few meetings, she still kept it up, just because she thought it was fun.

"…I could have sworn you were in the closet for a while…" Gram murmured, returning to her soup.

"You think that I *like* the fact that the small handful of people I have experienced physical attraction for have only been men? What I would *give* to be turned on by women!" I groaned, and Courtney nodded along with me, leaning against the counter.

"Women are pretty, smell nice, and are generally kind and considerate," Courtney added.

"Women won't follow you to your car at night," Gram said around a mouthful of soup.

"Trust me, Gram, if I was attracted to women I'd be happily tied down right now. It's a real inconvenience that men seem to be the ones who do it for me. Also, side note, did you notice that the new guy didn't smile once?" I turned towards Courtney specifically.

"Yes, I did. He seemed uncomfortable with introductions," Courtney confirmed, picking at her nails.

"Does 'new guy' have a name?" Gram asked, holding her

bowl up for Courtney to take to the dishwasher. Courtney came over to retrieve it while replying, "Adam-something."

"Adam, that's a decent name," Gram looked at a spot on the wall, "Adam...Adam..." It was as if she was trying the name out for size.

"...Addy," I chimed in.

"Ugh, no. He is *not* an '*Addy*'," Courtney shook her head in mock disgust. I laughed and closed my eyes to let out a very loud, fake sexual moan.

"Oh, *Addy!*"

Without skipping a beat Gram threw her head back too to add, "Right there, Addy-boy!"

"Ooughhh!" Courtney pretended to lean over the sink and hurl.

We both started howling with laughter, Gram holding her stomach and wiping a tear away from her eye. Courtney also started laughing uncontrollably, holding onto the sink to keep herself upright.

That was our vibe. A seventy-four-year-old living with two women in their late twenties, making each other laugh until we cry over a homemade bowl of soup. It made my heart happy, to watch this life I had lived happily in for years now.

"I swear to god if we ever befriend him, you will *not* call him Addy!" Courtney pointed an accusing finger at me. "He is way too muscled and manly for that nickname."

"Muscled?" I asked, wiping the tears from my eyes.

"Uh, yeah, did you not notice how he wore the hell out of his long-sleeved athletic top? There was no skin, but it was very form fitting and hid nothing," Courtney explained, returning to the table and reclaiming her seat. I thought about Adam's bicep poking through his sleeve and realized that she wasn't wrong.

"Muscles are nice," Gram chimed in, elbowing me in the seat, "So, do you think you would be interested in him as a partner?"

How many women in their seventies referred to anyone as a 'partner', and not something gender specific? She could have said boyfriend, but she went out of her way not to.

"I don't think so, I'd need to do some damage control because of how I behaved today. Plus," I looked over to Courtney with a smirk, wanting to bring the silly environment back so we didn't dive much deeper into the Adam topic, "I would need to be able to hold a conversation with my future partner without almost coming in my pants with one glance from them."

Courtney and Gram both cackled, laughing hysterically until Gram reached over to the shelving unit near her and pulled out a deck of Uno cards. The Adam topic dissolved, and soon Courtney and Gram were cussing at each other for playing draw-fours on the other repeatedly. We played Uno for over an hour, adding in our own house rules of course. Eventually, we called it a night, and we each went to our own rooms since Courtney and I both had early mornings tomorrow.

As I got ready for bed and crawled under the covers I found myself picturing my newest coworker again. The spike in my pulse surprised me when I thought about the simple shift of his light brown eyes landing on me. I realized what that sensation was, having his attention on me. It was thrilling.

When I thought about potentially seeing him at work again the next day I felt my gut start to twist with anticipation, and I noticed that I was holding back a physical smile on my face. After feeling mostly nothing for mostly nobody for a concerning amount of time, I was happy with the knowledge that I was able to behave normally under rare circumstances.

Here I was, a full-grown woman, proud of myself for developing a crush. Enjoying the fact that my body and mind responded in what I considered a relatively normal way to someone I could find attractive.

Then I thought about the expression on his face when he noticed me staring at his arm for an inappropriate amount of time. I realized that while I was laying there pulsing with energy knowing that I could be a normal, sexual woman, but that he probably would appreciate it if I kept my distance for the time being. I did not want to come off as some creep, and even if I did have a crush on him physically, there was a good chance our personalities wouldn't mesh just right.

I was kind of weird, and that was okay.

I didn't have to do anything about this crush. I didn't need to necessarily act on these exciting feelings I was experiencing. He never had to know. This could stay between Courtney, Gram, and me until our graves, or when I found someone else that I was attracted to that wasn't weirded out by my behavior the very first time we meet.

However long it would take for me to feel attraction for someone again.

I got instantly nervous. What if I didn't feel attraction again? *Don't be stupid, Beck. The universe can't be that cruel.* I scolded myself. The entire situation proved that I could be normal. I was just picky. Yup. I had a type. Dark red-heads. With freckles. There were lots of those in this world.

I rolled my eyes at myself and tucked the covers over my head, willing my brain to shut off and go to sleep. Tomorrow was a new day, and I needed to be on my best behavior around my new coworker.

Go me.

4

"*Hurry, hurry, drive the fire truck!*" I loved this song; it was fast and short. Of course, I had a favorite children's song. That was my job. I was with kids aged three and under for five days, some forty hours a week. If I didn't make myself pick a favorite children's song, I'd lose my fucking mind. We all sat in a circle while I led the songs, parents sitting behind their kids' seats, or their kids preferring to use them as a lap. The parents did a lot of hand-over-hand to prompt their kids into following the arm movements I was demonstrating.

"*Hurry, hurry, climb the ladder!*" I started the second verse if you could call it that. Each verse was 10 seconds tops. A couple of kids were getting fussy and whining throughout the song after a long day of Group, where we had them go to four different stations to complete different activities. It could be exhausting for a baby or toddler, and very over stimulating. I felt for them.

I quickly finished up the last verse and started the good-bye song, which was quick and a familiar signal to the kids that we were almost done and that they could go home.

After the song all the kids started reaching their arms out for their parents to take them away, ready to be done.

Same, kids. Same.

My client that I usually had right after Group canceled because they had some sniffles, and they wanted to be extra sure it wasn't anything more than allergies before bringing them to the facility, which was appreciated. We had a lot of different kiddos here with a lot of different challenges. Some of the medications these kids were on to help regulate seizures could cause a drop in their immune system's ability to fight off even a simple cold.

"Bye, Rebecca!" I heard one dad call. I internally cringed before glancing over and waving bye at his daughter specifically. She was maybe one and a half, had Down Syndrome and wore the cutest purple glasses that wrapped around the entirety of her head. She gave me a goofy grin before patting her dad's chest to get a move on.

For some reason, this dad felt comfortable attempting to subtly flirt with me during Group. He wasn't overly inappropriate or anything with his words or actions, but the looks he had given me made my skin crawl. Courtney and my other coworkers had noticed too and usually helped play defense in a way that wasn't obvious that I need a buffer from him.

"Stella did great today, Mr. James!" Courtney came up to his side to turn his attention away from me, because he seemed like he was going try to approach me when there was literally no need to. Courtney met with Stella one-on-one for Infant Stim, so they had way more of a reason to chat.

"Please, just Connor," He gave Courtney more of a polite smile, which continued to blow my mind. Courtney was beautiful and always had a smile on her face and a sunshine personality. She was blonde and had flattering curves and a light California tan on her skin. For some unknown reason,

Connor's type was tall pale brunettes with hearing loss (which, occasionally, gave me the best excuse in the world to ignore him).

"Daddy James still hasn't given up, huh?" Taylor asked, crouching down to help me put away the stuffed animals and toys I used as prompts during circle time.

"Weirdly no, but thankfully he is easily distracted," I replied. I heard a chirp in my left ear. Shoot. My batteries were dying.

"That's good to hear..." Taylor glanced over their shoulder to look at the thinning crowd as parents gathered their diaper bags and started heading towards the building exit, then they set their bright blue eyes on me, "Have you met the new PT?"

I felt my heart jump up into my throat. I kept my mouth closed and cleared it with no problem before nodding my head, "Actually, yes."

"What do you think?" Taylor pressed after closing the lid on the toy box and standing up swiftly, holding out a hand to assist me.

"What do you mean?" *Besides the fact that he's the most attractive man I have ever seen,* I thought to myself as I took their outstretched hand.

"He seems kind of quiet, I'm hoping he was like that with everyone and not just me, specifically," Taylor's dark brows furrowed. Taylor was an Occupational Therapist and worked a lot with the Physical Therapists at the clinic. They were very high energy and did not let anything get to them. So at first, I was confused as to why Taylor would be self-conscious about a new employee giving them the cold shoulder.

Then I remembered last week.

I was helping a client of mine walk to the front exit, holding their chubby hands where their mom was stuck outside on a work phone call. She had just mouthed the words, 'thank you' to me through the glass door when I heard Pat's voice travel across the waiting room to us.

"If you have a problem with them, feel free to find services somewhere else. All the other OTs have full schedules," Pat was generally kind and gentle, so to hear her voice have a hard edge to it was unsettling to me. I glanced past the welcome desk and saw her on the phone, shoulders hunched and a furrow in her brow. Her red lips were pressed in a dark line.

"I will not," Pat shook her head once even though whoever she was speaking to couldn't see her, "It is absolutely none of my business to know what specific set of genitals any of my employees have. It is absurd to me that this is that big of a concern for you—" That's when I realized that she was talking about Taylor. I smiled at the mom who was still on the phone and handed over her child, before making my way back through the waiting room as slowly as possible so I could continue to eavesdrop.

"—No. No. You're right. It sounds like we may not be a good fit. Which is a shame. I'm sure your child would have benefited greatly from our resources, but I am sure there are other facilities in the area that are more suited to address your bigoted concerns." Then Pat slammed the office phone down on the receiver before growling in frustration.

I was glad that someone who had an issue with Taylor wouldn't be coming into the office regularly. We had a waiting list of kids who needed our services, kids whose parents most likely weren't bigoted assholes.

When Courtney and I asked Taylor about it, they told us that the first OT session they had with that client was hilariously awkward. The parent kept addressing Taylor as a he or she, but then phrasing it as a question for Taylor to either confirm or deny.

Taylor didn't give a fuck either way, so they never corrected the parent. They could see the parents' faces get redder and redder the more they realized that Taylor was simply part of the LGBTQ+ community.

"He was quiet with Courtney and me, too. Though, that could be because I had a coughing fit when Pat introduced us," I scrunched my nose at the memory. Then I heard the chirp in my left ear again.

Did I leave spare batteries on my desk?

"That's comforting, I just…don't want any more drama, I guess," Taylor quirked their lips, making their septum ring twitch in an endearing way. I thought about the number of kids who had reached up and tried to rip it out of their nose and smiled.

"I doubt Pat would have hired him if she sensed even the slightest hint of hate from him, Taylor," I reassured, squeezing their calloused hand. Taylor was way more active than I'll ever be and had energy levels that competed with both Courtney and me combined most days. I glanced at their outfit, noticing that they chose to look more masculine today with a long sleeved grey thermal and black jogger sweatpants. Their brown hair was cropped short close to their scalp on the bottom and left longer on top for them to style. It was a cute haircut; one I've considered for myself. Courtney constantly begged me not to, because she loved my dark brown hair and how it slightly curled at the ends with a gentle wave in it.

"Yeah, you're probably right." Taylor squeezed my hand back before exhaling a puff of air up into their bangs.

Courtney bounded up next to us, having successfully dismissed Daddy James. My left ear chirped again.

"Do I have any spare batteries on my desk?" I asked Courtney, fidgeting with the tiny device in my ear.

"I thought I saw some in the top drawer last I went through it." She replied, fist bumping Taylor in greeting.

"Cool, I need to go switch them out." *Chirp.* Dang, I might need new hearing aids soon if they were just now indicating that the battery was low within minutes of the battery dying.

"Later-gator," Taylor waved while Courtney commandeered their attention.

Chirp.

Shit.

I pulled out the left hearing aid, hearing the vacuum of sound leave my ear canal. I blinked a few times, trying to let the minor dizziness fade, before deciding to remove the right as well. Ah, balanced. Much better. I enjoyed the world going almost completely silent, minus the small murmur of voices getting quieter as I walked away.

It could sometimes be peaceful not wearing hearing aids. It was incredibly helpful when I slept at night unless I was sick with a fever or had unusual ringing in my ears because the lack of sound made it so that I didn't startle awake as easily. I usually tried to enjoy the peace it brought me when the world went silent, especially after going through a noisy Group Therapy session with loud squealing kids.

I made it to my desk and found the package of batteries and decided to take it with me to the break room since I needed to refill my coffee.

Once I made it to the break room, smiling at coworkers along the way, I put the coffee pot on and reached into my pocket to put the devices on the counter. While the coffee brewed I also reached into the utensil drawer and pulled out a tool that I used to open up the battery chamber. I stashed a number of these tools all over the office. A paperclip worked too, but often those were flimsy and difficult to work with.

Plus, who carried around paper clips?

As I popped out the old batteries and started to replace the new ones in the device, I heard a low murmuring behind me. I had gotten used to ignoring voices when my hearing aids weren't in because everyone at work knew I was hard of hearing and that the best way to get my attention was by getting into my line of sight or tapping me on the shoulder. I felt a vague presence behind me but didn't turn round as I fumbled the pinky-nail-sized battery. It slipped through my fingers and bounced off the countertop once. Twice.

I tracked it with my eye and turned around to try to catch it as it jumped off the counter. I quickly reached my hand out, following the trajectory of it, and caught the small circular battery at the same time my hand knocked into someone stepping forward. As soon as my hand made contact with their body, I heard a low grunt. I quickly snatched my hand back as I took in the man standing in front of me.

I widened my eyes in horror as I realized I had just accidentally sack-tapped him. In the workplace.

I felt my soul leave my body.

Quickly, he buckled over, with one large hand gripping the edge of the countertop next to us and the other cupping in between his legs. Dark red hair obscured his forehead and eyes, but not the grimace and clenched jaw.

I felt my heart sink into my gut.

Fuck. Me.

"Oh! Oh no! I'm so sorry!" I couldn't hear myself that well, so there was a good chance that I was slurring my words in my panic. I quickly put the battery on the counter and reached back out to Adam, my hand grabbing his forearm in some pathetic attempt to soothe him.

"I'm so, *so* sorry!" I tried again. I hoped that I wasn't shouting too loud like I usually did when I couldn't hear myself. I got momentarily distracted by the fact that he wore a long-sleeved athletic shirt again. The material was soft and smooth but I could feel the muscles in his forearm flexing as he gripped the countertop.

Adam just nodded his head as he noticeably exhaled through his nose and started to straighten, slowly removing his hand from his groin. I quickly snatched my hand back, holding onto the wrist of it with my other hand as if I didn't have control of it.

I felt the ground vibrate and turned to see Courtney had stomped her feet a couple of times to get my attention, a slightly worried but mostly entertained smirk on her lips as her gaze bounced between our new coworker and me.

"What happened?" Courtney spoke but also signed for me. She must have tried getting my attention verbally, but when I didn't respond, realized I wasn't wearing my hearing aids.

I glanced back to see Adam's lips were moving, but he turned away from me to address Courtney. I had no idea what he was saying.

"I'm *so* sorry! I was trying to catch the battery and I think I hit him in..." I let my sentence trail off. Adam's head quickly turned to look at me, a small furrow in his brow. His light brown eyes looked like they had just stopped watering, probably from pain. His cheeks looked flushed, which made the freckles that dotted his nose stand out a bit darker against his skin. I turned to look at Courtney who was pressing her lips together in a tight smile to keep herself from laughing.

"Put your aids back on before you hurt someone else," Courtney spoke for Adam's benefit and signed for mine. I nodded and quickly turned to the counter to insert the batteries into the devices and shoved them in my ear. I blinked a few times to adjust to the sound being slammed back against my eardrum. The hum of the building's AC running made my skin crawl for a couple of seconds before I tuned in to Adam and Courtney's conversation.

"...of hearing." Courtney finished as she walked up to us and grabbed the coffee pot, that was now done.

"Oh, I didn't know," Adam responded, his voice deep. His voice must have been the one I heard murmuring behind me. When I wasn't wearing my aids, it was incredibly difficult for me to pick up high frequencies and noises. Courtney's feminine voice was nearly impossible for me to hear unless she was right next to me. Adam's voice is rough and low, which would make it possible for me to pick up on it without hearing aids. If I looked at his lips while he was speaking, I could probably have gotten the gist of what he was saying along with the murmuring sound.

His light brown gaze met mine again, the scrunch in his brow smoothed out a little, and I could see his eyes dart from either side of my head where my ears are.

"I'm so sorry, I was switching out the batteries in my aids and—"

Adam lifted a hand to stop me before saying, "It's fine, don't worry about it." Then the corner of his mouth picked up on one side. A smirk. He was smirking at me as if he also thought the situation was a little humorous. A smirk was a stepping stone to a smile, and I was so curious to see what the hard, sharp face looked like with a full, real smile.

I went momentarily silent. That smirk made my heart rate pick up again and words leave my brain. He raised a hand to casually run it through his hair, which looked incredibly soft. I felt my hand instinctively rise as if it had permission to touch it too, but quickly snatched it back before it got too close to him. He noticed my weird hand raise and the smirk disappeared from his face and a dark eyebrow was raised.

His eyebrows weren't exactly the same color as his hair, huh. They were a slightly darker shade of red. I wondered what he would look like with a beard, and what color that would be.

I had been quiet for too long. *Shit.*

I could feel heat radiating off my face. I knew I was blushing hard, and I couldn't stop it.

He was still looking at me as if he was waiting for me to say something.

Uh...

"Hopefully next time we run into each other I can act like a normal human," I blurted out. Then I squeezed my eyes closed and pinched the bridge of my nose because I was so pathetic.

I heard Courtney laugh, and I cracked one eye open to see his lips twitching on the corners.

"We'll see," Adam nodded at both of us, and with a quick, but small smirk, he left the break room.

No water or food or anything in his hand.

Why was he even in here?

"Well, that must have been super embarrassing for you," Courtney commented as she took a seat at the folding table in the corner and sipped from her coffee mug. Her blonde eyebrows were raised at me in a way that told me this would also be something she would forever tease me for.

"I think I'm going to throw up," I responded, resting both hands over my stomach.

"Please, don't." Was Courtney's reply.

I quickly grabbed myself a cup of coffee and joined her at the table. Leaning in close to her and speaking in a lower tone.

"I touched his junk. In the workplace." I took a sip of coffee and set the mug down so I could cover both of my hands over my face.

"You did not touch his junk…you slapped it." Courtney couldn't finish the sentence without her lips quivering from holding in laughter.

"It wasn't a slap! It was like a…" I vaguely repeated the gesture with my hands. My closed upturned fist knocked against my open hand.

"So, you punched it."

"No, more like a forceful nudge."

"With your fist."

"Yes, exactly."

"So, you punched him in the penis."

"Oh my god." I lowered my forehead to the folding table and stayed there, replaying the horrible moment in my head over and over.

I hope he doesn't report me.

"Do you think he'll report me to HR?" I asked Courtney, forehead still on the table.

"Who is reporting Beck to HR?" I heard Taylor's voice behind me and their heavy steps as they walked across the linoleum to where we sat at the table.

"Adam," Courtney replied with a dreamy sigh, I looked up to see her resting her cheek on her fist and staring off at the wall behind us, a glaze over her eyes. If I had to guess, she was picturing him shirtless or something. Taylor grabbed the chair next to me and tossed their brown paper lunch bag onto the table.

"What did you do?" Taylor inquired with raised eyebrows as they pulled out their sandwich.

I refused to fill them in so Courtney happily did so.

Leaving out no detail.

"…But in conclusion, I think Beck is safe from being reported," Courtney finished, taking some more gulps from her cooling coffee.

"You think so?" Taylor asked around a mouthful of food.

"Um, yes. The sexual tension when they both got a hold of themselves was *thick*." Courtney lowered her voice as she said this part, giving Taylor a knowing look. Taylor slapped their hands on the table and leaned into our conversation more.

"No!" Taylor whisper-exclaimed like they couldn't believe it.

"I can't help it! He's so good looking, it should be illegal." I tried to defend myself.

"And you think he's on the same page?" Taylor asked, crumbs spilling out of their mouth. They quickly wiped them off the table and onto the floor.

"Yes." Courtney responded at the same time I said, "No."

I turned to look at Courtney, who turned to look at me. We both blinked at each other, waiting for the other person to take back what they said.

Guess that wasn't happening.

"I'm not saying that I don't think I am good looking, too. I just don't think he's shown any indication that he's looking at me the same way I'm looking at him…" I sipped obnoxiously from my mug, making a lot of noise just to irritate Courtney.

She glared at me and snatched the mug out of my hand, making some coffee dribble down my chin as I laughed at her reaction.

"I think he isn't as inexperienced with attraction and

therefore knows how to handle himself better," Courtney shrugged, "But, I could be totally wrong."

Though the way her brown gaze slid over to Taylor in a conspiratorial way told me she absolutely thought she was right.

I huffed out a breath, still not totally convinced.

When Courtney discovered my secret stash of romance novels in college, she admitted that she had never really gone out of her way to read one. She seemed so genuinely curious about this secret hobby of mine that I felt compelled to give her some of my recommendations. I didn't think she would read them, I thought she was mostly humoring me.

Nope. She read them. All of them.

Often I would wake up in our dorm room to a light glow reflecting off the ceiling. I knew if I rolled over I would see her curled up with her iPad just binge-reading romance novels. I tried to tell her that she didn't have to keep reading them just to be polite, to which she rolled her eyes at me and said that she truly did enjoy reading romance.

"The sex scenes are the best part!" she would tell me, "Why doesn't everyone read romance? The *pining*, the *character flaws*, the *baggage*, ugh!" She would dramatically flop herself down on the bed after.

When someone in one of our general classes started to tease her for reading a romance novel out in public (they just had to look at the cover and title to figure out the genre), Courtney pinned them with a hard look and gave them a prepared monologue about how internalized misogyny had made it socially acceptable to watch movies and read books that are graphic or gory or allow bad things to happen to women. Then, as soon as a woman started to express her interest in consuming a story where generally good things happen to women, it was suddenly cheap and not taken seriously.

No one in our circles openly judged Courtney and me for reading romance after that.

All of this to say, Courtney grabbed my hobby of reading romance and took off with it without turning back. She loved setting people up, watching The Bachelorette, and daydreaming about various couples finding their happily ever after. It was also part of her motive for setting me up on blind dates and warning me when she thought a man was attractive. She was a schemer and had successfully gotten several peers to date each other—though, only about half of those ended up in lasting relationships.

So, I sat there at the break table, suspicious of my longest friend.

Not that the idea of Adam being into me as well wasn't thrilling. It made a type of energy buzz in my veins, but still.

"Well, time will tell I guess," Taylor shrugged while shoving the rest of their sandwich into their mouth, bidding us farewell with a mouthful, "Later, c-words."

Courtney and I both snickered as they got up and left.

My phone vibrated in my pocket so I pulled it out to see who could possibly be calling me. If it was a phone call, it was probably a robot wanting to steal my credit card information. Anyone who wanted to reach me either FaceTimed or texted.

Or sent me a funny video to watch.

Then I saw my mom's contact flash on the screen, and a ball of anxiety formed in the pit of my stomach.

I ignored the call and pocketed my phone.

"Who was that?" Courtney asked, seeing what I just did.

"My mom," I replied, my mood no longer anxious, just...numb.

"Oh, yikes," Courtney grabbed both of our mugs and took them to the sink, "Looks like we are rewatching *Ted Lasso* tonight!" She tried to cheer me up, knowing what kind of moods my family put me in.

5

I was curled up on the couch with Gram and Courtney. All of us were on a single three-person couch. With Gram being so lean we could all three fit comfortably. We each had our own blankets and Gram had her feet propped up on the coffee table with a pillow under her heels. Courtney and I had our legs curled up into each other as we drank our nighttime teas, happily watching Jason Sudeikis become kindness personified on the screen.

Gram reached over and gave my leg a comforting squeeze as we laughed at a classic back and forth between the two main characters of the show.

I was grateful to be where I was, even though my relationship with my parents was strained.

I grew up in a very strict religious household. Gram's son, my father, married a woman who was committed to her faith and he happily converted. Then they had me.

When I say strict and religious, I don't just mean strict church attendance and Bible study. I had been in therapy for the past five years because of the ideas and conspiracies I was raised with. It wasn't until I graduated from college that I fully realized my relationship with my parents wasn't healthy and that I needed to set boundaries.

Gram visited as much as she could growing up, however, she couldn't stand to hear a lot of the hateful teachings my dad would happily spew despite how she raised him, so I didn't get to know her as well as I would have liked. Once I decided to go to college (not a small religious one, to my parent's chagrin) I decided to try reaching out to Gram, and I was so glad that I did. Gram helped me through a lot of questions and concerns about who I was as a person versus who my parents expected me to be, and she taught me that it was okay to carve my own path in this world no matter how my parents raised me.

Just like her son was allowed to do.

My parents became very bitter and distrustful in my college years, telling me that the Devil was leading me astray and that my Gram was a lost cause and would only bring me pain and stress.

What actually brought me pain and stress as a child was being told that all my friends at school who were LGBTQ+ wouldn't make it to heaven and that I was expected to get married as soon as possible and pop out babies.

Babies I was expected to pop out without any sort of formal sex education, because of sinful thoughts and stuff.

When my graduation deadline was approaching my parents started reaching out to me again more and more despite my growing relationship with Gram. They kept sending me pictures and profiles of young men in our religious community and asking me if I'd like to be set up on a date now that I was done with college.

Because heaven forbid, I actually used my degree and did anything else than become a housewife.

Women had their specific place in my parents' world (such as, at the side of a "righteous" young man) and that was a world I absolutely had no desire to be part of. Hence, my choice to go out of my way not to visit them since graduating college and instead moving closer to Gram.

My dad was Gram's only family since her husband divorced her during the 70s when she spoke openly for women's rights. He then died in the early two thousands, so I had never really formed a relationship with my grandpa. Not that I wanted to, because it sounded like he and my dad had very similar ideas when it came to the roles of men and women (and no other gender).

Gram was a brainwashed hippy that ended up leading me down the path of darkness, and here we are. If it wasn't for Courtney and Gram holding my hand emotionally through my early twenties, I had no idea where I'd be or what I would be doing.

Every six months or so my mom still tried to reach out to me.

Sometimes it was a phone call, sometimes it was an email, and sometimes it was messages via social media. It started out innocent enough, asking how my job was going and how Gram was doing health wise. Then she always found a way to start preaching to me about what the current religious leaders were saying, and how I still had time to repent for my sins and come back to the fold before the end of days came.

End of days, because my parents were all about doomsday prepping. Not in the sense that they liked to be prepared in case of emergencies like floods and fires. No, they truly believed that the entire world would just explode one day when God flew across the sky, or something like that.

Don't worry, my family would be saved, of course.

My parents told me not to bother going to college or getting a degree because God would come and burn the earth before I had a chance to graduate.

So yes, many years of therapy and healthy boundary setting later, I was here in my happy simple life with my chosen family.

It was not easy, having little to no contact with my own parents. People who I grew up believing I could trust forever, putting them up on this pedestal only to realize literally every aspect of their beliefs and theologies were blatantly wrong, delusional, and degrading.

That's where Gram and Courtney came in. I didn't even have to answer the phone call from my mom to be put in a low mood, and I sure as hell didn't listen to the voicemail she left me.

"Oh, I forgot!" Courtney shot up from the couch and ran up the stairs toward her bedroom. She returned stomping down the stairs and hopped off the last step, holding up a small tincture in her hands as she walked over to Gram and me.

"I got this at the dispensary today," Courtney announced. If someone would have told me as a child that I would be openly consuming cannabis oil with my grandmother, I would have been horrified.

"Oh, what is it?" Gram asked, holding her mug out at the same time. Courtney pinched the dropper and added some to Gram's tea. I held my mug out as well.

"It's got equal amounts of THC and CBD, but it's a fairly high dosage, similar to if you took a full 10mg gummy, but a cinnamon flavor," Courtney explained while she dropped some into my mug, then I used the tea bag to help stir the contents.

"Mmm, I'm going to sleep so well tonight," Gram sipped her spiked tea and smiled happily.

I also sipped it, surprised that I wasn't tasting weed at all.

"It tastes good, doesn't it?" Courtney asked while spiking her own tea. Gram and I hummed and nodded our approval.

I wasn't a huge drinker, but marijuana had been able to calm my mind in a way that other methods just hadn't been able to. Transitioning from a constantly anxious child and teenager who feared the world, to a functioning adult, had been much easier since Courtney introduced me to marijuana in college. I was grateful to live in a state where it was legalized and easy to access, even if it did have a crazy high tax.

"This show is about to be ten times funnier," Courtney snuggled back onto the couch on the other side of Gram, pulling the blankets up to her chin, "Oh, also, Beck sack-tapped Adam today."

"What?" Gram reached forward and paused the TV, turning to look at me with wide-eyed concern.

Thanks, Court.

A night with Gram and Courtney was just what I needed to keep from spiraling into a mood. I slept great, thanks to the tincture Courtney gave us, and I woke up with a glow that allowed me to get back into my normal routine.

6

The next couple of weeks went by smoothly and I didn't get any more messages from either of my parents, which was a good sign. They used to be way more persistent to get my attention in years past but recently seemed to be getting the message. I think the last time I had spoken on the phone with my mom was half a year ago, and that call only lasted about 10 minutes.

It was the usual, Mom calling with her sweet voice asking about how my work and life were, asking how Gram and Courtney were doing. The normal family check in topics. Then when the conversation came to a natural lull, Mom started in with her latest interpretations of the Bible and I hung up on her without another word.

I could not be clearer about where I stood with them. My mom didn't reach out to me for a couple more weeks after that until I got an email explaining how I needed to stop overreacting to her knowledge of the Bible. Which I also ignored.

Then I got that phone call and voicemail from her two weeks ago, a voicemail I still hadn't listened to. However, the fact that I hadn't gotten any follow up communication was a good sign.

Having the concern about my parents trying to weasel their way into my life was a good distraction for my new work situation. The work situation was that my crush on my new coworker hadn't waned off in the slightest.

Courtney hadn't followed up with me about it, meaning she didn't tease me about actually having sexual feelings. Which was both nice but also unnerving. I felt bad whenever Courtney felt like she needed to tiptoe around me because she worried that I might unravel easily.

I had one appointment with my therapist, who I used to see weekly during college but now saw on an as-needed basis. I told her everything because she was my therapist and that's how that worked, and she was very happy to know that I was confidently feeling attraction towards another human being. She was never worried about what my sexuality was defined as, but more worried that my strict religious upbringing naturally programmed my brain to view sex as something wrong or unhealthy.

I mean, it sounded pretty textbook when you thought about it.

Thankfully, she helped me deprogram a lot of those unconscious thoughts and feelings toward sexuality, which I think is what helped me have a somewhat successful sexual relationship with my college boyfriend Spencer.

I asked what her advice was regarding getting over these feelings because it wasn't like I met Adam in a bar, or literally any place that was more appropriate than work. She just looked at me funny and gave me a smirk before telling me she would get back to me about it at our next session. Whenever that was.

The good news was that I haven't had any awkward run ins with Adam those past two weeks either. Meaning I didn't speak with him at all. I'd see him in passing since he was usually in the PT part of the building and I was good at staying in the Speech wing, but I haven't had to speak to him or provide anything besides a polite smile.

Not that he had ever smiled in return. I had mostly just been receiving chin lifts from him and, one time, an actual head nod.

So that's how that was going.

Today I wanted to actually speak with him, since one of our clients needed to adjust their schedule so that they didn't have to drive back and forth to the facility throughout the week for multiple therapies. The mom requested that we do speech first and PT right after so she could cut her driving down. Meaning that after Speech I would hand off the kiddo to Adam, and that would also give mom an hour and a half to run errands or get nails done or do whatever parents need to do to stay sane.

So, I sent out a text to the scheduler to let them know about the potential change and that I just needed to confirm with Adam. Though I doubted that it would be a problem since I saw that the time slot on Mondays was open on the team calendar.

I turned the corner and I saw the PT part of the building, which was just a large open concept area with half walls dividing the space here and there, so multiple PTs could have multiple sessions at once. Over on the red and yellow play mats, I saw that dark red hair of his first and then took in Adam as his large frame crouched down over a small client.

I blinked twice to let my eyes adjust and tried to calm my heart, which still picked up pace every time I looked at the man. Though that immediately proved difficult when I took in the scene in front of me.

Adam was crouching down on his knees in front of a baby. By the look and size of the kiddo, I would have guessed that they were between eight and ten months of age. Adam must have been doing some sort of initial assessment because he was shaking a colorful rattle with lots of dangle hoops and ribbons in front of the baby to keep the baby's attention. Adam's face was completely relaxed as he slowly moved the rattle side to side, encouraging the baby to move their head in the same direction.

My heart exploded at the sweetness of it.

After testing how far the baby could turn their head, he gently set the rattle down before mumbling a low, "good job" to the baby as he took their chubby ankles and gently tested their leg flexibility.

I was frozen in place.

Seeing Adam's large hands being so careful and sweet with a small human was enough to make my ovaries explode apparently. I was trying to breathe evenly through my nose, but when he took the baby and gently sat them up to test their balance, I had to stop myself from making an embarrassing squeak sound at the cuteness of it.

He was wearing all black. Another long-sleeved Henley shirt with black jogger pants that hugged his body. He wasn't wearing shoes, because the PT area had a lot of mats and foam equipment that could easily be torn up by sneakers, so his bright green socks stuck out in contrast to his dark outfit.

His thick hair looked like it had been trimmed lately, and I could see a light shadow of scruff around his jaw as if he hadn't shaved this morning. It was too short for me to determine the color, so I was still left wondering if it was going to be red or brown, or blonde.

Courtney was right the last time she brought it up because Adam was definitely muscled. I hated that I noticed since he was literally covered from ankles to wrists, and because I would be uncomfortable if a coworker noticed things like that about me and fixated on it. I tried to blink a few more times as if it would clear my vision and focused on his face again.

His light brown eyes flicked up and met my gaze as if he sensed me there ogling him. I could feel the heat of my blush color my cheeks as soon as he noticed me.

It was like I was in middle school all over again.

"Hey, uh, I can come back if you're busy," I jerked a thumb over my shoulder and took a step back, clearly hesitating.

"Did you need something?" Adam asked, glancing back down at the baby that he was now helping turn over onto their tummy. He gently let them collapse on the mat before adjusting their arms and legs to see how they could handle being in a crawling position. The baby stayed still, looking around curiously but not moving their legs. Adam took hold of their torso and started to slowly rock them back and forth to encourage the movement.

"I just wanted to ask you about your schedule. Emmett's mom wanted to lump her appointments together on Monday, so..." I trailed off when the baby looked up at me and gave me a large gummy smile, "Hi, sweetheart!" I couldn't help myself, I stepped a little bit closer and sat down on my knees in front of them.

"Who is this little one?" I ask, smiling back. They looked away from me for a moment before turning back, mimicking my smile.

"This is Claire," Adam responded, his low voice calm and soothing.

If I had any reservations about a male PT working with young kids before, those were all gone now. I had heard other therapists in the office talk about how well Adam worked with the kids and seeing him handle this infant was my own confirmation. I was skeptical because he didn't smile or act super friendly with other adults, but maybe he just liked kids better.

I completely understood why some adults didn't like kids.

I also completely understood why some adults preferred kids.

"Is Claire a new client?" I asked, wiggling my fingers at her. Adam turned her over onto her back again and held up the rattle for her to grab from him. I was immediately put on the back burner for her attention as she grasped the rattle with both hands and gently pulled the toy to her mouth.

"Potentially," Adam replied, "Her mom thinks she might be on the spectrum."

I raised my eyebrows at that, the child generally needed severe delays to be diagnosed with ASD that early. Neurologists liked to wait until the child was at least three or four years old before giving an official medical diagnosis because it was hard to be conclusive. Turns out, it was hard to tell if some behaviors are ASD-specific or if it was just the behavior of your average baby or toddler.

Adam raised a shoulder at my expression, "She isn't army crawling yet, and doesn't seem to have a desire to. She has been delayed with every gross motor milestone so far. She also stares at a lot of ceiling fans."

"Huh," I looked at the baby, who was still focused on her toy.

"So, Emmett's mom?" Adam asked, reminding me why I was there. I shook my head once and tore my gaze away from the cute baby to look at the handsome man in front of me. My gaze kept bouncing between his beautiful hair, his beautiful whiskey-colored eyes, and the freckles on the bridge of his nose.

"She wants to come in Mondays to meet with me, and then have Emmett meet with you right after. I saw that you had that time free on the schedule, but I wanted to double check with you in case you had promised that time slot to another client." I explained, my gaze landing on his mouth. I inhaled through my nose and glanced back down at the infant between us. She was looking up at the ceiling as she mouthed her toy.

"Yeah, that's fine." Adam nodded once and glanced back down at the baby. I heard footsteps behind me and saw his gaze lift to the person approaching over my shoulder.

"Sorry about that!" A woman's voice panted, "I didn't mean to be on the phone the whole time. How is she doing?" The mother set her bag down to the side of us and crouched down to our level. She was smiling brightly at Adam and then noticed me and held her hand out.

"I'm Mallory, are you a Physical Therapist too?" The woman had bleach blonde hair with a fake tan and wore a white tank top with acid washed jean shorts. Her blue eyes kept bouncing between Adam and me.

"Oh, no, I apologize. I just had a question for Adam," I made my way to scoot back and give them space, but then remembered her outstretched hand, "I'm Beck, I'm a speech therapist here."

"Oh, speech? Could I ask you some questions?" Her blue eyes widened at me pleadingly. Technically, we should have scheduled a formal appointment for me to assess her daughter, but I could read the strain in her facial features that told me she was genuinely concerned.

"Um, sure. I have some time," I adjusted my kneel and crisscrossed my legs as I glanced at baby Claire again. She was just too cute and had the same blue eyes as her momma.

"Claire isn't saying anything yet." I nodded my head once and made eye contact with the mom. Waiting. Nothing else. No actual question. Okay then.

"Are you concerned?" I asked, clarifying.

"Well, yes, the other kids at the park are at least saying momma and dada, but Claire just isn't. She's babbling, of course, but nothing specific," The mother physically deflated in front of me. I glanced down at the baby again, who had just randomly turned her head and noticed her mom for the first time and started wiggling with excitement.

Huh.

"Her motor movement isn't super concerning," Adam chimed in, reigning the parent back in for the assessment she actually paid for. "Her neck control is good, and she doesn't seem too flexible or too stiff. When prompted, she can…" I tuned the rest of Adam's words out as I studied Claire a little more intently. She continued to stare at her mom with the love that all babies show their parents but kept glancing around the room as well. It wasn't until Adam physically moved to adjust his seated position that the baby's gaze landed on him.

I leaned forward.

"So, she's just delayed for no reason?" The mom asked, not in a rude way, but in a way that told us she didn't know where to go from there.

"Not necessarily, there just aren't any obvious reasons that I can see in the forty minutes I have been working with her," Adam's voice was calm and collected. I looked around the room and saw the infant toy bin Adam must have gotten the rattle from. I reached inside and pulled out a different rattle that sang a little song when you pushed a button.

"But would you still be willing to work with her? If we made appointments to help her get up to speed?" The mother asked. Adam nodded his head and glanced back down at the baby, who has now focused on her rattle again.

"I'm sorry to interrupt, but can I try something?" I waited until there was a lull in their conversation before asking. Adam just looked at me with a curious expression while the mom nodded her head with encouragement.

"Please, you're the experts," The mother smiled at me and I smiled back. I reached for baby Claire and scooted a few feet back on the mat, making her mom and Adam out of sight. I smiled encouragingly at Claire and removed her rattle from her. Thankfully, she didn't wail.

I then placed the new rattle that played music above her head on the mat to where she couldn't see it and pressed the button to turn it on. When Twinkle Twinkle Little Star played, Claire just kept looking at me and cooing like babies do.

I moved the rattle to the side, and Claire didn't seem to acknowledge the rattle at all.

I then reached forward for the rattle and held it up in front of Claire's face, who went wide eyed and started happily wiggling when she saw the new colorful toy.

"Huh," I said out loud.

"What?" The mother asked.

As Claire was teething on the new rattle, I held both of my hands on either side of her head and gently snapped my fingers a few inches away from her ears.

Right side, she didn't acknowledge at all.

Left side, Claire turned her head and looked at my hand that had snapped.

I tried the right hand again, and she didn't move at all.

I reached over her and snapped my fingers above her head on the mat, and she didn't follow the sound.

"Have you had her hearing checked?" I asked, maybe a little more bluntly than I should have.

"She's been to see the pediatrician regularly, and she's up to date on all her vaccinations," the mother responded. That wasn't an answer to my question, but I understood it. Mothers received all sorts of judgment no matter how they parented, so excess information given by parents out of fear of being scolded for 'not doing enough' was common in this field.

"Do you know if the hospital where she was born did a

newborn hearing screening?" I clarified. In the state of California, it was law for hospitals to conduct newborn hearing screenings before being discharged from the hospital. It was how a lot of babies got diagnosed with hearing loss early on, which was important. Unfortunately, other states don't have those same regulations and it was common for kids not to be diagnosed with hearing loss until closer to age two or three when their speech delay was actually worth acknowledging.

"Can you call her name?" I asked.

"Claire! Claire, where's mommy?" Claire didn't acknowledge her mother's voice at all. She didn't even flinch in the direction her mom's voice came from.

After no response after a couple of tries the mom stopped calling for her daughter, physically deflating, "This is another reason why I am worried about her being on the spectrum. She doesn't respond to her name at all."

I snapped my fingers on either side of Claire's head again. Not even a flinch on her right side, but she checked in with my hand on the left.

"I'm not an audiologist, so take what I say with a grain of salt," I started, smiling at Claire who smiled back at me, "But I would recommend having her hearing checked. She isn't responding to distant sounds, and she is barely checking in with sounds on her left side. Does she usually look for you when you call her name?"

"...No, she doesn't..." the mother's shoulders sagged. This is the difficult part of my field. It was normal for parents to want their kids to be perfect, and I empathized with that. However the sooner parents came to terms with any sort of complication their child had, the sooner their child could learn and thrive despite those challenges.

"I can give you a couple of pediatric audiologists or ENT's names if you're interested, it might be worth at least ruling it out." I picked up Claire and set her down between my legs. I turned her around so she could see her mom and Adam, and then held my hands on either side of her head to snap my fingers again.

Even facing a different direction, Claire didn't respond to the snap on her right side but reflexively glanced to her left.

My hearing loss senses were tingling.

"So, you think she's deaf?" The mother asked. Again, I sensed no accusation or threat from her tone, just clarification.

"Not completely. I really don't know," I shrugged, scooting back to Adam and the mom, only keeping my gaze on the mom, "I doubt she's completely deaf, but she's clearly favoring her left side. If her hearing is unbalanced, that could be why she's experiencing gross motor delays as well."

Adam didn't say anything, but I noticed that his brow furrowed at my words. *Oh shit*, I was probably overstepping. I had basically hijacked his whole assessment.

"What does hearing have to do with gross motor?" The mother asked, reaching out for Claire when I lifted the infant up out of my lap.

"Maybe more than you think," I let out a sigh and wondered how much I should even say without an official diagnosis, but my gut told me I was right. "Let's say one of her ears is perfect, and the other ear is completely deaf. There are many studies showing evidence of imbalanced hearing affecting a developing child's equilibrium. Sound plays a big role in dizziness, balance, and all those things. Sometimes if the hearing is unbalanced enough, it can feel like constant vertigo."

I smiled at the mom, trying to be reassuring instead of instilling fear into her, "We have a number of deaf or hard of hearing kids here, and they all have similar gross motor delays as Claire. It's not that they won't ever feel balanced, but sometimes they just need a little help because they're dealing with something other kids don't have to. They are on their own timelines."

The mother, whose name still escaped me, nodded her head and looked down at Claire. I could see her brain working. She was probably cataloging every interaction with Claire that she could remember.

"Keep in mind, I'm not an audiologist, I'm a speech therapist, so I recommend going to an audiologist to either confirm unbalanced hearing or rule out hearing loss completely." My gut told me at least one of Claire's ears wasn't working well, I was honestly surprised her mom hadn't picked up on it. Though, I could understand how when you're with a child twenty-four seven that sometimes parents were just trying to get through the day. Naturally, she probably ruled out certain behaviors as just Claire's personality.

She noticed enough about Claire's behavior to suspect autism, at least.

"That's good to know, thanks for thinking of that," Claire dropped her rattle and then immediately reached for her mom's hand, pulling it towards her mouth.

Teething must be fun to deal with.

"No problem, sorry to hijack Adam's assessment," I gave him a sheepish smile, hopefully, to let him know that I was apologetic while also trying to make the mother comfortable.

"No worries, I wouldn't have even thought to check for that," Adam admitted, shaking his head once and going to stand. He then reached a hand out to help the mom up while I also stood. Having gotten the information I needed from Adam, I waved as I started to leave the PT area.

"It was nice to meet you!" I called to the mother as I departed. She gave me a shy smile but then turned her full body towards Adam. As soon as he crossed his arms over his chest to continue discussing the details of Claire's motor delays I made myself look away. I already saw myself staring too much at the muscles in his arms as they strained against the fabric of his long sleeves.

I made it back to my office before patting myself on the back for having a normal conversation with Adam, and a potential client's parent, without doing or saying something completely embarrassing.

I just had to take a few deep breaths and calm my heart now that I wasn't in his presence.

7

I never knew what kinds of conversations I would walk in on with Courtney and Taylor in the break room, but I truly wasn't expecting this one about a week later.

"I think she started to say 'good boy' or something, but then must have remembered I'm me, so she just started saying 'good, good...good' and just got stuck on that," Taylor chuckled while Courtney snorted. I pulled up a seat across from Courtney while Taylor sat at the end of the table.

"Did you say anything about it after?" Courtney asked, taking a bite of her sandwich. We both had tuna salad sandwiches packed that Gram made us. Along with a snack pack, as if we were off to elementary school instead of our adult jobs.

Because Gram was the fucking best.

"No, I don't really have a praise kink, so I don't think it would have mattered either way." Taylor smiled again as they took a large gulp of their Dr. Pepper.

"Ugh, I would be *so* mortified!" Courtney shook her head and finished off her sandwich, leaning back in her chair and tilting her head to the side before asking her next question, "...Do I have a praise kink?"

Taylor and I both glanced at each other, neither of us

knowing how to answer her. Courtney looked at both of us, clearly expecting something.

"How the hell would we know?" I finally asked. I thought I heard heavy footsteps behind me enter the break room, and Taylor and Courtney flicked their glances over my shoulder to see who arrived. I figured the kink portion of the conversation would wrap up with whoever entered the room, but I was wrong.

"Well, I like being acknowledged for my hard work, and my love languages are quality time and words of affirmation," Courtney explained.

"That's different from a praise kink," Taylor explained, leaning their arms on the table, "Do you like it when your partner tells you 'good job' when you're intimate, or do something they like?"

"I...think so? But doesn't everyone?" Courtney tilted her head to the side to ponder as the chair next to me scraped against the linoleum flooring. I was hit with a subtle woodsy scent that smelled really good. As I took a drink from my water bottle I looked to my left to see who was sitting next to me when Adam's beautiful face came into view, his glance flickering over everyone at the table.

I almost choked, but I powered through and cleared my throat after taking a sip and set my bottle on the table.

"I don't think I have a praise kink." Courtney continued when nobody said anything else to the contrary.

"We don't kink shame here," Taylor reassured her.

"Good to hear, so I think you all should share with the group what yours are so that I can figure out if I have unexplored kinks or not." Courtney leaned her elbows on the table and rested her chin on her two fists, glancing around at everyone. As if this was normal. As if all parties involved were close enough with each other to do this. Acknowledging the fact that Adam was sitting right next to me I quickly lowered my gaze to my sandwich and snack pack.

"Hmm..." Taylor stared down at the table for a moment, "Spanking. Definitely spanking."

"You like to be spanked, or doing the spanking?" Courtney clarified. My cheeks were burning. I could feel Adam's gaze on all of us as he unloaded his lunch, his elbow accidentally grazing my arm. I felt my whole body stiffen at the touch.

"If the person is into it, I like to do the spanking, obviously," I glanced up just in time to see Taylor wink at Courtney, who snorted in response.

"Spanking is pretty vanilla though," Courtney shrugged.

"We don't kink shame here," I repeated Taylor's earlier words to try to participate in the conversation an appropriate amount so that I wasn't unusually silent. Taylor lifted their knuckles for a fist bump from me and I returned the gesture. Then I realized my speaking up was a mistake because that set Courtney's sights on me.

"Okay, do you have any kinks to share with the class that isn't super vanilla?" Courtney asked me, her raised eyebrows and wide eyes letting me know that she was teasing me.

I felt a new wave of blush stain my cheeks and face, and I gulped down a dry bite of the sandwich before uncontrollably letting my eyes flicker over to Adam next to me.

He was just sitting there, a sandwich of his own in both of his large hands, his gaze meeting mine at the same time I glanced over at him. He was sitting so close to me. I could see the different highlights of red in his hair from where the sun probably bleached it, and I could see his nose freckles. As his light brown eyes met mine I stopped breathing for a few moments before glancing back to Courtney and rolling my eyes at her.

"C'mon, Beck, I know you must be wild in the bedroom. You're too kind and normal in the real world to not have any secrets like that." Taylor egged me on. I raised an eyebrow at them.

"Real world? So, when you're having sex you're no longer in the real world?" I asked, hoping to divert the subject. I couldn't believe I had just said the word sex in front of Adam when his arm was centimeters away from mine. We were basically breathing the same air. We might as well have been having sex.

Don't you dare fucking think about sex with Adam at work.

"Not if you're doing it right, no." Courtney nodded in agreement with Taylor. I quirked my lips to the side at that. I've never felt "out of this world" in bed. With Spencer, I was able to get off, and that was a relief when it happened. Though Courtney once told me that she had blacked out during one of her orgasms. I couldn't even comprehend that level of stimulation and I used a variety of vibrators regularly.

"So, is this what you guys do to make up for being around children all day? Just go straight for the adult topics?" Adam asked before taking a bite of his meatball sub.

The three of us all nodded our heads with various responses like, "Yup" and "Of course."

"Huh," Adam's brows furrowed a little at that, his voice

was low and manly, but his tone sounded almost…playful. "I guess I'm about to learn a lot more about my coworkers than I expected to."

"Yeeee!" Taylor stood up from their seat to bump knuckles with Adam who smirked in their direction. Again, I found myself wondering what a full smile from him looked like.

I finished my sandwich, but my pulse was thrumming in my veins from Adam's presence, and how at ease he felt at sitting with us. Almost as if he was going to be part of our work friend group. I started thinking about the possibility of talking to him every day and seeing him at lunch, and my heart rate started to spike again. Courtney must have noticed the shift in my mood because I caught her eye as she lifted a subtle eyebrow at me as if to ask, is everything okay?

I nodded once but decided to skip the snack pack. I threw it in the brown paper bag and decided to suddenly stand up and excuse myself.

Yup. I ran away.

To be fair, it was a tried-and-true MO. I ran away from my own family, after all, why should friends be any different?

***

A week or so later I was sitting at my desk filling out a report on one of my clients when the lights started flickering. I was listening to music in my hearing aids, so I wouldn't have heard a knock at the door. However, this facility was very accommodating and installed one of those doorbells that forgoes making noise and instead connects to the lamps. It made my office very deaf friendly.

I tapped my phone to pause my music and turned to glance out my office window. I saw Adam standing there and froze for a second. It was a second too long because I saw his dark brow furrow a little before I snapped out of it and stood out of my chair to open my office door.

"Sorry, I was in the zone," I apologized. I needed to stop apologizing. There was a week when Courtney would pinch me every time she thought I apologized unnecessarily, and after having multiple bruises on both of my arms she said I was hopeless and gave up.

"No worries, I just wanted to catch you up on Mallory and Claire," Adam leaned against the doorframe of my office, similar to how he held himself on his first day. I realized then that the woodsy smell I caught a whiff of in the break room was him. He smelled really good. I couldn't catalog the specific scent. Was it pine? Sage?

"Oh, alrighty," I went back to my chair and sat down to face him. For some reason both standing and holding a conversation with someone who I considered to be the world's most attractive man felt too difficult.

"She ended up seeing an audiologist and they did something called a sedated ABR?" Adam asked.

"Right. ABRs usually take an hour or two. Plus, they stick a ton of sensors all over the head, which is impossible to do on a wiggly infant unless they're asleep for it." I filled him in. He blinked at me once before nodding his head and clearing his throat.

"Yeah, so I guess you were right," Adam let his glance flick across my office before landing back on me, "She has severe hearing loss in her right ear, and only mild loss in her left. Unbalanced, like you guessed."

"That explains why she could hear some noise on her

left side," I nodded, leaning back in my chair, "So, are you going to meet with her then? Help her out with balance and crawling?"

"Yup, Mallory already set Claire up to meet with me once a week, but she probably won't start Speech or anything until she's closer to two." I nodded my head. The mom should start using ASL with Claire, but I had already offered a ton of unsolicited advice, and parents usually needed some time to adjust to the reality of having a kid with setbacks like hearing loss, so I held my tongue.

I smiled at him, happy it all seemed to be working out and that Claire was on the right path to get the help she needed.

The corner of Adam's mouth tipped up on one end; another smirk.

"Anyways, they probably wouldn't have discovered that if you hadn't been there while I was assessing her. So, thank you." Adam cleared his throat at the end and then shoved his hands in the pockets of his black joggers.

God, he was so good looking. It was unfair. He was just leaning against a wall, and I wanted to climb him.

"No problem, I'm glad I could help." I was. That was genuine. Adam nodded once, and when he didn't say anything else but kept his gaze on mine, I started to feel my flush start to creep into my cheeks again.

"Was there anything else...?" I sucked my top lip between my teeth, a nervous habit that made me look like a troll according to Courtney, but I was willing to potentially look like a troll if it helped me hold a conversation with Adam without coughing or hacking or saying something ridiculous.

"I, um," he reached up and rubbed the back of his neck

with his hand, and it made his arm muscles flex underneath his shirt. I bit my top lip a little harder than necessary, "…I'll just ask. I'm assuming you have hearing loss as well? I mean, Courtney told me you were hard of hearing…but I don't really know what that means."

I blinked at him. My top lip was released from my teeth as I took him in. He looked somewhat anxious, and I noticed that his forearm was flexing in a way that made me suspect he was tapping the back of his neck with one of his fingers. It looked like a nervous tic. Was this because he didn't know if I would be offended by his question or not?

"Was me sack tapping you because I didn't hear you walk up beside me not an obvious enough sign?" I found myself smirking at him, and I swore I saw a hint of a blush form on his sharp cheekbones, emphasizing his nose freckles a bit more. His light brown eyes glanced down at his feet as he sealed his lips shut in an attempt to smother the chuckle that erupted from him.

"It seemed pretty obvious then, but I just wanted to know more about it. We'll be working together, you know, so…" he let his sentence trail off as his whiskey-colored eyes lifted back up to meet mine. I felt my heart jump and then get stuck in my throat. He was curious about my condition, which made the immature part of me swoon because instinctively I wanted to interpret the curiosity as care.

Then I took in his words and realized he was probably just being practical. If one of his coworkers had hearing loss, he would probably need to make accommodations to work with them more efficiently.

Yeah. That's what was happening.

"I'm not completely deaf when I'm not wearing my hearing aids, but I only really pick up lower tones and voices. It's still nearly impossible for me to interpret words without me reading the person's lips as well though." I pointed to my own lips as if it was possible for him to not know what lips were.

"Ah, but I noticed that you wear hearing aids. So, when you wear the aids you can hear fine?" Adam asked, shoving both of his hands back into his pockets. He crossed one ankle over the other and I saw the toe of his shoe start to lightly tap the ground.

Definitely a nervous fidgeter.

"Fine is a good word for it," I smiled at him, because he was too handsome not to smile at, but also because I wanted him to feel at ease asking me about this. "It's not the same as someone with perfect hearing, it sounds a little more mechanical and there's static at times. But it's worth it to me to wear them still, obviously. Otherwise, I just wouldn't."

"…Can I ask when you were diagnosed?" Adam asked, his foot tapping starting to decrease in speed.

I almost let my smile slip from my face but tried to play off the slip as me thinking back to when I was diagnosed by letting my gaze land on the wall behind him and quirking my lips to the side as if I was thinking.

"I wasn't given an actual diagnosis until I was older. Closer to ten, I think," I tried to summarize the story as much as possible "I didn't grow up in a place with a lot of medical knowledge available, and the doctors think that my hearing loss was very mild before that. It wasn't until I got sick and had a high fever that the majority of my hearing was shot. I finally saw a doctor and was diagnosed shortly after."

Adam's eyes softened at that. It was a normal reaction, and that wasn't even the full story.

"Ah, I'm sorry," Adam's apology seemed sincere. His foot wasn't tapping anymore, though. Good. I wanted him to be comfortable around me.

Funny, considering until I could get my hormones in check, I wouldn't be comfortable around him.

"It's alright, it hasn't really held me back at all." That was true. The reason I decided to go get brainwashed by a "liberal hippy college" as my parents so lovingly put it, was because they had so many accommodations for deaf and hard of hearing students. That was something I hadn't experienced a lot of during middle and high school. Thanks to those accommodations I became more confident in my studies and was able to pursue a successful career that brought me fulfillment.

"That's great, I can see that," Adam glanced around the office for a moment before looking at me again. "Well, I'll let you get back to work."

"Sounds good," I threw him another smile before grabbing the edge of my desk to turn back around in my chair. "Now you know not to sneak up on me." I winked at him.

Oh god, I winked at him.

That's so uncharacteristically flirty of me.

Don't openly flirt with him at work, Beck!

Adam let out a low chuckle, "Yeah, now I know."

With one departing knock on the doorframe of my office, he left and closed the door behind him. I watched him walk past my office window down the hallway before turning back to my report.

I found myself smiling at my computer screen throughout my work, thinking about that private interaction with Adam. I winked at him and he wasn't offended by it, which was good. Did that mean he was open to flirting? Or maybe he didn't receive it as flirting? These are questions I would need to bounce off Courtney sometime, but I wanted to keep this little interaction to myself a little longer.

The good news was that I was getting better at talking with Adam at work. The bad news was that my body seemed to be getting more and more excited every time I saw him. As if I had some sort of hope that Adam would be interested in me the same way I was interested in him.

I guess it wasn't that out of left field.

I opened up social media and went to my own account, looking through all the pictures that included myself in the shot. I wasn't ugly, I knew that. I didn't think a lot of people in the world were truly unattractive, but I knew that my pale complexion and dark hair were a specific look people were into. My eyes were pretty; probably one of my favorite characteristics about myself. Also, I shared them with my favorite elderly woman in the entire world.

I was blessed in the boob department; I bounced between a B and C cup depending on when I wanted to pretend I was into exercise or not.

I had a narrower waist and wider hips than other women I knew, and some men were into the hourglass shape. Maybe Adam was into my figure as much as I was into his?

"No. Shut it down." I mumbled to myself, swiping out of the app and returning to my report. I hadn't had sex in a very long time, and I hadn't seriously dated anyone in even longer.

The thought of even attempting to start something up with my coworker who I would have to see every day, whether or not we ended up working out, made my stomach churn with fear. I didn't think I was versed enough in sex and dating to be able to handle that experience.

So, for the rest of the afternoon, I did what I thought I did best; shove Adam to the very back of my mind and move on with my day.

8

I had just discovered a new rock band and was listening to their album constantly. I wasn't picky with my music. I had a variety of rock, pop, indie, metal, country, rap, and R&B playlists. I loved finding the right music to reflect my emotions and feelings when I couldn't put them into words myself, and music had been a great escape for me when I was a child in a strict religious home.

You know, before the majority of my hearing was shot with one high fever. Music didn't sound the same with hearing aids, but it was better than nothing.

This rock band was called Carbon Cut and the more I listened to them the more I wanted to share their music with Courtney, who generally wasn't into rock. She was more into Sara Bareilles, Taylor Swift, and Harry Styles.

For now, Carbon Cut was making it easier for me to process the memories of my hearing loss diagnosis during my childhood. I kept getting bombarded by images of my parents assuming I was mentally incapacitated for not hearing their mumblings to me. How they would snap at me when I supposedly ignored their unheard demands. I specifically remembered my parents openly telling other kids and parents that they thought that I was slow.

I kept remembering how inadequate my family made me feel, people who were supposed to make me feel confident and safe. I recalled waking up one morning not being able to hear anything, and how my parents prayed over me in an attempt to allow God to give me my hearing back.

After a few days of this pattern, they realized that their prayers weren't being answered, and decided it might be worth taking me to a pediatrician, who then sent us to an audiologist.

Getting fitted for hearing aids had been fine, although the ear mold casting made my skin crawl for the five minutes it needed to set. I specifically remembered how overwhelming it was when I first put on the hearing aids, and I could actually hear everything for the first time. I never realized how loud fans and AC units were, or how often people lowered their voices out of politeness or privacy.

My parents gaslit me for the rest of my youth about how they had treated me early on, neglecting to take responsibility for my dissociative behavior as a young child.

You know, normal childhood trauma stuff.

When I was closer to thirteen, and Gram came for one of her rare visits to our small town, I learned that she too had hearing loss and had been dealing with it since her twenties. Something my dad had been aware of since he was a child but had failed to ever consider for his own daughter. That was probably the first time I felt truly connected to a member of my family. Gram not only showed me her hearing aids and shared her personal experiences with me, but she also told me about ASL and that I could go online and find videos to learn, in case I didn't have my hearing aids with me.

My parents never showed an interest in ASL or learning the language to communicate with me. Instead, they would just yell at me to put my hearing aids on.

I had tried to give them the benefit of the doubt multiple times. Whenever I would check in with them during college and tell them about how I was learning and how some classes had ASL interpreters or a scribe, my parents seemed genuinely shocked that those options were available, and that they were so helpful to me.

Then I would remember that they purposely went out of their way to isolate themselves and their family in a small town in the middle of California in the name of God, and thought it was better to prepare for the end of the world instead of gaining any sort of continuing education.

Or encouraging their child to get an education.

It was hard to feel empathy for my parents when I was constantly reminded that they purposely chose to stay ignorant of the world around them, in order to preserve a false sense of comfort and control.

I was spiraling and reprocessing all of this as I lay on my queen-sized bed in my bedroom. The room was covered in clutter that included books, knick-knacks from thrift shops, and a couple of spider plants. I was staring up at the ceiling that still had glow in the dark stars (that I stuck on myself years ago to make my inner child happy; thank you, therapy) when the light on my phone flashed. I also felt my comforter vibrate.

The flash only happened with specific notifications. Social media was exhausting so I put those notifications on silent, but the flash and vibrate combination was reserved for phone calls, FaceTime calls, text messages, and work emails.

I reached over and grabbed my phone to hold it up above my face, wondering in the back of my mind when the last time I dropped it on my face was, and if I was overdue.

It was an email, from Pat.

From: Pat Hayes
To: Therapist Staff (all)
RE: Mandatory Retreat

Hi all!

I know you have all been anxiously waiting for details on the upcoming retreat next month, and everything is finally scheduled and locked in.

We are going to Big Bear!

Don't worry, we will be staying in cabins that have plumbing and a working kitchen. It won't be camping as much as it will be an updated housing lodge in the middle of the woods.

We will be leaving Friday morning and will arrive at Big Bear Lake right before lunchtime. Then we will be having team building exercises like canoeing, a ropes course, and obstacle courses.

Saturday will be more team bonding with a fun (and mild) hike, and we will bus back to Orange County on Sunday morning to let you guys unpack and rest before work the following Monday.

This retreat is fully funded by one of our largest donor families, the Halls, and it is mandatory (but if you get sick, please don't come).

Attached is the link to the retreat where we will be staying, as well as a rough schedule of when all the activities will be happening.

There will also be an on-site doctor in the unlikely case of any medical emergencies happening. Please let me know if there is anyone you would like to bunk with specifically since there are not enough rooms for everyone to have their own

If you have any questions, feel free to email me or Christy.

Thanks! Can't wait!
Pat Hayes
Program Director

Well. That was interesting. Our last mandatory retreat was just all of us going to the beach and eating BBQ all day, so it was unexpected for this one to be two overnights in a location about two to three hours away.

I was also skeptical of the scheduling aspect because Pat was not generally the most organized person. She was a great director, as long as she delegated the specifics to other people. Unfortunately, she was also prideful, so delegation rarely happened.

My phone vibrated and flashed again.

Court-Knee: Big Bear! (Bear emoji, fire emoji)

I laughed and responded with a party emoji and fire emoji. The way communication had evolved during the twenty first century was brilliant. The fact that she was down the hall in her bedroom made the text conversation even better in my mind.

My bedroom door suddenly burst open and Courtney was flying towards my bed. I barely rolled out of the way quickly enough before she belly flopped onto the covers, a grunt following her landing.

"Ugh, why is your bed so much comfier than mine?" Courtney whined as she turned to face me.

"Because I make my bed? Because I don't eat popcorn in it and sleep in the crumbs?" We had been over this before.

"Nah, that can't be it. It's got to be the mattress."

"Courtney, we have the same exact mattresses. We bought our mattresses together." Then I frowned at her. "I think we need to spend less time together."

"How dare you suggest such a thing!" Courtney smirked and shoved me toward my headboard. I snorted and laughed. It was rare to find a friendship as close as ours, and though I teased her about us being too close all the time, I loved it. I was my truest self with Courtney and Gram. These connections I had managed to form for myself were very important to me.

"Okay, so you read Pat's email?" Courtney asked, sitting up and sitting crisscrossed on my bed. I scooted up until I was leaning my back against my headboard.

"Yup, you stoked?"

"Of course, but did you notice who donated the funds for it?" Courtney asked, pulling her phone out to I assume pull up the email again.

"Uh, yeah, some family."

"The Halls." Courtney clarified.

"Oh. Right. The Halls."

"You've met them before, right? When they toured the building?" Courtney asked, scooting over to me so we could sit beside each other. She showed me her screen with an internet browser she had pulled up on her phone. Pictured were a basic white family in fancy clothing, a blonde woman, and a dark-haired man with one red-headed son.

"Nope, I haven't."

"What? Really? They come at least twice a year. It's super annoying. None of the other donors come to make sure we aren't squandering their precious donations. Anyway, I'm getting distracted again. Do you know why I thought the last name was familiar?" Courtney raised her blonde eyebrows at me, waiting for me to guess. It took me a second, but I finally got there.

"Wait…isn't Adam's last name technically Hall?"

"Yes, except not technically. It actually is."

I ignored Courtney's jab and glanced at her phone again, right when she swiped the picture away and went to a picture of a shirtless, tattooed man walking out of the ocean.

My jaw dropped.

"Oh my god."

"I know!" Courtney flicked her blonde hair off her shoulder dramatically. "I'm such a super sleuth."

"Uh-huh." I took the phone from her so I could get a

better look at this picture. It looked like it was taken by a professional photographer. Adam was walking out of the ocean carrying a surfboard under his tatted arm, his black wet suit unzipped and tied at his waist, showing off just how muscular Courtney suspected him to be.

It was like looking at a surf model for Sports Illustrated. This could have been a legitimate ad for whatever brand of surfboard he was holding. His red hair looked amazing, even disheveled from the ocean. He wasn't smiling at the camera at all, but his eyes were shimmering due to the light from the sun reflecting off the water. I could barely look away from it.

"I had no idea he was the son of these two!" Courtney continued. I was barely listening to her. I was now confident I knew the reason why he always wore long sleeves at work was that one of his arms was completely tattooed from wrist to shoulder. He had a couple on his ribs and one on the opposite peck of the sleeve he had. They were all earthy, with mountains and trees and bears and birds. They were crisp and beautiful, not the muddy faded tattoos that were damaged by too much sun exposure that I usually saw in Orange County.

Today was the day I learned that I was into tattoos.

"You discovered this very quickly," I inhaled through my nose. Goodness, gracious. Adam was a very sexy chiseled, tattooed, red-headed man.

"Of course, I did. Look what else I found!" Courtney reached over to swipe again, and I saw another picture of Adam in a navy suit without a tie and his arm around a thin blonde.

She was small and beautiful but somehow had legs for

miles. It was obvious by the way he held his arm around her shoulders that they were a couple.

My heart sunk into my stomach.

"Who is that?" I asked.

"I think she's a model for some underwear company," Courtney responded with a wave of her hand as if it wasn't important. My gut churned at that.

So, Adam's type was thin blonde underwear models.

Why did I hate that?

I must have let my facial expression reflect my thoughts because Courtney quickly nudged me with her elbow.

"Hey…what are you thinking right now?" Courtney asked, noticing the change in my mood. I shook my head once and gave the phone back.

"Nothing," I responded, not looking at her.

"Okay…Oklahoma, what are you thinking right now?"

We stole this from the TV show *Ted Lasso*. "Oklahoma" was a safe word, meaning whenever someone said it, the other person had to tell the "God's honest truth" no matter what the situation was. Courtney probably used it more liberally than I expected her to, but she never pried too deep when she did decide to use it.

I sighed and looked at her phone which still had the picture of Adam and the pretty blonde. She even had a nice smile; her teeth were perfectly straight and white.

"…I guess it's just a bummer to see what Adam's type is, is all." I shrugged.

Courtney was silent for a few moments, and when I finally braved a glance at her she blinked at me a few times before speaking up, "You're worried you're not his type?" She translated my words in her mind quickly.

I shrugged, "I wasn't really expecting to be his type, or that whether I was or not would be relevant, but it is kind of a bummer to see him go for someone who is the opposite of me. In every way."

I had more curves than the girl he was standing with in the picture. My hourglass figure generally made buying jeans a nightmare, because they would be snug in the butt and hips but way too loose in the waist. My drive for doing cardio once or twice a month was usually fueled by my boobs not increasing in cup size, since I figured bouncing between a B and a C was large enough.

This girl was probably a steady B. The way she wore the golden shimmering spaghetti strap dress that fell just mid-thigh told me she probably didn't struggle to buy jeans as much as I did.

Not that I was ashamed of my body. I knew lots of guys loved curves. Hell, even I loved my curves if the clothes fit right. I knew how to love the way I looked.

That didn't help me feel better about what I assumed was Adam's opinion though.

"Oh, my sweet Beck," Courtney lowered her phone and wrapped an arm around me, "You have a huge crush on the guy."

"Well, I thought that was obvious," I mumbled. She sighed dramatically and wrapped her other arm around me as she shoved my face against her boobs, in the weirdest friendship hug ever.

"No. I was under the impression that you just thought

he was smokin'. Because he is. I didn't realize that you actually *like* him."

I mumbled my response into her boobs, but she couldn't understand me so she let me push myself away from her so I could try again.

"I don't *like* him, I don't really even know him enough to. I don't know what I'm feeling, I guess," I finished the sentence with a grumble. I pulled the collar of my t-shirt out so that I could pull it over my face in embarrassment.

"You're too fucking cute, stop it." Courtney grabbed my shirt and yanked it off my face, revealing my frown. She then grabbed my face and squished my cheeks together to remove the frown, and it worked. I laughed and palmed her face and push her away from me.

"Beck, I was mostly kidding before, but if you're into the guy enough to be this bummed about the possibility of him dating someone else, you should probably do something about it."

"I don't think I should."

"Why not?" Courtney leaned back and pulled her phone out to swipe back to the shirtless picture of Adam.

"Well, for one it looks like he has a girlfriend."

"Actually, that picture is from an article specifically stating that they broke up, so that's out." Courtney held the shirtless picture of him in front of my face again.

I couldn't not stare at it.

His stomach was so flat it almost made me self-conscious of my feminine little pooch.

Maybe I should go to the gym tonight? ...Nah.

"I don't think getting involved with someone at work is the best idea. That never works out."

"That's not true. There's a whole trope about workplace romances." Courtney pushed the phone closer to my face, so it almost smacked my nose. I stuck my tongue out to lick it and she finally pulled her phone back.

"Those books are fiction, Court."

"Loosely based on real life situations!"

"Loosely!" I laughed and covered my eyes with my palms. Arguing with her was always comical to me as if I was the more ridiculous one between the two of us.

"All I'm saying is, what if this is the time that it *does* work out?" Courtney sighed and leaned her head on my shoulder. "I don't think the universe is cruel enough to send the one guy in Orange County that revs your engine to the same place you work, only for you to *not* pursue him." Courtney patted my arm encouragingly while I sat there and contemplated her words for a moment.

"...I winked at him today."

"You *what?*" Courtney sat up at that.

I giggled and relayed the conversation with her, including my wink to make him less nervous, as well as my girly thrill at the prospect of him potentially being curious about my condition because he's curious about me as a person, and not just his coworker.

"This is good...this is good..." Courtney had her fingertips steepled together as she drummed them in contemplation. Her brow furrowed over her dark eyes.

"What's good?" I asked.

"Assuming your perspective of your interaction is correct, I think he's receptive like I've always suspected," Courtney explained, ignoring the eye roll I gave her, "Let's take this one step at a time."

I gave her a disbelieving look. In response, she pinched my arm so hard I yelped and smacked her hand away. I laughed as she scolded me and told me to, "Be serious!"

It was impossible to be serious with Courtney, but for her, I tried.

9

Emmett made huge progress during our speech session today. He may not have been signing on his own yet, but he recognized signs and was responsive to them. I made sure to shoot his mom a text updating her on his progress before I scooped him in my arms and carried him over to the PT part of the building. He was two years old and still wasn't crawling or walking. Instead, he did this cute little scoot thing where he sat on his butt and used his feet to tug his body forward. Kids always found the most creative solutions to their problems before actually doing the more effective thing. It was hilarious.

This was his first day doing back-to-back therapy sessions, and he had a tendency to get stressed out when too many demands were placed on him (honestly, same). I made a mental note to warn Adam about the risk of Emmett vomiting if he got too stressed, a common behavior with kids like him.

Emmett's chubby little fists were gripping my shirt and his legs hugged my waist firmly. I made sure to carry him in a snug grip to help him feel more grounded because transitioning was generally hard for special needs kiddos.

I also made a note to remind Adam to give him arm and leg squeezes if Emmett seemed to become over stimulated.

"You did so great today, little guy," I rested my cheek on top of his blonde head, and he leaned into me. He was one of the more affectionate kiddos in the clinic.

As we turned the corner to the PT area, I took a deep, steadying breath to prepare myself for the sight of Adam (now that I knew what he looked like shirtless), but instead, I felt my breath eject from my lungs against my will.

He was squatting down sanitizing play mats, his back to us. His black athletic jogger pants pulled tight around his ass. I cleared my throat as if he was doing something indecent and I needed to get his attention, but in reality, my throat had just dried up.

He turned to look over his shoulder at us and his light brown eyes made my heart skip a beat.

One step at a time.

"Special delivery!" I smiled at the discreetly tatted man and walked over to hand him the cute bundle in my arms.

Adam's gaze flickered over to Emmett, who gripped me a little tighter when he took in the sight of Adam's large frame.

"Hey, buddy," Adam's facial features softened, and hearing him change the tone of his low voice to be more accommodating and friendly for a young child made my lady parts scream. I was glad that Adam was educated enough about working with babies and toddlers that he knew to adjust the tone for them.

Since I primarily worked with children who had speech delays, it shocked me the number of parents who told me that they refused to talk to their child "like a baby." I didn't need them to clarify what they meant because during my sessions

I saw them interact with their child the exact same way they would hold a conversation with me.

Sure, some kids probably did thrive with that sort of communication style, but literally every other kid that I worked with needed more than that.

I was in the habit of reminding parents that they didn't need to make up words for the kids (and that it was actually better to use the correct terminology), but that most kids needed some sort of higher, softer tone of voice for them to pay attention. That was a very good indicator for kids to learn that they were being addressed directly, which was a stepping stone for their developing communication skills.

I wasn't sure what Adam's work history was, or if he previously worked with young kids or not. Based on his tone and how I saw him handle baby Claire though, I was starting to suspect that this wasn't his first rodeo.

"Maybe go a little easy on him today," I started when Adam held his arms out to accept Emmett. Emmett reached out to assist us with transitioning him, but his face was still clearly skeptical of Adam.

"Was Speech tough today?" Adam asked, snuggling Emmett up to his side like how I was holding him. Emmett couldn't take his eyes off Adam's face. He wasn't crying and he didn't look scared, which was promising.

"He did great today. He just hasn't had back-to-back sessions before, so he might get overwhelmed or stressed. If he does, and you hear him start to gag, I'd step out of the splash zone." I gave Adam a grin as his gaze went from Emmett to me at that last sentence.

"Splash zone?" Adam asked with one of his dark brows raised.

"He might stress vomit."

"...Stress vomit?" I noticed how Adam slowly leaned his head away from Emmett, who in response lifted a chunky finger and set it on Adam's nose. He was noticing Adam's freckles.

"Kids like Emmett are more prone to vomiting than others. He specifically has a history of vomiting when he's stressed or over worked," I took in Adam's raised brows. He kept looking from Emmett to me, and Emmett responded by giving him a cheeky grin after grabbing Adam's nose. Adam gave a small smile back at the little boy and then glanced at me one last time.

That small smile made butterflies take off inside my gut.

"Good luck!" I waved and spun around on my heel, a light skip in my step on the way back to my office.

I heard Adam's low chuckle behind me and I instinctively turned around to make eye contact with him one last time.

A small smile was still on his face as he looked away from me and started murmuring to Emmett, who seemed to be handling the transition very well.

Excellent, another normal coworker interaction with Adam in the bag.

One step at a time, just like Courtney said.

<h1 style="text-align:center">10</h1>

A couple of hours later in the day after I locked up my office and started walking out, I was surprised to see the basic white couple Courtney had shown me standing in the waiting room with Pat.

"Well, I don't know about that," the woman mumbled. She was taller than Pat, maybe closer to my height. She was wearing a black pencil skirt and a loose white blouse with heels. Her blonde hair was cut in a short bob similar to how Pat maybe intended to style hers. Her arms were crossed, and she held her chin a notch too high to be considered a polite posture.

"It happens." Pat shrugged once; her arms also crossed over her chest. Pat was generally a very friendly person, but I could sense the edge in Pat's tone as she interacted with this woman.

"Well, has your newest addition been working out?" the man asked. He had dark hair and was pale, with a hint of a European accent I had trouble placing. In general, I sucked at identifying accents.

Considering my hearing loss and inability to discriminate subtle sounds, that wasn't a surprise.

"Oh yes, he's doing very well," Pat nodded her head once,

her tone a little softer when directed towards the man instead of the woman.

"That's…wonderful." The woman's gaze turned away from Pat and landed on me, her light brown eyes looking all too familiar.

Ah, these were Adam's parents.

"Sorry to interrupt, I was just heading out." I smiled at the couple that supposedly donated a stupid amount of money to our non-profit. They were probably responsible for most of my paycheck.

"Oh, no problem! Beck, let me introduce you to Sterling and Edith Hall." Pat uncrossed her arms to grab my forearm and pulled me into the conversation.

Alright, so I guess Pat is desperate for a buffer.

"Hi, it's nice to meet you two." I smiled at them and held out my hand. Edith kept her arms crossed and looked down her nose at my hand, whereas Sterling smiled politely at me and gave me one firm shake. Just like how Adam shook Courtney's hand on his first day.

With obvious reluctance, Edith shook my hand afterward. Okay.

"Beck is one of our most in-demand speech therapists," Pat introduced me with pride, which made me feel a little shy. I tried to fight against the bashfulness and stand more confidently, my instinct telling me that that was necessary with these people.

"That's wonderful. It must be nice being so popular," Sterling sounded genuinely surprised, which in turn surprised me. I thought it was weird to look at me for three seconds and seem shocked that people enjoyed working with me.

"I don't know, sometimes it can be overwhelming. I don't always have all the answers that parents expect me to, but I'm always willing to learn for them." Why did I feel like I was in a job interview?

"Odd, considering you had no issue offering medical advice to a client you weren't even evaluating," Edith added, condescension dripping from her tone. I quickly turned my gaze from Sterling to his wife, who was looking down on me from her high horse.

She was definitely rough around the edges.

"I what?" I lifted an eyebrow at her, confused at her accusation.

"Ah, there he is!" Sterling outstretched his hand in the direction of the corridor behind me. I got the sense that he was trying to change the subject, so when I turned around, I wasn't too surprised to see that Adam was on his way to exit the building through the waiting room as well. As soon as he caught sight of his parents, he stopped in his tracks. His gaze flicked over everyone, clear hesitation written in his body language.

There was an awkward moment of silence, so I decided to be super helpful and tried to fill it.

"What happened to your shirt?" He wasn't wearing his long-sleeved athletic wear, instead, he was wearing a plain white t-shirt that showed off his earthy tattoos on his right arm.

Adam looked down at his shirt and then back at me,

"Turns out, I was in the splash zone." I thought I saw his lips twitch with the hint of a smirk.

I covered my mouth with my hand before I said, "He really puked on you?" I snickered. Adam nodded his head and decided that approaching the circle was fine.

"Hazard of the job, I'm afraid," Pat smiled at the two of us. I looked back at the Halls, Sterling smiling warmly at his son while Edith's sour expression hadn't changed at all.

"To be fair, you tried to warn me." Adam lifted a shoulder and gave me a small smirk of his own before turning his attention to his parents. "What are you guys doing here?"

"We wanted to check in and see how things were going," Sterling replied coolly, his hands in the pockets of his slacks.

Adam's dark brows lowered at that response.

He was clearly suspicious of his parents.

"Well, I see you've at least managed to last this long," Edith chimed in, my head snapped towards her with a visible frown on my face. I felt Adam's body stiffen next to mine at his mother's words.

"What does that mean?" I asked.

Being raised as sheltered as I was, I had a few "gaps in my social skills" according to Courtney. This was something I had learned and corrected over the years but, in this moment, I decided to be rude and not pretend that Adam's mother didn't say something very weird.

I understood that when you were in a social setting and someone you didn't know made snide comments like, "You've managed to last this long," it was generally best to brush it off and make it seem like everything was fine for the sake of everyone's comfort. Especially if the person you were stepping on eggshells around was a major donor to your employment, and the reason you could pay rent and buy groceries.

I knew this as an adult, whereas when I was a child, I would just ask blunt questions for clarification's sake. Like I was doing now.

When Edith's head turned in my direction with an expression that made me believe she was questioning my audacity to address her rude remark, I kept my expression cool. "Tell me, what qualifications do you have to tell a client to see an audiologist? Or that their child might be deaf?"

Fuck, how did she find out about that?

"I didn't think anyone needed to be qualified to suggest that a child should check in with a doctor," I replied, not looking away from her gaze. Adam's light brown eyes always seemed warm and dreamy to look at. It was weird that his mother had the same eye color, and yet her eyes are noticeably cold and harsh. I did not enjoy looking at them nearly as much.

"Still, it was dangerous to voice such a thing to a brand new client. We don't want to risk any unnecessary, expensive, lawsuits," Edith responded.

"Hey." Adam's low voice was a warning. I wondered how much power was behind that warning when I saw the hand Adam had gripping the strap of his backpack. His middle finger had started to tap against the strap in a steady rhythm.

Right, he was a nervous fidgeter.

"We are always at risk for unnecessary lawsuits. We work with children of sensitive, emotional parents," I countered, raising an eyebrow at her. My cool expression was melting into something along the lines of, what the fuck is your problem?

Edith's gaze bounced between Adam and me before she continued, "Then maybe it would be best to not risk voicing our opinions to those emotional parents."

I blinked at her a couple of times as I heard Adam exhale an annoyed breath. At the same time, Pat took a turn to stiffen beside me.

"...Even if it means the child may be untreated for something as serious as hearing loss?" I replied. My voice sounded a lot cooler than my feelings. I was starting to get very irritated with this woman. Was she bored? Is that why she had this pathetic attempt to try to tear me down at the end of a long day?

"Investigating whether a child has setbacks such as being deaf, or blind, or anything else, should be left for the child's pediatrician to deal with. This facility is for providing therapies, not diagnoses." Edith's challenging gaze never left mine, even when Sterling rested a hand on his wife's lower back. It looked like a silent plea for her to stop. I could tell he was trying to cool his expression even though his wife was kind of being a bitch.

Alright. I'm tired. I'm done.

I snapped my fingers as if an epiphany just came to me, "You know what, you are totally right." My voice was sincere, out of the corner of my eyes I saw Pat and Adam's heads turn towards me as I continued this weird ass conversation with Edith Hall.

"I'm sure you were only trying to be helpful," Edith

continued. As I expected, now that I stopped challenging her, she was immediately more agreeable, "But it might be beneficial to remember that you didn't go to medical school. That's all."

"I totally get it," I nodded my head as if I actually thought she was a smart person. "I mean, noticing significant behaviors in children that are almost identical to my personal experience growing up with hearing loss means absolutely nothing, right?"

Edith frowned and glared at me, and I couldn't stop the little smirk that picked up on the corner of my lips.

"I don't think that Edith meant—"

"I don't think that's what she meant either," I interrupted Sterling, who quickly snapped his mouth shut. "I am not a doctor, but I am a certified therapist. It is in my job description to look for clues or behaviors that will better help us understand what the child is experiencing. That way, as their therapists, we can provide *exactly* what the child needs," I narrowed my gaze at Edith, who stood frozen in her spot while she shot daggers at me with her eyes. "It might be important to remember, though, that words have meaning. So maybe, before you start attacking me for doing my job, you should be more careful with the words you choose."

Adam started to gently cough into his fist, but I swear I heard the words, "Oh shit" get mumbled from him.

"There's also the possibility that I misheard you, my hearing aids have been acting kind of wonky lately. But based on what I read from your lips, I seriously doubt it." I stopped smirking and pulled my phone out of my pocket to check the time.

I put it back into my pocket and took in Edith and Sterling's expressions at my little jab.

Yes, I too have hearing loss, you fetuses. I'm an educated adult, capable of taking responsibility for my actions, such as telling a mother to take her child to the audiologist.

My hearing aids weren't obvious. They were smaller and hidden in my ear canal, so it usually took people by surprise when they learned that I used hearing aids in both of my ears. It was probably why Adam was surprised to learn that I had hearing loss myself. Most people expected to see the large chunky devices that hooked over the top of the ear, but the technology was advancing, and I personally liked the inner ear devices better.

"On that note, I need to head home. I have a bus to catch," I held two fingers up to my forehead and gave the Halls a sarcastic salute before turning to Pat. "I'll see you tomorrow!"

"Travel safe," Pat gave me a conspiratorial smile, her arms recrossed over her chest.

I didn't wait for the Halls to say anything else before I walked past them through the front doors. I took a deep breath as I let the fresh air embrace me before I continued. I was halfway through the parking lot when I heard my name being called behind me.

"Beck! Wait!" I froze in place at the sound of the all too familiar voice. I heard his footsteps crunch the loose pavement until he was next to me before I turned to give him an embarrassed smile.

My behavior was suddenly catching up to me.

I nervously put both of my palms to my cheeks.

"Oh shit. I was so rude," My smile dropped from my face, and my cheeks started to flush when Adam slowed to match my pace and rested a large hand on my shoulder to stop me.

His hand was warm, and electricity shot from the spot on my shoulder where it rested. The only thing that my brain was able to produce were the words, *Adam is touching me* repeatedly.

"That was wonderful. Seriously." Adam gave me a smile, and I froze. It was a full, real smile. It was handsome and made my heart skip a beat or two. His teeth weren't perfectly straight, the front ones curved in a little bit as if he'd taken a hit to them before, but they were white and mostly even and wonderful.

I wanted to lick them.

Who the fuck wants to lick teeth, Beck?

"I can't believe I acted like that," I said, as Adam's large hand squeezed my shoulder, and his woodsy scent finally caught up with us. I was feeling an overwhelming number of emotions right now. Mainly embarrassment for being rude to the people who funded what I assumed was most of my paycheck, and sexually frustrated from the proximity Adam was to me right now.

He was touching me for fuck's sake.

As if he read my thoughts, he released his grip on my shoulder and nodded his head away from the direction I had been walking, "I heard you mention catching the bus, but can I give you a ride home instead?"

I blinked at him and slowly lowered my hands from my face.

"I insulted your parents, and you want to give me a ride in your car?"

Adam raised an eyebrow at me, "I want to apologize. I'm the reason my mother even knew about Mallory and Claire. We were all out at dinner one night and she asked me how the job was going, and I told her about you and how helpful you were that day. I should have known she would have seen your advice as an intrusion instead of the success story it is. But—you already knew that they were my parents?"

Oh shit.

Busted.

Own up to it without sounding like a creep.

"You and your mom look a lot alike. You have the same eyes…And last name." I tried to go for an innocent expression, hoping I didn't reveal any hint of the fact that I had seen his shirtless pictures online. And that I had stared at them for an embarrassing amount of time.

"Ah," Adam nodded as if that made sense, "You knew who she was, and still called her out on her demeaning, overstepping bullshit. Yeah, I'll definitely save you a bus trip for that."

He jerked his head in the direction of his car again and started walking towards it. I shook my head and followed him almost robotically because I wasn't about to pass up a free ride from Adam.

Was it the kind of ride my hormonal self would have really liked to receive from Adam? No. But riding in his car was probably the closest he and I were ever going to get.

11

"Holy fuck, tell me everything!" Courtney squealed, jumping over the back of the couch and landing on the opposite end from where I was sitting.

Gram was on the living room floor doing downward dog. She wrapped up her yoga routine, then settled down on the mat cross legged to listen to my story. Courtney had gone to a new gym she wanted to check out after work and Gram had an early bird's dinner date with one of her friends. So, when they finally walked into the door of our townhome I waited until everyone had removed their shoes and changed into comfy evening clothes before telling them how I was transported home from work.

I appreciated the excitement they both gave me, even if it felt a little overwhelming.

"He drives a Tesla," I started with. I wasn't too surprised, based on how loaded his parents must have been. I didn't know why they were loaded, or how famous they were. I hadn't seen anything on the internet about them since Courtney showed me those couple of pictures a few days ago.

"Environmentally friendly, nice," Courtney gave a thumbs up as she reached for the popcorn bowl on the coffee table.

"What did you guys talk about on the drive home?" Gram

asked, stretching her legs out in front of her and bending towards her feet.

I snapped my mouth shut and stared wide-eyed at Courtney. Embarrassment took over me, because I wanted to talk to them both about this, but also never talk about it.

Two very conflicting emotions.

"…What? What happened?" Courtney asked, picking up on my obviously anxious body language.

"We didn't exactly talk…" I chewed on my top lip; nervous troll face on full display for them in the safety of our own home.

"Oh my god, you hooked up?" Courtney squealed, jumping to conclusions. Gram straightened and started clapping her hands with joy as if she wasn't seventy-four years old and dealing with arthritis.

"Did you use protection? You need to protect yourself from germs, young lady." It sounded as if Gram was trying to act like a parental figure, instead of the grandmother/soul sister she was.

"By 'germs' your grandma means STIs," Courtney explained unnecessarily. She shoved a handful of popcorn in her mouth and waved her hand for me to keep going.

"No, we didn't hook up…we didn't talk or anything. He got a phone call as soon as we got in the car," I finally released my top lip to explain, "He stayed on the call the entire drive. Then he gave me a head nod when he dropped me off."

"Ouch," Courtney cringed before shoving more popcorn in her mouth, "He didn't even bother to call the person back?"

"No…it sounded kind of personal and important. I tried to look out the window a lot to give him privacy. Well, as much privacy as I could sitting in the passenger seat." I lifted a shoulder and then leaned my head back against the couch. Maybe I should have taken my aids out to create actual privacy? No, that would have been weird.

"Who was the phone call with?" Courtney asked. I shrugged.

"Maybe his accountant or someone? Adam's responses were very short and to the point, so I really have no idea what the conversation was about. He just listened to someone else most of the time." I remember seeing Adam clench his jaw a couple of times throughout the conversation. He didn't seem like he was happy about the phone call, at least.

Darn, the more I elaborated on the situation, it really wasn't that cool or exciting of an experience with him.

"Why did he offer you a ride in the first place?" Gram asked, rolling up her yoga mat.

"Oh…" I cringed at them, "I met his parents today."

"Seems a little premature to meet the parents at this point, but okay." Courtney reached into the popcorn bowl and grabbed air, frowning.

"Yeah, well, I'm kind of wishing I didn't, they didn't seem like nice people." I frowned and ended up relaying the gist of the story, focusing more on Edith's body language and tone when discussing how she thought I needed to stay in my lane. Gram and Courtney both made twisted faces when I got to that part, which gave me some satisfaction that Adam's mother was clearly a disgruntled woman.

Then when I got to the part where Adam was happy to offer me a ride for basically giving his mother the verbal finger, Courtney snorted with laughter while Gram frowned.

"Sounds like he isn't close with them," Gram murmured, her brow pinching and increasing the number of wrinkles on her forehead.

"Yeah, I doubt he is…" Courtney looked between the both of us expectantly and then, when we just sat in comfortable silence, she loudly groaned and pulled out her phone from her pocket and started tapping away frantically, "I guess I'm the only one willing to investigate this!"

"Nobody felt the need to investigate this," I reminded her.

Gram held a finger up, "Actually, I want to investigate this." I wasn't that surprised. Gram wasn't close with her only child, because their relationship wasn't possible with how different their personal theologies and lifestyles were. If there was a chance she could encourage someone else to keep a relationship with their parents, she would take it.

I felt true sympathy for her.

"Hmm, did you guys know what Adam did before he started working with us?" Courtney asked. Gram and I both shook our heads at her.

"His mom did say something super cryptic about Adam 'sticking this out' or something like that," I added. Courtney nodded her head and kept thumbing away at her phone.

"Okay, so according to this article, Adam and his ex-girlfriend broke up a year or so ago." Courtney's eyes didn't leave her phone screen.

"Where are you finding this?" Gram asked.

"Well, I tried his social media, but he doesn't have any. There are only fan pages dedicated to him. This is a small, local gossip article writing about the very public breakup they had, and the pictures taken of it seem to confirm the story."

I blinked as I took in those words. "Fan pages?"

"Yeah, I guess he was on his way to the Olympics." Courtney's blonde brows furrowed a little bit, "Oh, sorry, that's why I asked if you guys knew what he did. I always get distracted."

"Olympics?" Gram asked, getting her back on track.

"Yeah, I guess he was very into surfing. But for whatever reason he stopped competing...wait..." Courtney was quiet for a little bit, typing and swiping while Gram and I were waiting patiently in the silence.

"...Adam has fan pages?" Like, he was a celebrity? What the hell? Did I just get a ride home from work from a potential Olympian?

"Yup. Don't worry, they're not good. Very little content besides just the same pictures of him shirtless posted multiple times."

"There are pictures of him shirtless?" Gram started to crawl over to where Courtney sat on the couch. She may be old, but she was never one to turn down looking at an attractive person. Especially if that attractive person was a shirtless man in his prime.

"Yes, and I'll totally show you them, but one second I'm onto something," Courtney's eyes were glued to her phone.

"...Is it weird that we are stalking him on the internet like this?" It was the age of social media, and unfortunately, if you were relatively famous or in the public eye, you simply didn't have that much privacy anymore. I still felt a little icky about it though.

"Hmm, you're right." Courtney snapped her phone shut and quickly pocketed it, even when Gram tried to snatch it out of her grip, "I'm going to ask him about it at work on Monday."

"What? Courtney, no."

"It's too late!" Courtney lifted her hands as if it had already been done.

"No, it's literally not." I laughed and shook my head at her. She just lifted her nose in the air and jumped off the couch as she started to head for the stairs.

"The deed is done!"

"What deed? You literally haven't spoken to him or any-thing!" Gram threw a throw pillow at Courtney's retreating figure, grumbling something about missing out on abs.

"It's done!" With that, Courtney ran upstairs, and Gram and I didn't see her again for the rest of the night.

12

The weekend went uneventfully. Gram got very into a show called *Yellowstone* so we spent most of Saturday and Sunday just roasting the shit out of Kevin Costner's cheesy lines and how toxic the masculinity in the show was. Gram had a huge crush on the old man, so we ordered a ton of takeout and made a girl's weekend of it. Some edibles were taken. On Sunday night Courtney gave Gram and me more of her tincture to help us sleep well and wake up refreshed in the morning.

Except I'm pretty sure Courtney accidentally squirted a little more than I usually took in my sleepy time tea, because the afterglow I was feeling the next morning was just strong enough to make me grateful that I knew the bus schedule for work.

I was glad to take the bus with Courtney, who was reading one of her romance novels on her iPad because my head felt just a little too light to hold a conversation that early in the morning. It made staying focused during my one-on-one sessions with kiddos slightly more difficult. So, to combat that, I told the parents that I wasn't going to push their kids super hard that day and instead gave them a break to let them feel happy and comfortable in my office space.

It was a real thing, kids needed breaks. Sometimes, though, those days were spontaneously squeezed in when I was still slightly hungover from doing too many legal drugs the night before.

My mouth was still dry, and I found myself drinking lots of water all morning.

I was feeling a little better around lunch time, and when I joined Courtney and Taylor in the lunchroom (because we were clingy and decided to schedule all our clients so that we could take lunch together at least three days a week), I was completely unprepared for her ongoing investigation on our newest coworker.

"You!" Courtney lifted her plastic spoon to someone over my shoulder. We were in our usual seats. Courtney on the chair against the wall, Taylor on the end, and me with my back to the door of the break room.

I was startled by her sudden shout and jumped in my seat.

"Jesus, Court. I'm still recovering from you overdosing me last night," I rubbed the bridge of my nose a little bit, as my heart nearly jumped out of my chest.

"Sorry," she barely glanced at me but then continued to keep her gaze on whoever was approaching the table and pulling a chair out next to me.

I recognized that masculine woodsy smell at once.

"Me?" Adam's deep voice asked as he lowered his large body onto the folding chair. He unpacked his lunch, another meatball sub.

"I have some questions," Courtney's eyes narrowed

accusingly at him. I immediately remembered our conversation from Friday night and my cheeks filled with heat.

"Courtney, no." I shook my head at her, but she just rolled her eyes and continued to point her spoon at Adam.

"I just wanted you to know that I have been looking you up on the internet," Courtney started, throwing it all out there. Taylor laughed while I groaned and covered my forehead with my hands, lowering my gaze to the table.

I swore I could feel Adam's eyes on me, but I refused to meet them.

"Find anything interesting?" I heard him ask. I removed my hands from my forehead and picked at my sandwich, feeling mortified for my friend and wondering how pissed Adam would be.

"I did, actually," Courtney smiled triumphantly, possibly motivated by Adam's somewhat cool tone of voice. "I'm sorry about your breakup, by the way."

I felt Adam go still next to me for a second before he mumbled, "Thanks," and took a bite of his sub.

Damn it, Courtney.

She glanced at me, and then at Taylor, as if she expected us to have anything to add. Though the look Taylor gave her in return seemed conspiratorial. I wondered what that was about.

"…Was that all?" That came from Adam. I found myself smiling a little at Courtney, it was a good sign that Adam seemed to be acting casually about Courtney's invasion of his privacy. Hopefully, he wouldn't be too offended by our snooping.

"Nope. Though, your fan pages need some work," Courtney scooped a large spoonful of her snack pack into her mouth before continuing. "But it looks like you're not competing anymore."

"Competing?" Taylor asked.

"I used to surf competitively." Adam shrugged, eyes glancing at all of us at the table. I looked between us and noticed that the toe of his shoe was lightly tapping again.

Another nervous tic.

Maybe he wasn't feeling as casual as his voice sounded.

"Can I ask why you stopped?" I couldn't help but ask. Hell, I was curious.

Adam's whiskey-colored eyes slid over to me and he blinked once before answering, "Wasn't feeling it anymore."

It was silent at the table for a little bit, so I filled it in by just saying, "Oh, okay," and focusing on my food.

"Why weren't you feeling it anymore? Too stressful?" Taylor asked, leaning their elbows on the table.

"Something like that." Adam kept his gaze on the table.

"...Whoa, slow down. It's hard to digest all this information you're spewing at us." Courtney rolled her eyes at him, and I kicked her under the table. She glared at me, and I glared back at her. Taylor and Adam watched the whole exchange with interest.

"I'm not exactly sure what you want to know," Adam added, glancing between the two of us. I got the sense that he wanted to de-escalate the glaring match Courtney and I were having with each other.

"While I was stalking you," Courtney leaned her elbows on the table and steeped her fingers together, "I happened to notice that your breakup with a woman named Eloise was right after you quit surfing."

"I didn't quit surfing." Adam's dark brows pinched together the slightest bit. "I just quit competing."

"Eloise is a pretty name…" I mumbled to myself.

"It is," Courtney agreed before glancing back at the redhead, "Were those two events related at all?"

Adam's toe tapping paused for a moment, then resumed before he said, "Yes. She didn't like the direction my career was turning. So we ended things." He added a casual shrug, though it seemed a little too forced.

Taylor and Courtney were quiet for a few moments while they processed, so I said, "I'm sorry, that sucks."

Because I'm eloquent like that.

I got the smaller chin tilt from him in acknowledgment.

"I had a relationship end because the guy didn't want me to get my septum piercing," Taylor said with a shrug.

"Why are human beings the worst?" Courtney asked.

"We aren't the worst. We are *taught* to be the worst. I believe humans are generally good people." I tried to defend our race, while also shifting the conversation off of Adam.

I was *this* close to becoming someone I would consider to be "the worst," but then in a moment of bravery, I escaped my parent's clutches and educated myself about the world we lived in.

"I would have to disagree with you, Beck. My evidence being the entirety of world history." Taylor shook their head at me in a way that told me they thought I was cute and naive.

To be fair, I was naive about a lot of things. I was work-ing on it.

"The sins of world history aren't entirely the fault of the human race," Adam added after finishing his sandwich. "I think it's mostly the fault of entitled men, specifically. Who just happen to be human."

We all sat in silence as Adam casually dropped that bomb.

I stopped breathing and stared at his sharp profile blatantly. I had a feeling Taylor and Courtney were doing the same.

"Women are generally more willing to negotiate with each other without making a war out of it," Adam continued, folding up the wrapping of his sub. My heart was racing again, and I couldn't stop looking at him.

I watched the way his lips moved as he simply announced to the table that he was a feminist. I watched the way the horrid break room light bounced off of his red hair. The way the freckles on his nose stopped their journey before crossing over to his cheekbones.

The way his beautiful light brown eyes slid over to me and glanced over my face, probably wondering why I was gaping at him. He must have finished talking and noticed the heavy silence coming from the three of us.

"I think you just fried Beck's brain," I heard Taylor tease.

"You fried all of our brains," Courtney stepped in, prob-ably to help me snap out of it.

"I'm...sorry?" Adam's dark brows pinched together, con-cern covering his features.

Meanwhile, I think I was praying.

Universe? Deity? How could you do this to me? How is this

stupid sexy man also a proud and open feminist? Does he have no flaws? What am I to do about this insanely inappropriate level of attraction I am feeling toward him?

I blinked, blushing again, and finally turned away from him. Courtney was smiling brightly at Adam and me.

"Adam, nothing is sexier than a man who isn't afraid to put appropriate blame on men," Taylor explained around a bite of their food. I couldn't tell you what they were eating. I had too many thoughts and emotions coursing through my body.

"Ah," Adam nodded once, his lips twitching as if he was fighting another smile.

Who fights smiling? Just fucking smile. Let those emotions out.

He nudged my arm and leaned towards me, and I think I looked mildly panicked because he stopped himself before leaning too closely. "By the way, I apologize for taking that phone call on Friday. That was rude of me to drive you home and make you sit in silence."

"It's no problem! You're allowed to answer your phone." My voice was definitely higher than normal. I gave him a tight-lipped smile and tried not to focus too much on the spot on my arm that he nudged. It felt warm like it was still recovering from the contact with him.

I felt like I was in middle school and going through puberty again.

"Was it an important call?" Courtney asked, clearly not interested in letting Adam keep anything about his life private.

"Not really, more of an inconvenience than anything."

"Well, I think that in order to make it up to Beck it would

make sense for you to drive us all home in your fancy electric vehicle," Taylor leaned their elbows on the table and wiggled their eyebrows at all of us.

"Is that how that works?" I asked, trying to save Adam from having to carpool our band of misfits home from work.

"Fine, but maybe you could let me drive it around the parking lot after work?" Taylor crossed their fingers on both hands and widened their bright blue eyes pleadingly at Adam, who chuckled before nodding his head once.

"Yeah, sure."

"I can't wait to drive your car!" Courtney bounced in her seat as she cleaned up her lunch.

"Wait, what?" I asked, not realizing Courtney was part of the deal too. She grabbed my lunch, which I still had a few bites left of, and stood up from the table to dump it all in the trash before running out of the room. Taylor laughed maniacally and followed her out.

I just blinked at the doorway behind me for a moment before turning back to Adam, who was staring at me.

"I'm sorry they bullied you into letting them drive your nice car." I couldn't hold his gaze, instead, I kept looking at his nose freckles. And hair. And jaw. And lips.

God, I wanted to feel those lips on mine.

"It's fine, I don't mind." He winked at me before balling up the rest of his trash and standing up from the table. Were we friends now? Friends who winked at each other. Friends who bullied the other into driving their vehicle. The idea was both exciting and disappointing. Did I want to be friends with someone who I inappropriately thought about last night as I took care of some things in the privacy of my bedroom?

Probably not, but it didn't look like I really had a choice in the matter anymore.

Adam had found a way to weave himself into my day to day at work, and my stomach fluttered with daily anticipation now.

Remember, Beck, other grown adults figured this dilemma out in their youth.

I blew out a frustrated breath and finally stood up from the table, realizing that I needed to be prepared for this new chapter of my life where Adam seemingly fit in our group at work. I had no control over that anymore.

13

The end of the workday came, and everyone met up at my office before going out into the parking lot to drive Adam's shiny black Tesla.

During this time, I learned that Adam specifically drove something called a Model 3 and that he chose this model because the other ones were on back order and he didn't want to wait a year for his new car.

Rich people problems.

Taylor drove us all around North Irvine, Courtney riding shotgun and making everyone listen to her playlists while Adam and I were stuck in the back seat, which was much more spacious than I would have guessed for a car that size.

While Taylor gave me a heart attack with sharp turns and unnecessary acceleration, I learned that Adam was economical in his car choice. He thought it was a good idea for most gas vehicles to become extinct in exchange for energy efficient travel, and that those who were worried about the electric grid in California being overwhelmed didn't know that anyone who owns electric vehicles usually charged their cars overnight, when usage and costs are at its lowest.

We talked about the hypothetical bullet train from LA to San Francisco that kept getting brought up every few years, but would most likely stay a fairytale. Adam was convinced that the bullet train would never get built, because he believed that politicians and higher ups didn't actually want travel to become more cost efficient.

To back up this theory, he mentioned how toll roads weren't supposed to cost anything anymore, but that the state continued to charge fees for them because they didn't want to give up that income.

It sounded a little tin-foil hat to me, but I would forever be skeptical of conspiracy theories due to my upbringing. I just loved this unique opportunity to get to know Adam outside of work.

When we were stopped at a red light, Courtney turned to face Adam and me. "Since we are technically not at work anymore..." she wiggled her eyebrows.

"— We *actually* aren't at work anymore," Taylor corrected her, making Courtney and I laugh for a few moments before she regained all of our attention.

"Anyway, I vote we all go out to sushi," Courtney grinned right as my stomach decided to make the loudest, most grotesque grumble. Because Adam's stupid fancy electric vehicle didn't have a loud engine running, everyone heard it. They let me know that they heard it by turning to look at me with raised eyebrows, Taylor's eyes meeting mine in the rearview mirror.

"Not a word," I narrowed my eyes at everyone and dared them to make fun of my hungry stomach.

"Sushi it is," Adam declared, giving me a smirk before

unbuckling himself and reaching forward to type in the name of a restaurant he had in mind in the GPS.

His butt was so close to me as he leaned forward, and I couldn't look away from it.

Finally, he sat back down and buckled himself back in before we all headed to get food.

***

We were picking plates off of the conveyor belt next to our booth when Adam noticed one of the top ten most embarrassing things about me.

"Do you not know how to use chopsticks?" Adam asked, noticing the plastic fork I snagged from the hostess stand. I'm pretty sure that they were reserved for kids, but fuck that.

"No, I just prefer forks," I countered, handing him the small Vegas roll he nudged me for. The booth was fairly small, and his thigh was mostly pressed against mine while Taylor and Courtney sat across from us, looking just as squished.

"That's a lie," Courtney grinned after gulping down her water, "Beck refuses to learn how to use chopsticks."

"What? Are you twelve?" Taylor asked, adding to the embarrassment.

"Why do I need to learn how to use chopsticks?" I asked, defending myself since nobody else at the table would. Adam was chuckling next to me; I could feel his body shake with laughter via his thigh.

"I don't know, maybe for when you're at a sushi restaurant? Where did you even get that fork?" Taylor countered, reaching behind Courtney and grabbing some seared salmon.

"Oh, that looks good," Adam mumbled, following Taylor's lead and reaching behind me to grab the second plate of seared salmon when it made its way closer to us. His body was putting off an insane amount of heat, and his forearm brushed against the back of my neck when he stretched toward the conveyor belt. His chest was fully pressed against my arm and shoulder, and I had to fight every cell in my body not to lean into that firm chest.

I'm pretty sure he held his breath because his face was so close to my head.

He finally retrieved the plate and pulled back from me as far as he could, which meant that our legs were still touching.

I felt my pulse race from the unexpected close contact, and I looked up to see Courtney smirking at me from around the rim of her glass.

We would definitely be dissecting that experience later.

"I found it as we passed a bin of them on the way to the booth," I explained, clearing my throat and trying to still my racing heart.

"You stole it out of the bin that had a sign specifically saying, 'for kids twelve and under'?" Courtney clarified, snickering.

"You know what, I don't like your attitude," I balled up my straw wrapper and tossed it at her forehead. She picked it up and tossed it back at me. I quickly tried to dodge it by turning to the side and shielding my face, making playful eye contact with Adam who was watching us with a smirk.

"Here," Adam spoke after Courtney and I stopped throwing trash at each other, he was opening a fresh pair of chopsticks, "Give me your hand."

It took me half a second to realize he was talking about

me, and I silently obliged as he broke apart the chopsticks and attempted to mold them into my fingers.

It felt weird. The chopsticks, specifically. Adam's warm hands gripping mine and trying to get my fingers in the right placement did *not* feel weird.

It felt warm and lovely.

"There," Adam was still staring at my hands as another smile graced his facial features, "Now just use your finger to adjust the top stick."

I didn't do what he asked, so he looked up at me to see if I heard him. Before he could ask if I was okay, I cleared my throat and looked at my hand in an attempt to execute the motion.

I had never been to any sort of Asian restaurant until college when Courtney took me out to one. My family didn't eat out a lot, mostly because they felt like they would be shamed for praying in public over the food that the servers would bring out to us.

You know, because the world was corrupt and constantly trying to take away white people's God-given right to pray over their meals in public. I had no memories of anyone shaming us for that, but paranoia was my parent's MO, so that was that.

"Aw, little Beck is growing up!" Courtney cooed, pulling her phone out to take a picture. I ended up giving her a flat, annoyed expression as she quickly took a couple of pictures to document my first mildly successful experience with chopsticks, probably to show Gram later when we got home.

It wasn't until later that evening, after Adam dropped us

all off at home, that Courtney showed me the pictures she had taken that day.

She had discreetly taken pictures of Adam and me discussing the public transportation issue in the backseat of his car, and I ended up grinning at the fact that we both looked equally engaged in the discussion. Both of our bodies were turned to face each other, our knees inches away from touching.

The next couple of pictures were of Adam and me at the sushi place, his hand wrapped around mine as he guided me to hold chopsticks properly.

My expression was annoyed, his was soft with a smirk on his lips, eyes on me.

It made my heart skip a beat.

"Look at how he's looking at you, Beck," Courtney nudged me as we sat in my bedroom that night, "You two will have the cutest little red-headed babies."

I scoffed and pushed her phone away.

"He's looking at me with pity because no one had ever gone out of their way to show me how to use chopsticks before." I lifted a brow at her.

"Hey! Not true! I totally tried to teach you how to use them!"

"Tossing chopsticks at me and saying, 'now hold them, no, not like that, hold them differently,' is *not* teaching me!" I laughed at the various memories we had of that interaction happening multiple times during college.

"Whatever," Courtney palmed my forehead and shoved me back before standing up from my bed and heading towards the door, "I'm just saying, baby steps!" She blew me a kiss and danced out of the room, shutting the door behind her.

Baby steps.

Today we had a successful conversation *not* about work.

Technically, we held hands for a few moments during the chopstick lesson.

I brushed my left hand over my right, still able to recall the feeling of his hand over mine. I liked it, and I didn't realize how much I was starting to miss the familiar touching that came along with companionship. The freedom and comfort of being able to touch your partner like that consistently.

As I drifted off to sleep, I found myself wondering if Adam was also someone who missed familiar touch with a partner.

Hey, I noticed that you have nobody to hold hands with. Maybe we could hold each other's hands? Maybe make out? Maybe screw each other's brains out? No? That's fine. I'll just go bang my head against a wall out of embarrassment instead, no worries.

I sighed at my own thought process before pulling the covers over me and falling into a deep comforting sleep.

14

"Fuck."

"We're at work."

"Shit."

I didn't care that we were at work. When my office door was closed I felt free to speak my mind, which was currently repeating curse words over and over again.

"That seems a little dramatic," Courtney reassured me, walking over to my desk where a gift basket of baked goods currently sat.

"They haven't done this before. It's concerning," I repeated. Courtney turned to give me a compassionate smile before investigating the package contents for herself.

When I first saw the basket on my desk I smiled; excited because I expected it to be either from Gram or Courtney or maybe one of the parents of my clients. I dug around in the homemade pastries, immediately recognizing them, and I felt my heart sink into my butt. When I saw the note sticking out of the top with my mother's handwriting, my suspicion was confirmed.

My parents knew where I worked.

They hadn't sent me a care package. Ever. Not even when I was at college and I purposely gave them my home address.

Once I started to draw some firm boundaries, I didn't bother filling them in on the details of my personal life, like where I worked. I figured reminding them that I was choosing a career that made me happy and fulfilled would upset them. It was just a reminder that I left their religion and didn't marry the first available Godly boy from my hometown.

How did they figure out where I worked?

Did Gram tell them?

They knew where Gram and I lived, because Gram was always friendly and happily willing to engage in conversation the rare times my dad reached out to her, so it was possible.

"Did you read the note?" Courtney asked, plucking it from the basket and unfolding it.

"Nope." I couldn't. I stopped as soon as I saw my name written in my mother's handwriting. When I saw that it was folded multiple times and that it was more likely a letter than a simple note, I texted Courtney for backup.

It was the end of the work day and we were both staying late to fill out paperwork for our clients, so even though we were closed in my office we still had the majority of the building to ourselves. I appreciated the sense of privacy since my parents had somehow found a way to invade mine.

"I'm gonna read it," Courtney announced, not asking permission. I shrugged. I didn't care if she read it. The words would probably make my skin crawl less if they came from Courtney's sunshine voice.

"Ahem," Courtney sat on the edge of my desk and pretended to clear her throat for the theatrics of it all. I folded my arms and sat down in my office chair, fidgeting from side to side. *"Rebecca,"* not the nickname that I preferred, which also showed how distant we were, *"I hope you like this delivery we have put together, I tried to include your favorites."* Half of the pastries had shaved coconut on them, something I hated very much and had vocalized to my parents multiple times during my childhood. My mother sure loved coconut, though. *"I thought I would fill you in on some life updates since I have been unable to get a hold of you the last few months. Our neighbor John has recently gotten married to Margaret Smith—*is she one hundred years old?" Courtney shook her head at the poor girl's name and continued to read, *"and they now live in a cute little apartment a couple of blocks away from home."* Courtney just looked at me and, when I didn't say anything, she continued, *"His parents are hoping to expect more grandchildren soon—*what? Why?"

"That's the next step, obviously. Go on two or three dates, get engaged, marry a couple of months later, procreate as soon as possible, and raise perfect God-fearing children." I shrugged as I felt acid in my mouth. I wondered how many kids I would have now if I had stayed trapped in that toxic, sexist environment.

"I hate that. But wait, they really got married after just a couple of months of dating?" Courtney stared wide-eyed at me. It was comforting to know that Courtney was raised relatively 'normal'. In the real world (the world outside my parents' head) people didn't get married that quickly. They dated and learned about their partners before committing to something so serious. Sometimes Courtney forgot how wild my old culture was.

"If you were celibate and couldn't have sex until marriage because God would smite you, you wouldn't waste time either," I shrugged and then waved my hand for her to continue.

"Right, right," Courtney nodded as if that was totally normal. "*Your cousin Paul is working for Mr. Robinson's warehouse full time and is finally expecting his first child with Rachel, they are due in just two months.*" Ugh, Paul and Rachel had struggled with infertility for years, and I secretly thanked whatever deity existed that they couldn't procreate because that child was screwed no matter what sex they had when they are born. "*Do you remember Josh Patterson?*" My skin crawled.

Josh Patterson was my age and had his sights set on me for about five minutes in high school. There was a second where I was flattered by his aggressive attention, because I was fifteen and discovering what "horny" was, but then quickly realized that he was scum. Not because he was having sex with a handful of girls at school that weren't part of our religious community, but because he would go behind their backs and lie to everyone in our congregation about their relationships. He would tell stories about how the girls would throw themselves at him, and how he had to be responsible and turn them down. Sometimes he claimed he would invite them to pray the sinful thoughts they had away.

Some of those girls I highly respected and got along with, even though I was the weird religious girl of the group. That whole clusterfuck was one of many dominos that began to fall with my religious deconstruction.

"He has been asking about you," Courtney continued, glancing at me, seeing my ill expression, and looking back at the paper, *"I thought it would be a good idea for you two to catch up, so I gave him your number."* That wasn't okay, not that my mother cared. *"I called Gram and she filled us in on your current situation, including your occupation. I hope you'll return my calls so we can catch up, I miss you and love you so much. Let me know if Josh gets in touch with you.* And then there is what looks like a Bible verse at the bottom, want me to read that too?"

"No."

"...Your mom is the one who thinks she sees the future, right?" I nodded my head. My mother's religious schizophrenia aside, my blood was boiling with rage. How could Gram betray me like this?

"I'm going to kill Gram."

"You absolutely will not! I'll punch you so hard if you lay a hand on that sweet old lady!" Courtney folded up the note and shoved it back into the gift basket. I groaned and rubbed my hands down my face.

"Obviously I'm not actually going to hurt my only blood relative that I actually get along with," I turned in my chair and laid my forehead on my desk while gripping fistfuls of my hair, "Why can't my mom just leave me alone? Why can't she let me go?"

Courtney was quiet, knowing the question was mostly rhetorical. Though I wouldn't be opposed to knowing what was going on in my mother's brain, as scary of a place as that must be.

She was truly delusional if she thought I would respond or get in contact with someone like Josh Patterson. I remembered telling my mom the truth about what was happening at school with Josh at the dinner table one night. My dad had interrupted the conversation, shutting it all down as nonsense because Josh was a man of God and there was no possibility that he would lie like that.

Because Josh happened to grow a penis in utero, his words were regarded as truth, whereas the non-religious uterus owners were just over emotional from his (non-existent) rejection.

"Well, it sounds like we should ask Susan," Courtney tugged on my arm to get me to sit up before taking the gift basket in her hands, "I'll go dump this, these are covered in coconut, and I know you won't eat any of it anyway."

My friend of however many years knew me better than the woman who had given birth to me. Courtney chose to care about me as a person, to get to know me, and try to understand me. She learned ASL (on top of our already heavy college coursework) for me. She didn't want me to conform to her personality or lifestyle but wanted to help me feel most comfortable in my own skin.

If I was doomed to have a chaotic relationship with my parents, I was grateful to have Courtney by my side through it all.

"Thank you," I thought she could hear the emotion in my voice, because she smiled at me before sauntering out of my office, giving me a few moments to myself to cool down. My body suddenly felt heavy, and it took all my energy to leave work and face my grandmother.

*****

A week or so later I finally started to feel myself get out of my slump. Receiving that unexpected package from my mother pulled me into a dark place for a little bit, which happened whenever my parents were constantly present in my mind. It sucked because they were my parents and I would always love them, but distance from them had truly given me the most peace.

Something they, apparently, would never understand.

The discussion with Gram that night had gone as well as it could. She was open and honest about speaking with my dad on the phone a day or two before. If it was my mother who called, Gram probably wouldn't have answered, because she also doesn't like being constantly shamed for her sinful lifestyle by her. Gram was so desperate to save any sliver of bond between her and her son, that she was generally willing to answer whenever he spontaneously decided to call her. She admitted to telling him the name of where I worked, and she assumed he googled the address for my mom to send her stupid note and care package. After reading the note, Gram scoffed and apologized profusely. She admitted she should have known better, and would remember to keep me out of it whenever my dad decided to grace her with a phone call.

I forgave her and we hugged it out.

Then we all got high and watched *The Bachelorette* with Courtney.

The remaining work week had been a fog for me, and

the worst part was that I knew I was in a slump. My body language made it super obvious to everyone around me, but it already took all my energy to pretend everything was fine with the clients I met with, so I had nothing left to pretend for everyone else.

Little Maddy had been making great progress the last couple of weeks, happily engaging with the AAC device and becoming much more intentional with her communication. Since I was able to still be the fun bubbly Miss Beck for the kids, I let myself be depressed in the presence of my small circle of friends.

Taylor would occasionally pat my back when passing me in the halls at work, or whenever they sat next to me at our table during lunch. Adam must have noticed my mood too but didn't engage with me at all about it. I was convinced Courtney said something to him, considering the vibe one day last week when I walked in late to the break room for our usual lunchtime (that Adam now participated in every day). The room went quiet as soon as I entered. I wasn't paying attention to the words being said when I walked in, but based on the sudden silence and compassionate looks all three of them gave me, I was sure Courtney had filled Adam in on the situation with my parents.

Taylor was filled in a couple of years ago when I fell into a similar funk over a similar interaction with my parents.

I had felt my heart pick up once in the last week. I had felt Adam's gaze on me. It was when I was handing him Emmett for his PT session and something had sparked to life inside me, but as soon as I left Adam's presence the slump was back.

I had a good weekend after my slump week, Courtney

and I went to the beach and went on a small hike. It was her way of encouraging me to come back to myself after giving me space to grieve my non-existent parent-daughter relationship.

So, by the time I was back at work the following Monday, I had a real smile on my face. That was until I helped a new client find their way back to the front of the building to exit, and saw two familiar women standing at the front desk.

One of them was Edith, Adam's mother.

Her gaze sharpened as soon as I entered the room, and I realized Adam was standing on the opposite side of the front desk, a frown on his face as he lifted his head to meet my gaze. Papers were scattered on the front desk everyone circled around.

"Morning," Adam greeted me with the smallest smile in the world. I felt bad for how I acted last week, so I smiled back at him and nodded once as I waved goodbye to the clients I had just met with.

"Rebecca." Edith greeted me, using my full first name. Nice.

"Hi—I'm Eloise!" A thin blonde standing next to Adam's mother smiled brightly at me and held her hand out. My stomach sank. This was the ex-girlfriend.

Adam frowned harder while I approached Eloise to shake her hand. This was probably so weird for him. I hated that my parents even sent a single package to my workplace, so I couldn't imagine what it must have been like for him to have both his parents and ex show up, too.

At the same time, no less.

I remembered the conversation I had with Courtney and

Gram a few weeks ago regarding the possibility of Adam not being close to his family.

"Hi, you can call me Beck," I held my smile for her. Damnit, she was truly beautiful in person, even in her cargo pants and grey tank top. She was casually dressed down but still glowing, like bubbly blondes usually did.

Adam had good taste.

"Busy day today?" Edith asked. I couldn't tell if she was trying to dismiss me, or if she was simply referencing our last weird-ass conversation in this very room.

"Super," I replied with another salute, similar to the one I left her with last time. I wanted her to know that her presence didn't intimidate me.

I had my own shit to deal with.

"Are you coming on the work retreat in a few weeks?" Eloise asked, genuine curiosity flooding her tone. Her voice made me want to make her happy. I wondered if she had that effect on everybody.

"You mean the mandatory one?" I replied, raising an eyebrow.

"Mandatory for therapists, yes," Edith clarified. I didn't bother giving that a response. *I* am *a fucking speech therapist, bitch.* Clearly, I was feeling defensive in Edith's presence. Though, Eloise hadn't met me before and probably didn't know if I was part of the therapist team or administration.

"Yay! I hope you all have fun; I'm trying to come up with a reasonable itinerary," Eloise beamed as she picked up a piece of paper and handed it to me. "We have been bothering Adam with his opinion on everything, but I'd love to get others' opinions too. I don't want the retreat to only be team bonding activities."

Any second now butterflies would just fly right out of her ass. She was that kind of person. I blinked at her before glancing at the piece of paper. Her words were catching up to me.

"You're planning the retreat?" I asked, glancing at the list of activities she gave me, but not reading any of them.

"Yup! I was having brunch with Edith when she told me about Adam's new job. I love what you guys do here and I wanted to help support you all on your 'mandatory' vacation." She was even cute when she used air quotes with her fingers, what the fuck? "Since the Halls are footing the bill, I offered to help organize it. Pat seemed relieved when I spoke to her about it." I'm sure Pat was. Again, detailed planning wasn't her strong suit.

I nodded, pretending that I wasn't overwhelmed by the epitome of human sunshine this early in the morning. "Cool, thanks for your help. I'm sure it'll be great," I smiled at her and glanced at Adam, who just continued to look uncomfortable.

She beamed at me and took the paper back to set it on the desk.

"You're busy, so I'll let you go. But it was lovely meeting you!" I truly believed she had a "lovely" time meeting me. Eloise gave me a farewell hug and released me before I had the chance to realize what was happening and hug her back. She smelled like roses. Of-fucking-course she did.

"It was nice meeting you, too!" I didn't bother acknowledging Edith with more than a nod and a polite smile, but

I waved at Adam who slowly lifted a large hand of his in farewell.

God, he was so handsome. I must have been in a real depression last week to forget something so constant in my thoughts.

Whoops, I was staring at him too long.

I could tell because he looked at me as if he expected me to say something. Why else would I linger like this? Thankfully, Edith and Eloise were already leaning over the papers on the desk and murmuring to themselves.

Instead of coming up with something to say to make this moment not weird, I blushed and turned on my heel, and left.

Excellent, I may have been out of my depression, but I was back to being an embarrassment of a woman. Oh well.

15

Thwack!

I shouldn't have been surprised by what I saw when I walked into the break room later on, and yet here I was.

"That sounded like it hurt!" one of the occupational therapists giggled at the sight we were all witnessing.

Courtney and Taylor were standing in the middle of the small (and crowded) space, squaring off at each other. They both had their lips sealed tight and their cheeks full of something. A flour tortilla in one of their hands.

Courtney's cheek was red as if she had just been slapped.

Unexpectedly, Courtney swung her hand and slapped Taylor in the face with her flour tortilla. Taylor stayed still, groaning through their closed mouth and squeezing their eyes closed.

Laughter erupted around the room.

What the fuck did I just walk in on?

"Don't! Don't you dare spit out that water!" One of the PTs chastised Taylor, who was turning red and looked like they were holding back laughter.

I thought I remembered seeing something like this on social media.

"The tortilla challenge?" I asked the room, and a couple of people responded with various versions of "yes".

"I tried to discourage them," I heard a low voice to my right, I glanced over to see Adam leaning against the back wall a couple of inches from me, "But obviously that was useless."

"Obviously," I agreed, smiling at him and turning back just in time to see Taylor slap the absolute shit out of Courtney's face.

Courtney managed to make a high-pitched squeal afterward, bending over and trying her best not to laugh.

"Guys. Not cool. This isn't professional." I heard Pat's motherly voice chastise my best friends behind me, and I stepped out of her way so Courtney and Taylor could see her. My arm grazed Adam's, which was crossed over his large chest, and I felt like my skin was burning from the contact.

"Yeah! Not professional!" I chimed in, earning eye rolls from Taylor and Courtney.

"But we all placed bets!" One of the therapists whined. Pat glanced around the room and looked back at Taylor and Courtney, resignation on her face.

"Fine, wrap it up," she crossed her arms and leaned on one hip while Courtney surprised everyone by slapping Taylor's face when they weren't expecting it. The room erupted with laughter, which made Taylor squirt a couple of drops of water from their lips.

Courtney pointed, eyes wide and jumping as she gulped down the water in her mouth before shouting, "I win! I win!"

Taylor ran over to the sink and spit out the water in their

mouth before bending over it and cackling. "That last one was so unexpected!" they cried, holding their gut and laughing.

I was laughing too, and a couple of therapists were wiping tears from their eyes as everyone fist bumped. I had no idea who all bet on Courtney and really didn't care.

"I want a rematch!" Taylor held up a fist in mock rage as the room started to clear out, now that the show was over. Courtney snickered and shook her head.

"No way, you'll be way more competitive next time since you lost this time!" We all made our way over to the table, and I pretended not to internally squeal when Adam casually pulled my usual chair out next to his after he already sat down himself.

Cool it, Beck. He was just being nice and knows where you always sit.

"What about you, Beck? You up for a casual tortilla slapping?" Taylor asked, turning their chair around and straddling it backwards before leaning their elbows on the back of it.

I shook my head before answering, "No way," and pointing to my ears. No chance in hell I could have tolerated that kind of thing.

"Oh, right, your ears would hate that, huh?" Courtney asked after realizing my reasons for saying no.

"What? Really?" Taylor asked, curious.

"Yup. If I was wearing my aids while my cheek and ear were slapped like that, I would go blind for a few moments from shock." I wasn't lying. One time a cranky kid I was working with slapped me on the side of the head with a paper storybook, the ringing in my ears lasted all day even after I ripped my aids out. I couldn't focus my eyes for half a minute after the original slap.

The hearing aids struggled to process the noise the slap made; it was as if I was hearing the slap last forever for that solid minute.

"Huh, good to know." Taylor shrugged before rummaging into their paper lunch bag and digging out their food. Courtney pulled out the extra snack packs that Gram had snuck in our lunches to give to our work "buddies" as she likes to call them. She slid one over to Taylor and I slid one over to Adam, who accepted it as if it was a totally normal thing we had done before.

It wasn't, but the fact that he accepted the children's pudding without question (and that it was never brought up again during lunch as the conversation continued) created a comfortable, warm feeling in my chest. I glanced at the newest addition to our friendship circle out of the corner of my eye periodically. One time he caught me staring at him and gave me a polite smirk when I gave him a friendly smile first.

I could do this.

I could be friends with this man. Sure, I still struggled with the fact that he made my blood pulse with want. I also struggled with the fact that these feelings hadn't decreased since I had spent more time in his presence. It wasn't painful anymore, though, just a new normal I could deal with.

Though if I had to be honest with myself, normal totally sucked.

The more I got to know Adam the more I liked him. He hadn't done or said anything incredibly off-putting like I had. He cared about the environment and wasn't pretentious enough to protect his precious car from the excitement of our friends. He was great with kids. Whether or not a woman wanted to have kids of her own, I felt like it was a universal truth that seeing a grown man handle kids with love and care was a huge turn on.

He seemed to accept Courtney, Taylor, and me.

Just like we all accepted him.

He fit in our circle. He laughed at our antics, added small quips of his own when the moment was right, but also respected my emotional capacity when I was very obviously struggling. Adam was here, waiting to pull my chair out for me when I decided that I was ready to be more socially involved again.

Maybe one day, months or years from now, I could broach other things with him. Things of the, "you're so fucking hot and perfect that it makes my heart hurt," variety. That is, as long as some other thin blonde underwear model didn't interest him first.

Baby steps, Beck. You got this.

<h1 style="text-align:center">16</h1>

I did not have this.

I didn't have any of this.

This, I did not have.

I left work today a little later than usual because I loved saving all the boring paperwork for the end of the day when it was quiet in the office. As I was leaving the building and walking through the parking lot towards the bus stop, I saw a flash of red hair near a shiny black Tesla and my attention was immediately grabbed.

Correction; I saw a flash of red hair and a naked back, and my attention was immediately grabbed.

Because Adam was changing his shirt next to his car.

Just out in the open, in the parking lot, with very few parked cars to obscure him from anyone's view.

So I stared. Like a pervert.

I stopped in my tracks and just blatantly gaped at him.

I stared at his naked back, that I really wanted to rake my fingernails down.

If a woman needed to change her shirt in a parking lot and a man inappropriately ogled her while she did so, the feminist in me would rise with fury, because women should be allowed to do quick emergency shirt changes like that without becoming the center of some man's sexual fantasy.

Kettle, meet pot.

The worst part was that he caught me staring at him. Right as he was pulling a short sleeved grey t-shirt over his sculpted shoulders and tugging it down his torso, he looked over his shoulder and made direct eye contact with me.

My mouth was open and everything.

I know this because as soon as we made eye contact I snapped my mouth shut and tried to come up with any reasonable excuse for my behavior.

But we both knew there wasn't one.

I figured the next best option was just to apologize profusely, "I'm sorry! I'm so sorry!" I was acting as if I'd accidentally sack-tapped him again. I spun around to give him some privacy, but then realized it was too late for that and he already had his shirt back on, so I turned back with a look of guilt on my face.

Adam just chuckled before adjusting his shirt, "It's fine, no need to be sorry. I'm the one changing in public." I shook my head and smiled at myself. I was acting like such a *girl*.

"I'm still sorry, please don't report me to HR."

"Please don't report me to HR for flashing you," Adam smirked at me; he was teasing again. Apparently, we did this now.

I pretend to zip my lips closed, "No one has to know."

"Perfect," Adam opened his driver's-side door. "It'll be our little secret." Then he winked before disappearing inside his car.

I thought of that wink while I was lying in bed that night. Gram and Courtney were probably peacefully asleep in their rooms, and my libido was out of control. I kept replaying the scene over and over. The wink, the dark shirt showing off his tattooed arms, the playful glint in his eyes, and the wink. Did I mention the wink? It felt significantly more sexual than his last wink. Or maybe I just haven't had sex in a long time.

That was definitely possible.

However, I was safe in my bedroom. My imagination was limitless. I didn't have to worry about controlling my thoughts because I wasn't in the workplace. I could fantasize all I wanted to here.

I snuggled under my comforter, feeling safer, and squeezed my eyes closed. I was still stuck on the loop, except now Adam was nodding his head towards his car in invitation for me to join him. I was way more confident in my fantasies than I was in real life, so I didn't hesitate to get into the passenger seat. We drove in silence to his apartment, which in my mind was modern blacks and greys and the height of luxury, because why not?

I may be confident in my fantasies but I never made the first move. So Adam did—because it was my fantasy and I could fantasize however I damn well pleased. As I was grabbing a glass of water at the sink, I felt his large presence walk up behind me, his hands grabbing my hips.

His mouth found my neck and traveled up to my ear, whispering dirty things to me.

"…It'll be our little secret…" I felt his lips smirk against the shell of my ear before his tongue traced the shape. I shivered and pushed my ass back into his groin, feeling how hard he was already. In my fantasy, it was only fair he was as hot for me as I was for him.

I pictured his large hands snaking around my waist, over my stomach, and starting to lower towards the waistband of my leggings. I reached over to my nightstand drawer to grab my little bullet vibrator.

Sometimes I pictured him working the vibrator on me, sometimes I imagined that his fingers are making me feel how the vibrator felt. Currently, he was sucking on my neck as he pushed me into his kitchen counter with his hips, grinding his erection into my ass.

A heavy thud hit my bedroom door, followed by Courtney cursing. I jumped.

"Hey! You busy?" I heard her call from my bedroom door. She clearly tried to turn the knob and walk in unannounced, but I had the forethought to lock it. Courtney had yet to accidentally walk in on me masturbating and I wanted that streak to continue. I immediately turned off my vibrator and felt a wave of embarrassment wash over me.

"Very!" I let my irritation blanket my tone.

"...Really?" Courtney asked. "I just had a quick question!"

"Court. For the love of God, go away!" I groaned and flopped back on the bed.

"...Oh. Were you...having DIY time?" She knew I was. This wasn't the first time she had rudely interrupted me. I had done the same to her (on accident, and less maliciously) so it wasn't one sided but usually, I wasn't being interrupted while fantasizing about a very real person in our life. It felt even more embarrassing than it usually did.

"Court…" I grumbled at her, my orgasm seeming more and more distant.

"Paddling the pink canoe?"

"Court."

"Dialing the rotary phone?"

"Ugh."

"Auditioning the finger puppets?"

"Go. Away."

"I can't. I have more. Getting lost in the deep end? Womansplaining yourself?"

"Fuck it. The moment's gone." I threw my bullet at my door while she started cackling and made her way down the hall. It was 11pm, and there was no way I could calm down enough to try to finish what I started…right?

I sat there in the darkness for a couple of moments. I could hear when Courtney went back to her bedroom and shut the door, and the likelihood of her visiting my bedroom again was non-existent now that she knew how I planned on spending my evening. Too bad I couldn't possibly get my head back in the game after that.

…Or could I?

I closed my eyes and took a couple of deep breaths to relax my body, and the sexiest red-head in the world appeared behind my closed lids, smiling devilishly at me.

If there was a hell, it was *so* worth the risk.

I slowly crawled out of bed and retrieved my bullet.

17

"Hey, roomie!" Taylor called out to whoever was behind me at the end of Group Therapy.

"Roomie? You have a new roommate?" I asked, turning around to see Adam smirking and shaking his head.

"For the big weekend, yes." Taylor held out their fist for Adam to bump. I remembered Pat sending out an email a couple of days ago reminding everyone to tell her who they would be comfortable bunking with at Big Bear. Rooms were limited but each one had two twin beds to accommodate everybody.

Obviously, Courtney and I listed each other.

"Oh, fun." I smiled and thought about that one time Gram had walked out of the bathroom completely naked a couple of days after I moved in with her, that horrible image controlling the way my body usually reacted when Adam's presence was close.

My breathing was under control and only a little blush flooded my neck and cheeks. Progress.

Now I just had to work on my pulse.

"Are you rooming with Court?" Taylor asked me.

"I think she would stab me if I even pretended that I wanted to room with anyone else."

"It's true. I would." Courtney appeared in our circle, waving goodbye to one of her clients. I glanced over to see which she was waving to and saw Daddy James. Ugh.

I tried to look away, but it was too late.

"Hey, Beck!" I hated my nickname on his lips. It sounded forced, like the way he consistently tried to force my attention on him. I plastered a smile on my face and stepped away from our circle to address him, smiling at little Stella in his arms.

"Hey, Mr. James."

"Connor." He corrected. I just smiled at him. As soon as I called him by his first name he would think that we were more than acquaintances. Courtney had encouraged me in college to trust my instincts, especially when men were involved. As someone who was raised to fear the world in general, I was actively trying to not be fearful of everyone and everything. However, after being exposed to situations in college that could have turned out dangerous if she hadn't been there to guide me through them, I learned that it was okay to have a healthy caution with men. Courtney encouraged me to follow my gut instinct because women were usually right about that sort of thing and it wasn't worth the risk.

My gut was telling me that Daddy James was icky.

That had never changed.

"Stella did great during circle time!" I said in an attempt to keep our conversations on an appropriate topic. Daddy James nodded and snuggled his daughter closer to him in pride. Stella usually struggled with sitting still and focusing on the songs and signs. Like every other kid in Group Therapy. Today she sat in her chair all by herself at least seventy-five percent of the time. A huge improvement worth noting to her parent.

"She did! Hopefully, those skills will transition over to preschool," Daddy James kissed her forehead and turned to look back at me.

"How is the preschool evaluation going?" I asked, hope spreading in my chest as I remembered that Stella was going to turn three in the next couple of weeks. While I would miss her cute face, I felt relief knowing I would only have to deal with Daddy James a little longer. When our clients turned three, the state aged them out of the Early Intervention program we ran. Meaning the state no longer covered the cost of therapies, and that whatever school district the child was part of would step in to provide support. Usually, that meant starting preschool, hopefully with trained therapists visiting the child's class and helping them one-on-one. Sometimes parents liked the therapies we provided better than what the school district offered and continued to come here while paying out of pocket or through insurance. Our services certainly weren't cheap, so not a lot of parents had that as an option.

"Great, actually. The school psychologist has already been dropping hints on what preschool program Stella would thrive in, so that's comforting," he smiled, and I beamed at Stella. I was excited for her.

"That's so nice to hear! Sometimes the evaluation process can be stressful, or the school district doesn't reveal anything until the IEP meeting," I explained, glad that that didn't seem to be his experience.

"Yeah," he was done talking about this, I could sense the

shift in his demeanor as he glanced around the room and seemed to hover closer to where I was standing. It took everything in my body not to step back to recreate the appropriate amount of distance between us. That would give off the vibe that I was intimidated by him, and for some reason, my gut was telling me not to do that.

"So, listen, I don't want to be too forward—" he started. Oh god. It was happening. By saying that I knew *for a fact* that he was about to be way too forward.

"What's up?" I cut him off, hopefully throwing him off his game. It didn't work.

"When Stella graduates from Early Intervention, we will no longer be clients here," he explained. I knew this. It was as if he was speaking in slow motion, each word making my anxiety rise along with each painful second that passed.

"Right," I tightened my smile, trying not to show the stress building inside me.

"So, once that happens," he cleared his throat before showing me his teeth with what I suspected he thought was a dazzling smile, "I was wondering if you'd be interested in getting coffee with me sometime?"

There it was. The official request.

"Oh," I pretended to be surprised and stared at him for a few moments as if Daddy James asking me out hadn't ever been on my radar. "Um, that's super nice of you, but," I glanced over at my friends standing a few feet away, wondering if any of them could save me from this, "I don't think that would be a good idea."

"Why not?" He asked.

Shit, good point.

Looked like I just needed to be straight forward.

I inhaled a little and gave him a friendly smile, "I'm flattered, but I am going to have to say no."

"Oh, are you seeing someone else?" he asked as if that could be the only possible reason I said no.

"I'm not." I didn't elaborate, because I shouldn't have to be dating someone else to say no to a date. The conversation should have been over.

"Oh, well that's a bit of a relief," he smiled sheepishly at me, the nerve. "You sure you don't want to just get one little coffee with me?" Ugh. Men. I should have just lied and said I had a boyfriend. Men were quicker to back off if they thought the girl they were interested in was already committed to another man. If the woman simply wasn't interested and said no, men are more willing to apply pressure to the situation until she finally caved and said yes. It was archaic, and manipulative that men have more respect for an imaginary boyfriend than for a woman's right to choose who she dates.

"I'm sure. Thank you for asking," I hated that I felt like I had to coddle him for my own safety, especially in a professional work setting, "But my answer is still no."

"Ah," he hung his head low as if my rejection was devastating. It wasn't. He was attractive enough, he probably didn't have trouble getting dates. "I figured it was worth asking anyway. Let me know if you change your mind."

"Sure." I wouldn't.

He nodded once and smiled at someone behind me before turning around and leaving with his daughter. I exhaled a breath of relief that that whole interaction was over as I turned around to face my friends, who were all watching me intently. They clearly heard the whole exchange.

"Well, that was terrible," I mumbled as I rejoined them.

"It didn't seem that bad, I think you handled it well," Taylor encouraged, patting me on the shoulder.

"Thanks," I patted their hand before they released me.

"He wasn't as pushy as he could have been," Courtney chimed in, "So there's that."

"There's that." I agreed, glancing over at Adam but being too chicken to hold his gaze. For some reason, I was feeling embarrassed to have to turn down Daddy James in front of him.

Why was that?

Did I want Adam to know that I wasn't interested in guys like Daddy James? That's something I would have to unpack later. We chatted a little bit about how Group went that day, and when we were all getting ready to disperse and resume our work day, we were intercepted by Pat speed walking towards us.

"Adam! Do you have a minute?" Pat asked, glancing at all of us as well.

"Sure," Adam replied. Taylor patted him on the back once as they passed by and continued toward their office.

"It's in regards to your mother," Pat started.

"Oh. Then I lied. I'm very busy," Adam quipped back.

I barked out a laugh at that, which made both Adam and Pat look at me as Courtney and I walked past them on our way to our offices.

"Sorry, that was hilarious," I shrugged as I met their gazes. I thought I saw Adam's lips pick up on the corners.

"I'll try to make it quick," Pat smirked at him as they continued their conversation, their voices lowering a little bit.

How weird it must have been to have your parents so involved with your full-time job as an adult. To have your own independence, but still see or hear about your parents in your work bubble.

I couldn't fathom that.

***

Later that afternoon when I was listening to Carbon Cut on the bus ride home, I felt my phone vibrate with a notification. I had my phone set to ignore calls it didn't recognize, because somehow my number was on the list of every scammer known to man, so I was surprised to see a notification for a voicemail pop up on the screen. I paused the music I was listening to, mildly annoyed because this new band was starting to become my jam, and pulled up the transcript of the voicemail.

"Hey Rebecca, this is Josh Patterson—"

Delete.

Was I a little curious about what that guy was doing with his life? Mildly, but not enough to justify listening to a voicemail of his. The fact that he had my cell number made my stomach churn, so I was hoping that never responding to him sent the correct message.

It was so easy to ignore people nowadays. I loved it.

I resumed listening to my latest musical fixation, leaning my head back against the bus window and taking in the lyrics of the band. I really needed to get Courtney to listen to them.

I was so happy I discovered them. Even though it was an all male rock band, their target audience was clearly women. Sure, that could be said for all male bands, but their lyrics were what drew me in. Their songs were modern, in the sense that they weren't all about sex or drugs or heartbreaking relationships. Some were, obviously, but at least half were not. Carbon Cut's songs had way more depth to them. They had the musical energy of pop punk, but the message of modern feminism.

I had a sneaking suspicion that all the band members were feminists themselves.

If a song praised a woman, it did so respectfully. Speaking highly of her mind and character, not just her body. There were also a few songs that seemed nerdy. Discussing climate change through a universally understood medium, music. It was so creative, I found myself listening to their album repeatedly. They were my go-to.

Though pop punk wasn't Courtney's genre, once she heard their lyrics, I'm sure she would become a fan.

Another notification popped up on my phone, this time an email.

From Eloise. Ugh.

Hello Everyone!

My name is Eloise Bane and I am your activities coordinator for the upcoming retreat! I have been working closely with members of your team and have come up with, hopefully, a fun activity schedule!

> Attached is a waiver, this is mandatory for everyone participating and will be requested before loading up the buses. Please fill it out as soon as possible and bring either a printed copy the day of or email it back to me here.
>
> I can't wait to meet you all there!
> Eloise Bane

Fuck. Even her email was cheery and filled with sunshine and rainbows. Just knowing that she was involved left me feeling confident that every detail of the retreat was planned so that each individual employee would leave feeling truly appreciated for their work.

I hated that the only reason I was bitter about her existence and involvement was that Adam had dated her. Past tense. As in as far as I was aware he was currently single.

Sure, it wasn't like I was actively pursuing Adam either, but I still felt this barbaric competition with her. I needed to work on that. It was important to me that women didn't continue to make unnecessary enemies of each other because we needed each other more than we needed men.

Maybe I could up my cannabis oil dosage in order to relax and not be annoyed every time she opens up her perfect mouth during the trip, it would be worth experiencing the possible lingering afterglow.

***

Time passes differently as an adult.

When you were a kid things either lasted forever or they happened too quickly. There was little in between.

As an adult, time passes at a more steady, comfortable pace that makes it easy for someone to miss important moments entirely.

I remembered having crushes in high school and looking forward to simply seeing the person in passing. Whether it was in the hallway, across the cafeteria, or even entering the parking lot, I looked forward to little glimpses of the boys who made my heart race faster than normal. I never approached one or did anything about my pitiful little crushes as a teenager, mostly because my parents forbade any sort of dating. Though I did remember having big feelings, even if they were fleeing. Feelings that reminded me a lot of my feelings whenever Adam was in the room, and my heart raced just as fast as it did in high school. My teenage crushes never lasted more than a few weeks, but when they were there, I felt like my body would burst with the stress of it.

This crush I had on Adam was different.

I did look forward to seeing him in passing at work, or next to each other during lunch, but because I was now able to hold a basic conversation with him, I didn't feel like I was going to burst from stress anymore.

Maybe it was because he had been part of our lunch routine for a couple of weeks, or maybe it was because having Courtney and Taylor buffer any awkward moments I created with Adam made me feel a little more comfortable. Like a built-in safety net. Either way, I was proud of myself

I was officially able to interact with an adult man I was sexually attracted to without falling apart.

It was the little things in life.

Currently, Adam and I were hanging out in my little office, something that made me panic the first time it happened. Now I was used to Adam's presence in there.

We discussed clients together, like Emmett and Claire, because it was important for us to be on the same page regarding the child's development in order for us to provide the best care possible. Adam was just updating me on a scheduling situation with Emmett when Courtney and Taylor started hitting the silent doorbell on my office, making the lights flicker on and off repeatedly.

"The door's open. You can just come in," I shook my head at their antics and turned in my chair to face them, giving Adam my profile. Adam was leaning against my desk, and because he was taller and larger than me, I always felt crowded by him. Maybe I was just hyperaware of his presence, and that would never change, but I was still grateful Courtney and Taylor came in to unintentionally buffer again.

"We have a message from Pat," Taylor announced, "There is a Miss Bane here to meet with a Mr. Hall." Taylor winked at Adam, probably enjoying the fact that they got to deliver the news that Adam's ex-girlfriend was back.

Over the last couple of weeks, Adam had slowly spoken up more about that whole situation, specifically about the fact that he did truly hate that his mother and ex-girlfriend managed to embed themselves here.

I remembered his body language specifically, how he sat next to me at the break room table with a clenched fist and jaw. His foot tapped uncomfortably at the turn of discussion. Eloise had just dropped by earlier that day to ask Pat and

Adam their opinions on food since we were being served three meals a day at the retreat.

"It feels like a lot of what your ex-girlfriend comes here to ask you and Pat about could easily be written in an email or text," Taylor observed as Adam took his seat.

He just nodded once.

"She seems super excited about the retreat," I chimed in, in an effort to divert the conversation to something less accusatory as Taylor wanted.

"She's excited to be my mother's little minion," Adam grumbled, taking an angry chug from his water bottle.

I was only mildly distracted at the sight of his throat working before his words registered with the table.

We all stared at Adam, waiting for him to elaborate, but he didn't. Adam usually didn't speak unless spoken to, and when he did he used very few words.

"Wait, do your ex-girlfriend and mom hang out a lot? …On purpose?" Courtney asked, surprise coloring her tone.

"Yup," Adam replied, emphasizing the *P*.

"Yikes," I mumbled, mostly because I wouldn't want any-one I was romantically involved with to be buddies with my own mother.

"That sounds horrible," Taylor agreed.

"It got worse the longer Eloise and I dated…it was part of the reason we broke up," Adam lifted one tense shoulder, staring at his salad like it offended him.

"Gross." Typical Courtney, always so blunt. "So, is it super uncomfy that they both just waltz in here whenever they want?"

"Very," was Adam's curt reply.

I nodded, my sympathy building for him. He clearly had some sort of relationship with his mother that he valued enough to struggle to keep intact, otherwise, I couldn't see why he didn't just ignore her like I did mine. Other people's family dynamics were always intriguing to me.

"At least she seems nice," I offered. Even though I was super bitter about her sunshine personality, I tried to focus on the positive. Eloise might be a stage five clinger, but at least she wasn't gross about it.

Or maybe she had a collection of Adam's fingernails hidden in a jar in her closet. Who's to say, really?

"She's unbearably sweet," Courtney agreed around a mouthful of her tuna sandwich.

"Do you think she still has feelings for you?" Taylor asked, taking on Courtney's blunt line of questioning. I guess it made sense. If Adam was going to be so careful about the words he spoke, being blunt was probably the best way to get information out of him. Also, I was curious as hell what he thought the answer to Taylor's question was. I'd seen the way Eloise looked at Adam, and frankly, it was probably a look I gave Adam when I wasn't being careful. *Wanting.* The difference was, Eloise had Adam and lost him. Whereas, I believed that I would only have Adam in my imagination.

"I don't know," Adam replied. Dang, I guess that mystery still remained.

"If she told you she wanted to get back together, would you?" Courtney pressed. This time she swallowed her bite before asking.

"…No, I wouldn't." Adam shook his head once.

Why did that fill me with so much relief? I had to focus on not exhaling the breath I had been holding too loudly.

Fast forward to now, inside my office. Taylor and Courtney were a little too happy about delivering the news to Adam that Eloise had yet again made an unscheduled visit, and I felt a little bad for him.

"I'll be out front in a minute, let me finish up with Beck first," Adam replied, nodding towards them in what was clearly a dismissal. Taylor and Courtney both saluted us and walked out of the room, Courtney raising her brows at me a little. This was her way of reminding me that, yes, Adam was alone with me in my office and yes, I was undoubtedly thinking dirty thoughts about it.

The thing was, mine and Adam's discussion was pretty much over before those two came in and blinded us with the lights. I glanced back over at Adam who was rubbing the bridge of his nose with his fingers, clearly stressed.

"I'm sorry," and I was.

Adam glanced up at me with his golden eyes, "What for?"

"It must be stressful, having her show up unannounced. No matter how friendly she is with everyone. I wouldn't like it if any of my exes or parents did." I gave him a friendly smile because that's what we were now. Work friends. If we were regular friends we would hang out outside of work, which we absolutely did not do. Not since the sushi day. Work friends were still allowed to talk about what stressed us out, and right now Adam was stressed about Eloise.

"Yeah." It was all he said for a few moments as he hung his

head and rubbed the back of his neck with one of his hands, his muscles flexing under the material of his shirt.

He was still sticking to those long-sleeved shirts in the workplace.

"She called me the other night," Adam spoke up, making my heart race a little bit more. We never really spoke about anything important (unless it was work related) when it was just us. Usually, Courtney and Taylor were the ones constantly pressing him for information about his personal life, while I just sat back and tried to play defense when he seemed too annoyed by it. The fact that he offered that unsolicited information to me caught me off guard, but I did a good job recovering.

"Oh yeah?" I asked, trying not to sound too interested. I didn't want to scare him off if he was trusting me at the moment.

"...She wanted to talk to me about the possibility of getting back together," Adam spoke to the floor, his red hair hanging over his forehead, "She spoke for an entire fifteen minutes straight, stating her case and delivering evidence as to why she thought we should. Like she was in some business meeting."

I had absolutely nothing to say about that, but he stopped talking and was still sitting here, so he was probably wanting some sort of vocal interaction from me.

"...She just...monologued at you for fifteen minutes?" I asked, I figured clarifying the details of the conversation was safer than asking the questions I wanted to ask.

Did you say yes? Do you want to get back together with her now? If you do, what changed from a couple of weeks ago?

"Yeah, she waited until I answered the phone and just…talked," Adam lifted his head to look up at me, and he looked tired. "It was painful to sit through because I have no interest in getting back together with her."

Oh, thank god.

What are you thanking God for, Beck? It's not like he's saying he wants to start anything up with you. Could your pathetic hormones even handle the possibility of that? Probably not.

"Did you tell her that?"

"Yes, but…I don't know. She's still involved here, with my mother's encouragement. I think I'm worried she's going to try something at the retreat. She took my rejection a little too well." He made a face that made me suspect he was chewing on the inside of his cheek, and his foot tapped a little on the office carpet.

"Well, you have us," I replied. "Courtney and Taylor have been buffering for me with Daddy James since the beginning. I'm sure we could all buffer for you and Eloise if you'd like."

Adam quirked his lips to the side, "Daddy James?"

"Stella's dad."

"I know, I was there when he asked you out."

Why did I blush at that?

It wasn't like I did anything wrong. It was an unsolicited request for a date in the workplace, one that I shut down with relative ease. It didn't stop Daddy James from looking at me a little longer than necessary during Group Therapy today, though.

Thankfully, it was Stella's last day. I'll hopefully never have to interact with him again.

"Courtney came up with the nickname and it stuck," I explained, realizing that was why he was questioning the name. "But for months, before you started working here, we all knew it was coming. I would constantly feel his eyes on me. Taylor and Courtney would divert his attention so I could make a quick escape."

Adam looked at me a little longer than my body was comfortable with, and I started to fidget in my seat before I heard the annoying *chirp* of my hearing aids.

I was changing the batteries twice a week now. I needed to make an appointment with the audiologist to have the devices looked at. I probably needed new ones at this point.

"Ugh, stupid things," I murmured as I leaned back and opened my desk drawer, grabbing my spare batteries and tool.

"Pardon?" Adam asked. So proper. I wondered if he was raised by a British butler like I pictured all wealthy people in the world were raised.

"I need to change the batteries really quickly," I explained, glancing at him as I removed one aid and then the other. All background noise in the room went silent.

Adam's eyes quickly widened as he stepped back from my desk and covered his groin with both of his hands.

I dropped my mouth open in shock and started to shake my head, desperate to reassure him his privates were safe, right when he couldn't hold it back anymore and started laughing.

Not that I could hear it super well, but I could see it. How his mouth busted into an open smile and his hand came up to cover it, his body hunching a little in that rhythmic motion that laughter creates.

He was teasing me.

"Very funny," I spoke, probably mumbling the words more now that I couldn't hear myself. I looked up at him after I popped the dying batteries out of the devices so I could try to see what he said.

"I thought so," he crossed his arms over his chest and resumed his position against my desk. I smiled at him and shook my head as I finished replacing the batteries and closed the chamber. I quickly stuck both devices back into my ears, blinking at the sudden intrusion of noise. I turned to him and realized he watched me do the whole thing. I was about to say something, but when Adam leaned forward and reached a hand close to my face, I held my breath.

God, he smelled so good.

"I just," he paused his sentence as his fingers gently brushed some of my dark hair back behind my shoulder, his skin barely skimming my ear, "I didn't know they made hearing aids this tiny. The kids in the clinic who wear aids don't use the tiny ones you have."

Ah, he just wanted to look at the device in my ears. He wasn't flirting with me. *Calm down, Beck.*

"They're kind of a choking hazard for little kids," I replied, trying not to sound breathy or lean into his touch, "But I like them, they are less bulky."

"That must be nice," Adam's face was so close to mine, even though he was looking at the side of my head and not my face, my heart was beating so rapidly he could probably see my pulse. Time was slowing down, because it felt like Adam spent an eternity just staring at me. I glanced at him out of the corner of my eye, and I saw his whiskey-colored gaze meet mine. He definitely wasn't looking at the devices anymore.

"Ahem," I heard Pat clear her throat behind me, and though my body desperately wanted to push back from Adam and shout "Nothing is happening!" I knew that would look more suspicious.

We weren't doing anything inappropriate; Adam was just looking at my hearing aids. He also didn't pull back immediately. He just looked over my shoulder to where Pat was. By the way that his face hardened a little, I had a feeling someone else was standing with Pat at the moment.

"Are we interrupting?" My brain must have been playing tricks on me because I could have sworn Eloise's voice had a slight edge to it. When I turned around to take her in though, she looked calm and collected, with that permanent smile set on her face.

"Nope, I was just checking out her gear," Adam replied, straightening. Pat looked almost relieved at his reply.

"Eloise just wanted our input on the hike really quick," Pat explained, looking just as put out by Eloise's presence as Adam did. Huh, I wondered if she was getting on the administration's nerves as well.

"I was just passing by and thought I'd pop in," Eloise explained, her entire focus now back on Adam. Oh man, she had it bad.

Is that what Courtney thought whenever she saw me look

at him? Probably. The truth was, the more time I spent with Adam, the more I realized I actually *did* have it bad. I was constantly daydreaming about him, what his touch would feel like, what kissing him would feel like. It felt like my crush had turned into a full-blown case of obsession.

I was too happy to see him at the beginning of the work day and too disappointed to go home without the possibility of bumping into him when the work day ended.

I had no idea how I was going to handle two overnights at the large cabin that we were going to be staying in. No doubt we would be in each other's constant company a lot, especially since he would be rooming with Taylor during the trip.

***

A couple of days passed, and I was sitting on our living room floor where Gram was helping Courtney and me pack for two overnights at a luxury cabin in Big Bear. Both of our small suitcases were open in front of us with various items thrown around the room.

"Pajamas, warm and cold?" Gram asked, reading off the list I made.

"Check!" Courtney and I replied.

"Toiletries? Toothbrush, hairbrush, tampons?" Gram continued.

"Check, check, and check," Courtney replied, throwing a couple more tampons in. Neither of us were supposed to be on our period this weekend, but better safe than sorry. Plus, it was always good to keep some on hand in case another fellow uterus owner needed them.

"Condoms?" Gram asked, brows raising at this item as she looked at us accusingly.

"What? Who wrote that?" I asked, leaning over to check the list Gram was reading. Sure enough, the word "condoms" was thrown in the middle of it.

"I did, obviously," Courtney replied, pulling a sleeve of rubbers out of thin air and adding them to her bag, "I have high hopes for this trip."

"Really? Do tell." I laughed as I continued to pack my own clothes.

"What if there is a super hot trail guide? What if the cook at the cabin is also super hot and dying to have sex with me? What if I run into a mountain man in the woods and get swept away to his sexy cabin, and I was naive enough about this trip not to bring protection?" I was laughing at Courtney when she paused and made direct eye contact with me before saying, "What if you and Adam finally hook up?"

I snorted, nice and loud.

"Oh, good point," Gram agreed, ripping off two of the condoms from the sleeve in Courtney's open suitcase and tossing them into mine. Courtney smiled, feeling victorious no doubt.

It said a lot about your dating life when your grandmother was hopefully packing condoms into your suitcase.

"Adam and I aren't going to have sex on this trip," I assured them, adding socks over the newly added contraception.

"Not with that attitude, you're not." Courtney clicked her tongue at me, and I laughed. She was ridiculous, but I loved her.

"Courtney, you and I are sharing a room during this trip.

Would you really want me to try to seduce Adam and bring him back to our shared room? Do you really want to know what I sound like in bed?"

Gram pinched the bridge of her nose in mild disgust while Courtney just shrugged, "I would just bunk with Taylor in their room if Adam was in ours."

I rolled my eyes. She had an answer for everything.

"Better safe than sorry," Gram chimed in, tapping the stack of socks that the condoms were hidden under. I rested my hand on top of hers, squeezing once, and continued packing while Gram continued to recite the list for us.

We would be leaving tomorrow morning, Friday, and the bus ride would be about two hours long. I was finally getting used to being in constant close proximity with Adam at work, for no more than eight hours a day. I was getting a little nervous about the fact that I would be spending over forty-eight hours with him. Not that we would have to be in close proximity the entire time, but with the number of employee bonding activities Eloise had planned for us, it was safe to assume I would have to endure his handsomeness and delicious smelling soap most of the hours we were there.

I glanced nervously at the condoms hidden under the socks. *I should really take them out, it probably wasn't healthy to even entertain the idea...*

I added more underwear to my suitcase, right over the socks, burying the condoms even more.

18

The bus smelled like someone had smoked an entire pack of cigarettes on it. I was sure that by the time the bus dropped us all off after two and a half hours that we all smelled like secondhand smoke, and I desperately wanted to shower.

Unfortunately, Pat and Eloise didn't give a shit and directed us all to unload our luggage to our bedrooms and meet back within a half hour.

That's right, Eloise rode with everyone on the bus. It was weird. I had filled Courtney and Taylor in on the need for us to intervene with Eloise and Adam, and it was like The Avengers assembled around him.

Courtney and Taylor made their way on the bus first, then Adam followed them. We were the last group to check in and load our bags into the storage, so since I was technically the last person on the bus, Eloise tried to physically step in front of me to follow Adam.

I could tell that she had every intention to sit by him on that bus.

So, I hurried my steps and physically bumped into her arm, ensuring I stayed behind him and that she had to enter the bus after me.

She gave me what would have been an undisturbed facial

expression to any normal human being, but because her constant bright smile was not on display, I wondered if it was considered a glare for her. I smiled and said something along the lines of, "Oops, sorry, I'm such a klutz," with all the sincerity I could muster and followed Adam to his seat.

As soon as we were seated, Adam settled against the window with me sitting in the aisle seat opposite Courtney and Taylor. Adam leaned over to whisper a very seductive, "Thank you," near my ear. I noticed how careful he was not to blow too much of his breath toward the hearing aid.

It probably wasn't that seductive, but to my raging hormones and overactive imagination, that's how my body received it. I had to suffer the entire bus ride trying not to think dirty thoughts about Adam whispering other things in my ear, or about the fact that our thighs were touching each other exactly like that one time at the sushi restaurant, because he was a tall and large person and bus seats generally didn't accommodate adults his size.

"Man, I needed this." Adam leaned his head back in his seat, his Adam's apple (ha) emphasized on his neck. I wanted to lick it.

"Hmm?" I asked, making sure to look at his face when he replied.

"You know, a change of scenery?" Adam turned his head towards me to look down at me with slightly hooded eyes. It made me think he was tired and probably going to nap on the drive to Big Bear.

"Oh, of course. It's always nice to get away," I smiled politely at him, trying not to focus too much on the parts of our bodies that were touching each other on the squished bus seat.

"Especially from helicopter parents..." Adam yawned at the end of this sentence before settling into his seat and folding his arms across his chest, man spread activated. Seconds later he leaned his head on the window and closed his eyes before quickly dozing off.

I, however, had no chance in hell of sleeping. The thought of accidentally laying my head on his shoulder was too humiliating to tempt fate. I stayed stiff as a board while Adam slept almost the entirety of the drive there. My skin was buzzing with nervous energy every time his leg or arm or elbow nudged mine throughout the drive.

I might have jumped up a little too quickly when we finally came to a stop and it was time to disembark the vehicle because Courtney raised an eyebrow at me as she started to stand up at a less enthusiastic pace.

The cabin was large (which was good because there were about thirty of us on this trip), and the exterior siding was all wooden logs. It reminded me of my old linking-logs set that I had growing up. It looked exactly like you would picture a cabin at a place called Big Bear, with a large, covered porch surrounding the first level of the two story building.

We all rushed to find our bedrooms and dump our luggage, quickly filling water bottles and packing snacks before we had to head back out. Courtney and I both bought matching fanny packs specifically for this trip because we were super annoying people and because we wanted a convenient way to keep snacks on us 24/7.

The fanny packs had a hideous camo print on them, and as

we rejoined the group and started to trek our way down towards the woods where the ropes course was, we made fun of our fanny packs so others would feel comfortable to as well.

"I'll try not to lose sight of you in the woods, I wouldn't want you to get lost," Courtney teased as she linked one of her arms through mine.

"Who is getting lost?" I heard Eloise ask as she quickly caught up to where the four of us were walking.

"Hopefully not Beck and I, but with these camouflage fannies, we might just accidentally blend in with our surroundings." I giggled at Courtney's stupid joke while Taylor groaned at us with annoyance and rolled their eyes.

I looked over my shoulder to see Adam walking behind us, with Eloise taking up residence right next to him. Whoops.

"For a second, I thought your torso was cut off from your hips. It looked like there was a transparent strip dividing your body from itself," I added, pulling Courtney away from me so I could take in her outfit.

We both wore khaki shorts that were fairly short, definitely not something I would have been allowed to wear growing up. It was warmer this far inland. Drier, too. I was grateful for the booty-shorts because I was already missing that ocean breeze I had become so used to.

Courtney had her blonde hair in a perfect ponytail while rocking a bright yellow tank top, I had my dark hair in a less perfect ponytail and was wearing a plain white tank top. It was thick, so my skin-colored sports bra didn't show through.

We were looking cute, minus our fanny packs.

Eloise had a full face of makeup, nothing sparkly or bold, but she was wearing enough makeup to pull off a flawless natural look. She wore camel-colored shorts similar in style to what Courtney and I wore, along with what looked like brand new hiking boots and a cream tank top that made her skin look tan. Her ponytail was a little extra with her hair French braided until it reached the knot of her pony.

If there was a chance that I could learn to appreciate her and become friends on this trip, I would like to ask her to do that same fancy ponytail for me. It was cute.

At the moment, that seemed unlikely.

"I can't believe you guys are wearing those things," Taylor shook their head at us. They were wearing an athletic t-shirt and cargo shorts, along with tube socks and hiking shoes that had clearly been used thoroughly during their lifetime.

"I can't believe you wouldn't buy one for yourself," Courtney tsked her tongue at Taylor. I was there at the thrift store. There were three, and even though we FaceTimed Taylor at the store asking if they would be willing to wear them with us, they firmly stood against the look.

"They're...cute..." Eloise's nose scrunched as she glanced at Courtney and me, now separated and posing dramatically throughout the walk. We were falling behind the rest of our coworkers.

"We know they're hideous, you don't have to pretend," I smiled at Eloise, pausing my stride and pressing my fists on my hips in an attempt to proudly display our fashionable find.

"Then...why are you wearing them?" Eloise seemed genuinely confused. I guess I understood, it was odd for late twenty-somethings to buy a fanny pack simply because we thought it was hilariously ugly.

"It brings us joy," Courtney walked ahead of us to jump in

the air and click her heels together. It was perfectly executed, except when she attempted to land, she didn't know that she was above a patch of wet mud, and slipped directly onto her butt.

Taylor and I started cracking up.

Tears were falling down my cheeks from laughter as Adam walked around us cackling at her hilarious failure and helped Courtney back up.

"Oh no! Your shorts!" Eloise cried, holding her cheeks as if the mud that was now covering Courtney's butt was a travesty.

"Ah, it's fine," Courtney flapped her hand as if to dismiss the whole thing, and then flipped off Taylor and me instead. We were still trying to catch our breath.

Eloise's lips were twitching as if she also was trying to hold in laughter.

Courtney looped her arm through one of Adam's, sticking her nose up in the air as if she was done with us, and my laughter immediately died down.

How was Courtney already comfortable wrapping onto Adam's arm like that?

Was I friends enough with him to touch him like that?

I shook the intrusive thoughts away and grabbed onto Taylor's and Eloise's arms, settling in between them and continuing the hike down the hill towards the ropes course.

The ropes course was newly built, so it looked like it had hardly been used at all. The course guides were younger—maybe early twenties—and kept all the directions short and to the point. It took a few minutes to get everyone's gear buckled and learn how to use the various carabiners needed to make it across.

"I was worried for a minute that these wouldn't fit with our fashionable fannies, but thankfully they do. Crisis averted." Courtney smiled at me as she noted this, tugging her straps until everything was nice and secure. We gave each other a high five and then we clinked our helmets against each other for shits and giggles. We both turned to look at our friends, noticing Taylor had no issue putting together their harness as if they had done this sort of thing a dozen times.

Adam had a frown on his face as he tightened the last of his straps, his light eyes darting at the ropes course ahead of us and quickly darting away. He looked stressed, and Eloise wasn't even standing that close to him. In fact, she was off to the side chatting with Pat.

I wondered what that was about.

We were the last to arrive at the ropes course, the last to get all suited up, and the last to climb up and start. It was a beginner's ropes course, thank god because my balance was pure horse shit. This was proven as I wobbled and swayed consistently throughout the first course, and it was only about fifteen feet up off the ground. Thankfully there was safety netting under the entirety of the course, but that didn't comfort my balancing skills at all.

"Beck, I think you should wiggle the ropes some more. I would hate to continue doing this without the constant fear of falling," Courtney's dry humor was topped off by her turning around to give me an eye roll. She was following behind Eloise, who kept looking over her shoulder to check on us all. Adam and Taylor were behind me holding up the rear.

"Hey, Court? Maybe...shut the fuck up?" Then I wiggled the rope that she had a grip on maliciously because I was a child.

"Girl, chill! We could technically fall from this!" Courtney scolded me in between her giggles.

"Again, not *technically*, you *actually* could fall from this! That's what our harnesses are for, idiots," Taylor called from behind us. That made Courtney and I laugh even harder, I had to stop in the middle of the ropes bridge to try to get a containment on my laughter.

"We should keep moving," Adam's voice spoke up from behind me. I turned to look up at him with tears in my eyes and a goofy grin on my face that quickly faded when I took in the sight of him.

His face was hard and stern, and both of his hands were gripping the ropes so tightly that his knuckles were white. His brows were lowered into a pinch, and he wouldn't make direct eye contact with me.

I had a sneaking suspicion that Adam wasn't having as much fun as Courtney and me on this course.

"Sorry," I threw a flippant grin at him to attempt to lighten the mood before turning back and following Courtney to the platform.

The course probably took two hours for all of us to complete. We were a large group and some of us were slower than others (like Courtney and I), and it took a while to ensure everyone started the next section of rope safely secured. My legs and arms were starting to get sore from balancing and pulling myself across course after course.

Taylor wasn't even out of breath, the physically fit asshole.

We finally made it up to the last stretch of rope, which also happened to be the highest section of all. The safety net underneath was a concerning distance from where we all stood up high on the platforms.

Like every other station on this course, our small group took our sweet time and let the rest of our coworkers start the course in a more timely manner. Eloise always went first, Courtney following her, then me, then Adam, then Taylor who was being a surprisingly good sport about waiting on our slow butts.

"Shit," Courtney mumbled as she took her turn to cross the last stretch, she was much more hesitant this high up.

"You got this! Believe it, achieve it!" I encouraged her with a friendly smack on her ass.

"Believe it, achieve it…believe it, achieve it…" Courtney murmured to herself as she kept her eyes on her feet and shuffled along the wobbly ropes bridge. Eloise had already jumped up onto the last platform and had turned around to check on us before starting her climb down the ladder, where the rest of our coworkers were waiting for us.

"You go ahead," Adam murmured behind me. He looked like he had been in a sour mood the entire time, which I think helped Eloise keep her distance from him.

"You sure?" I heard Taylor ask. I turned around to smile at Taylor as well.

"You've been stuck behind us the whole time. You go," I smiled at them as they quickly latched their carabiner to the course. They had no problems going ahead of us, apparently.

"Finally! You guys are slow as hell," Taylor complained,

throwing a teasing wink my way before confidently maneuvering their way toward Courtney, who was still midway through the course.

I cupped my hands and called out to my best friend, "You better hurry, otherwise Taylor will mow you over!"

Courtney responded by keeping both her feet and hands attached to the ropes at all times and shuffling quickly across the bridge, a movement that looked both awkward and hilarious.

I laughed at her before latching my carabiner and turning to face the grump of the day, "We are *so* close to being done with this." I had a feeling his grumpy mood was because he didn't think this was fun at all. To be fair, this ended up not being that fun after two hours of maneuvering obstacle courses made out of rough rope. I didn't see myself ever doing something like this again.

Adam just nodded at me, his light eyes meeting mine for half a second before looking down at how high up we were.

I took the first couple of tentative steps needed to start the bridge, and I called out to Taylor, "Alright, T. Amateur hour is over, time to show you how it's done!"

Taylor had gently shoved Courtney along to help her finish the bridge in a timelier manner and was climbing up onto the last platform as I addressed them. They responded by just turning around to laugh at me directly.

Well, fuck you very much.

I took a few more steps, starting to feel more confident, before calling over my shoulder to the frowning red-head, "On a scale of one to ten, how likely are you to *never* do this again?" I smiled at myself as I took a deep breath before continuing on. I had about three quarters of the way to go.

How the hell did Courtney and Taylor sprint across this thing?

"I'm going with a solid eight point five, personally," I added, realizing Adam hadn't responded to my pathetic attempt at small talk.

Before continuing I decided to check on the grump. I looked over my shoulder to see Adam standing stock still, having paused his progress a few feet behind me. He was staring wide-eyed at his feet.

"…Adam?" I asked, trying to hide the concern in my voice.

He didn't acknowledge me at all, not even with a glance. He was painfully frozen, gripping the ropes and not moving a single muscle. His brow was pinched together, but he wasn't glaring at anything anymore. His face looked incredibly pale all of a sudden.

He looked terrified.

Oh shit.

"Hey," I called back to him, turning around fully. Everyone else was finished and we were the last two to complete the course. I shuffled back over to Adam, who seemed to grip the ropes even tighter when he sensed my presence and finally tore his eyes away from the ground below us.

"Don't look down," I told him when I met his gaze. He huffed through his nose and his eyes immediately dropped back towards our feet, "Hey! I'm serious! Don't look down. Look at me."

He was breathing sharp, short breaths through his nose now. His lips pressed so tightly together that they were almost white. I scooted closer to him until I could rest both of my hands on his, holding the ropes tied to either side of us.

It was in the high eighties this far inland, and Adam's hands were cold. Not a great sign.

"Adam," My voice was calm and controlled, with a hint of authority I usually used for my more disruptive clients, "Breathe in through your nose, out through your mouth. Eyes on me."

There was a strange phenomenon that happened when one person happened to be freaking the fuck out and I wasn't. Courtney called it the Mom Friend Override. I would never correct a waiter for bringing me the wrong dish I ordered, but if Courtney had been the one to get the wrong dish, I would have asked the waiter to exchange her food on her behalf. I wouldn't even hesitate.

If I was too nervous to advocate for myself, Courtney's Mom Friend Override would kick in and she would speak up for me.

The same scenario was happening now. I was previously nervous about being this high up off the ground, but now that I could see Adam was clearly in distress, my anxiety seemed to vanish.

I needed to act as some sort of anchor here.

Adam reluctantly lifted his whiskey-colored eyes to meet mine, showing me more of the whites than he usually exposed.

"Good, breathe," I reminded him, keeping my foot on the ropes and sliding one step backward, holding his gaze.

He hesitantly followed my movements. In hindsight, it was nice of Courtney to show us her dorky shuffle that allowed us to keep both hands and feet attached to the ropes at once. It seemed to give Adam a sense of stability.

"I heard that they were going to serve us sandwiches for lunch today," I thought maybe talking about something that wasn't standing above fifty feet off the ground would be helpful, "I doubt they have your favorite, though."

He kept his gaze on my face, I could tell he was struggling to keep himself from looking back down at the ground with the glacial pace we were making, "My favorite?" He asked, his voice rough from nerves.

"Meatball subs," I smirked at him, "You eat them, like, seventy-five percent of the time."

"...Almost as much as you eat tuna," Adam quipped back. His lips tipped up in a weak smirk before flattening again.

"And pudding cups," I added, looking over my shoulder to see how much farther we had to go. Thankfully we were approaching the halfway mark, but Courtney and Taylor were still waiting for us on the other end.

"Everything okay?" Taylor called out to us, probably just now realizing that things definitely weren't okay. Adam looked over my shoulder at them and frowned, a hardness tightening around his eyes. I squeezed his hands underneath mine once and regained his attention.

"Mind your business!" I called back to Taylor while keeping my eyes on the large man in front of me, "Oklahoma, what are you thinking right now?"

"Oklahoma? What?" Adam asked, his body movements still seeming robotic.

"It's our safe word," His eyes widened at that, "Not like that!"

All the color that had previously drained from Adam's face was probably flooding the entirety of mine because *of course* he would think sexually. I tried to recover, "It's from a TV show! My favorite, actually. Any time someone says the word 'Oklahoma' the other person is supposed to tell the 'God's honest truth' no matter what."

Adam's dark brows furrowed. Thankfully not out of fear, but of confusion. Excellent, my distraction methods seemed to be making progress with his anxiety levels.

"Huh," was all he said, I could see that I was starting to lose his attention, so I tried again.

"Oklahoma, what is *your* favorite TV show?"

For a moment he squinted up at the sun shining down on us before looking back at me and saying, "I can't think about that right now."

If he was a toddler, I would have congratulated him on how well he was able to communicate how he was feeling. Since he was an adult, I just felt sympathy for him for being so distressed.

"I see you as a guy who rewatches *The Office* all the time. Maybe *Sons of Anarchy*," I smiled at him as I squeezed the tops of his hands again. He barely lifted the corner of his mouth as we got closer to the end of the bridge.

When I felt my foot hit the platform I turned around and climbed up onto it, turning around to find Adam still stuck just before he could climb as well.

There was about six inches of space between the ropes and the platform, and that's where Adam's eyes were.

"Hey, big guy," I called down to him, reaching with my

arms to physically grab his jaw and tilt his head up and away from what I'm sure he pictured as his sudden death. His eyes were wide with fear until they met mine, then they started to focus a bit more and his breathing started to become more even.

"Want a hand?" I heard Taylor ask from my side. I scooted over so we could each take one of Adam's hands and help him step up onto the platform where Courtney and Taylor had watched the entire thing.

What I wasn't expecting after Adam crawled onto the platform was for him to almost tackle me to the floorboards.

He never got up off of his hands and knees. Instead, he released a large exhale and blindly tugged the hand that was holding mine toward his body. Then he wrapped both of his large arms around me, laying down on his side and taking me with him.

I made an *oof* sound as we settled against the floorboards.

Every muscle in his body was stiff, and as he buried his head against my shoulder, I realized he was shaking, his breathing still choppy and unbalanced.

My heart crumbled.

"You're safe." Mom Friend Override activated, "You made it. You're safe. Take some deep breaths."

He was gripping me so tightly that I tried not to let my strain show through my voice. I could feel his breath gush out of him in waves against my shoulder and collarbone. I managed to wiggle my arms free and wrap one around his shoulder and one around his waist, rubbing my hands all over his back to help him feel grounded.

I also had the opportunity to reach my hand up and brush my fingertips along his hairline.

I fucking knew his hair would be stupid soft.

"Take your time, no rush," Courtney's soft voice came from behind me. I could see in my peripherals that Taylor was staying close by to where Adam and I were bundled on the floorboards.

"Hey! Are you guys heading down soon?" We heard Eloise call from below. Adam's arms seemed to reflexively tighten around me at the sound of her voice.

"We're enjoying the view!" Taylor replied without missing a beat. We were so high up at this point that the rest of our coworkers probably couldn't see Adam and me embracing each other on the floor.

"…Well, you probably shouldn't stay up there too long. It's time to have lunch soon!" Eloise replied. I looked up to see Taylor give her a thumbs up instead of a verbal response.

"…I'm sorry…I'm sorry…" Adam's voice was small and dry as if he was gasping for air. His grip on my torso loosened a little bit before tightening again.

"Don't be sorry. You're fine. You're safe." I gave him a reassuring squeeze back, which probably took a lot more effort on my part since I wasn't nearly the size he was.

The four of us stayed up there for a while longer. It could have been five minutes; it could have been half an hour. I had no idea. All I could focus on was Adam's breathing, the way it felt to have his arms desperately wrapped around me, and how I suddenly was given permission to not only embrace him back but also draw soothing circles on his back and shoulder. How if my hand crawled up towards his neck and hairline he seemed to lean into the touch and relax a little.

Eventually, his panic attack finally seemed to subside.

He slowly, slowly released his hold on me. It seemed to take an incredible amount of physical effort for each of his fingers to undo their grip on my shoulder and waist. Eventually, he untucked one of his arms from underneath me and rolled onto his back, his arms folding over his eyes.

It was at this moment that I couldn't stop myself from admiring him again. He was wearing a white t-shirt today, which showed off the sleeve on one of his arms. For some reason, seeing his arms flexed this way looked incredibly attractive.

Not the time to ogle him, Beck.

"I'm sorry," Adam mumbled, his voice starting to regain normalcy.

"Don't be sorry," Taylor piped up. Along with Courtney, they were sitting crossed legged, looking out at the trees and nature around us.

"We all need a little grounding sometimes," Courtney added, pulling her phone out of her butt pocket and checking the time, "I could feel Eloise's FOMO from here."

"Eloise can suck a fart," I replied, reaching out to squeeze Adam's wrist with my hand.

At my rude response, Adam lifted his arms and looked at me, shocked, before laughter erupted out of him. Taylor and Courtney started howling too, which I think helped ease some of the tension that was radiating off of Adam.

We helped each other up and made our way down the

ladder, back to solid ground. Adam took his steps a little more carefully, but once he finally touched the ground his entire body seemed to relax.

"C'mon, guys!" I heard Pat call us from the far distance. Everyone else seemed to be gathered towards the top of the hill where the cabin was, and I thought I caught a whiff of food in the air.

Oh man, I was so hungry.

"Anyone want to race?" Taylor asked, hopping on the balls of their feet with every step they took. I could tell they were still thrumming with energy because for some reason the ropes course wasn't enough exercise for them.

Instead of responding, Courtney smacked their ass and took off up the hill, making them laugh as they chased after her.

Adam and I were normal and didn't feel the need to run up the hill, so we continued walking at a leisurely pace. I peeked a glance at him out of the corner of my eye. His hands were shoved in the pockets of his joggers as he stared at the ground. He looked almost defeated, and I suddenly wanted nothing more in the world than to make him feel better.

I decided that I should just start talking, maybe that would help him get out of his own head, "Whenever I have panic attacks, it feels better to eat and then take a three-hour nap." I shrugged and kicked a stray rock, in an attempt to look super casual about this.

Out of the corner of my eye, I saw Adam's head turn towards me, pausing a few moments before saying, "You have panic attacks?"

"Of course. Everyone has panic attacks." I nudged his arm with mine to create a sense of camaraderie.

"…I haven't had one in a long time," Adam started, "Not for a year, at least."

"It sucks when they sneak up on you, right?" I looked up at him, taking in the way his red hair glistened in the sunlight. Color had returned to his handsome face.

"Yeah…" it took a few moments for him to add, "The last one I had was before my last surf meet."

I lifted my eyebrows at this. I still knew very little about his previous occupation.

"What happened?" I asked. I was thrilled that he was opening up to me about this. It showed an incredible amount of trust, which I would never take for granted from him.

"According to my therapist," Adam started, adding at least ten points of sexiness simply by acknowledging that he went to therapy, "I ignored too many things going on in my life and allowed them all to blow up the moment I felt too much stress." He lifted a shoulder.

"…What things?" Shit, maybe I was pushing too hard.

"The usual; helicopter parents. My mother trying to be involved with every aspect of my adult life. A girlfriend who needed everyone to like her and would do anything to make my mother happy. Feeling like my life and choices weren't my own," he released a long sigh as if it felt good to get this off his chest, "I think that's why I quit competing. I realized I didn't feel joy or purpose from it anymore. I was just going through the motions because it was expected of me. My mother always wanted an Olympian for a son, and Eloise wanted to be on the arm of one…but I felt like a shell."

My heart swelled for this man.

His relationships with these women in his life were all starting to make more sense now, and I couldn't believe that Adam was comfortable talking to me about this. It was an honor, considering at the very beginning I never thought that I could handle holding a simple conversation with him without my hormones bursting through my skin.

"...So, you hit the reset button on your life and decided working with babies and toddlers was way cooler than being an Olympian?" I grinned at him as he looked down at me with a smirk.

"After a long wave of depression, where I hardly left my apartment and wondered what I was doing with my life, yes. I decided to put my degree to good use." he gave me a smile then, "And I'm glad I made that choice for myself...because my job is awesome."

"Fuck yeah, it is!" I lifted my hand for a fist bump, something Taylor would probably do in the moment. Adam laughed while meeting my fist and then wrapped an arm around my shoulders and pulled me in close to his body.

Oh god, he was hugging me.

A side hug, but a hug.

A hug that didn't happen during the throes of a panic attack.

"Thank you, for helping me back there," Adam mumbled during a squeeze. "In case you haven't realized, I'm scared of heights. I will probably be embarrassed for the rest of my life, but I appreciated the assistance. Also, sorry for, um, tackling you."

I grinned and wrapped one of my arms around his waist

because apparently, that's how close we were as friends now. Perhaps it was because he saw how physically affectionate Courtney, Taylor, and I were with each other. If Adam was going to be part of our friend group, it only made sense that he hugged us as much as we hugged each other.

Even if my racing heart was confused and hoping that he was hugging me for purely selfish and romantic reasons.

"Don't apologize, I'm happy to be a personal weighted blanket. It always feels good to be given a spontaneous bear hug." I released his waist, and he released my shoulders, and when I glanced up at him something had clicked into place in my brain that both thrilled and terrified me.

I think I'm falling in love with you.

The thought was intrusive and shocking. I physically gasped at the realization of it, stumbling over my own feet and barely keeping myself upright. An embarrassing and vulnerable moment that Adam was now a personal witness to.

"Whoa, you alright?" Adam asked, gently grabbing my shoulder to steady me. His touch scorched my skin, sending thrilling waves of electricity throughout my body. I nodded and pasted a casual grin on my face as I gently tugged my arm free of his grasp.

"Yup, just clumsy sometimes," which wasn't a total lie. Like baby Claire, I was also prone to moments of unbalance.

"Alright," Adam subtly lifted an eyebrow, looking a little more suspicious than I liked. He must have noticed the sudden change in my mood. We were almost at the top of the hill where the rest of our coworkers were starting to head towards the cabin's outdoor dining area.

Eloise caught sight of us and started to make her way over. I looked up at Adam to see him release a slightly annoyed sigh at the sight of her.

I gently tapped his forearm to regain his attention. "Not to be too sentimental, but," I glanced over at Eloise again, remembering what little he had said about their relationship, and feeling a swell of emotion rise inside of me as I quoted a phrase I had heard from somewhere, that felt weirdly fitting at this moment, "…I just…I hope that someday, you can find a partner who speaks your language…that way you don't need to spend the rest of your life trying to translate your soul."

There was a very real possibility that I was projecting.

Adam blinked at me, clearly caught off guard by my unsolicited relationship advice. I gave him a weak grin and squeezed his forearm before walking away in search of Courtney and Taylor. I passed Eloise just as I caught the look of suspicion on her face as she eyeballed both Adam and me.

I was in huge fucking trouble.

19

I made things weird the rest of the day.

Thankfully, Pat and Eloise kept the day's itinerary casual, so we pretty much just ate food and played outdoor games like volleyball and bocce ball. Around late afternoon Pat retrieved a large rolling cooler from the bus and disappeared into the kitchen. Minutes later, she emerged with the cooler filled with ice, soda, and hard seltzers.

"We spend so much time around kids for work, I figured it would be nice to make the weekend feel more adult," were the words Pat used to justify the alcohol.

I didn't drink any, feeling unnerved by my earlier revelation.

It was all coming together. The way my heart would pick up speed any time Adam entered a room. How my day to day at work was now broken up by when I would run into him and when I wouldn't. How I constantly was daydreaming about simply touching him, and how I valued our one-on-one chats more than the average friendship.

I was getting ahead of myself.

It couldn't possibly be healthy feeling all these big feelings after getting to know him over such a short amount of time;

it must have been due to my inexperience with physical attraction and boundaries.

It was as if Adam pulling me in for a side hug was the last puzzle piece that clicked into place, cementing the growing infatuation and attraction I had for him over the last few weeks into real, adult feelings.

I couldn't wrap my head around it, and the thought of that being my new reality terrified me.

So, after giving him unsolicited relationship advice after the ropes course, I went out of my way to keep my distance from him. I would follow Courtney and Taylor around, trying to be subtle about it. I would choose seats specifically by Courtney or Taylor, instead of our usual seating arrangement where I would find the seat next to Adam. If he noticed my avoidance, he didn't act like it, which brought me relief.

The downside of my avoidance was that Eloise was taking full advantage of it, leaving it up to either Taylor or Courtney to be Adam's buffer. She was acting oblivious to Adam's uncomfortable body language, which was wild to me because it seemed so obvious whenever she entered the same space that he was in.

"You're being weird," Courtney murmured to me when we were all settled around one of the large campfires that evening.

"What? How?" I was proud of myself for how genuine my confusion sounded.

"I've been watching you for weeks, Beck," Courtney scooted closer to me on the log we were sharing, in an attempt to keep the conversation private. "And I've seen how you can't stop yourself from eyeballing him," she nodded her head vaguely towards Adam, who sat a few logs away with Taylor and Eloise, "but suddenly, you can't even look in his direction. You're glued to my side. What's up with that?"

"I…" I shrugged, "I'm just trying to not be so obsessive, I guess." It wasn't entirely a lie, but Courtney narrowed her eyes at me as if she knew I was leaving something out. I quickly looked away from her and watched some of our coworkers attempt to roast marshmallows over the large fire.

"It's just…" I turned back to her, to see her shaking her head at me, meeting my gaze before continuing, "It seems pretty shitty to support him during one of his most vulnerable moments at the ropes course, only for you to avoid him immediately afterward."

My heart sank into my gut at her words.

Courtney was completely right.

She must have known that her words hit their mark because she dropped it and pulled out her phone to scroll through the pictures she had taken throughout the day. We didn't have the best service out here, but depending on where we were at the campsite, we could get a couple of bars.

I glanced over to where our friends were sitting, only to unexpectedly make direct eye contact with the most beautiful pair of brown eyes I'd ever seen.

Adam was staring at me.

I felt my heartbeat pick up speed, an all too familiar physical response to his attention and held his gaze. Eloise was sitting as close to his side as possible, holding her own marshmallow stick towards the fire and seemingly chatting nonstop. Not that Adam looked like he was paying a lick of attention.

I attempted to give him a friendly smile across the fire.

One corner of his mouth tipped up, and ease relaxed into my shoulders. Hopefully, he didn't think I was giving him the cold shoulder *because* he was so vulnerable with me earlier, but I was stuck on how I should be handling the situation going forward.

Clearly, if I spent too much time in his direct presence and we continued those little side hugs and friendly touches, I was prone to falling in love with him. This was a problem because as Courtney had said previously, dating your coworker was generally a no-no.

Separation and distance seemed like the logical solution to that problem. Courtney was also right though, because it was incredibly shitty to avoid him after bonding the way that we did. I felt trapped between two impossible scenarios, which did nothing for my racing heart.

That evening we all said our goodbyes as we filed to bed, exhausted from the traveling and physical exertion. Pat and Eloise kept reminding everyone that we all needed to wake up bright and early the next day in order to do the hike. Eloise assured everyone it was a beginner's leisure hike, only about five miles long (which Taylor translated to mean that it would take about two, maybe two and a half hours long to complete).

That meant nothing to me. So that night I found myself in our small bedroom that reminded me of the more stereotypical grandparents' house, preparing my ugly fanny pack and backpack as if we were going to be without plumbing and food for most of the day. The room was small and narrow, just large enough to fit two twin beds with a single nightstand in between them, a tall dresser, and two paintings of what looked like elk. Dark wood paneling covered all four walls and the ceiling, matching the wooden floors. The beds had brown and red flannel covers on top of them. Courtney was sitting on one of the beds brushing out her hair before bed.

"Trail mix, band-aids, water..." I was murmuring to myself as I packed everything together.

"Condoms..." Courtney added dryly.

"Ha-ha," I flipped her off over my shoulder. After double checking everything I thought I may or may not need, I set my bags by the door. This way I could sleep in as late as possible because all the packing had been done the night before.

I removed my hearing aids and set them on the nightstand. There was one window in the room that we left open a few inches, and the distant sound of cicadas and other wildlife faded into silence with the loss of my hearing aids. I exhaled a relieved breath as I snuggled into the musty bed, a few feet away from where Courtney lay in hers.

I looked over at her to wish her goodnight when she started signing to me.

I want you to be happy.

I smiled at her; *I want you to be happy too.*

Allow yourself to be happy, Courtney responded with a small frown on her face. I blinked at her, not entirely sure what she meant by that, but nodded at her anyway. She gave me a single nod as well before rolling over and pulling the covers over her shoulders.

I lay there in the dark and silence for a few moments,

trying to process all the events that have led up to me spiraling about my feelings towards Adam. Spending more and more time with him certainly hasn't helped, but that was not his fault.

If the situation was reversed, and I had recently gained a close friend that suddenly closed themselves off from me because they couldn't control their feelings, I would be sad or heartbroken.

Would Adam really be heartbroken, though?

I pictured him being more bummed than anything.

It wasn't like he and I were best friends, like Courtney and I, but it seemed obvious the more time we spent together the more comfortable he felt confiding in me. I did not want to lose that safety net for him. I let my thoughts of anxiety run freely, eventually morphing them into the daydreams that I usually had of Adam, before finally drifting off into a deep, deep sleep.

20

The next morning, I decided that it was best to confide in one of the two people in the world I could talk to about anything.

"I think I'm falling for Adam," I blurted out as Courtney and I were getting dressed. She was in the middle of putting on one of her brightly colored shirts over her head before making a shocked noise in her throat and getting stuck in it. Eventually, she tugged it over her head and slipped her arms through, turning to look at me wide-eyed in reaction to what I just said.

"*Falling* for him?" Courtney asked, making sure she heard me correctly.

I heard a few distant voices come in from our still cracked window and decided I felt safer signing to her.

We had a moment after the ropes course, I explained with my hands, *and he hugged me. It was friendly, nothing romantic happened, but it was like an anvil got dropped on my head.*

Courtney smiled at how I decided to sign that, by spelling out the word anvil and dramatically miming it falling over me and crushing me. ASL was an awesome language.

I like him too much, I finished, exhaling with the relief it felt to get the words out in the open. Courtney quirked her lips to the side and looked at something over my shoulder (probably the ugly deer paintings) and thought about her words before responding.

One time in college we were discussing something of great importance to me, not that I could remember the topic of conversation years later. During the discussion, Courtney did a similar thing where she quirked her lips to the side and stayed silent. I couldn't handle it. I was twitching with anxiety about what her response was going to be. I eventually asked her what she was doing, staying silent like that, and she just looked at me and said, "I'm thinking before I'm speaking."

I flipped her off and told her that that was cheating, and we had laughed about that interaction multiple times since.

Not now, though. Now I was waiting patiently for her to give even a sliver of advice.

Courtney lifted her hands to continue our conversation in ASL, *you should ask him out.*

I rolled my eyes at her and turned to clip on the ugly camo fanny pack.

"Hey, I'm serious," Courtney spoke with my back turned to her.

"I am too, Court," I glanced over my shoulder and bent to grab my backpack. "I fucked this all up. I'm already in too deep with him. Starting something like that will most likely just end up with me eating inhuman amounts of chocolate and sobbing into my pillow. Then I'd have to wipe my eyes clean and deal with seeing him at work every day." I nibbled on my top lip; troll face activated.

"Yeah, that could totally happen," Courtney shrugged as she clipped her matching fanny around her waist, "Or, he could be the one."

I paused as I went to sit on the bed and slip my hiking boots on. "There is no such thing as, 'the one'." I reminded her. This was a callback of one discussion we had after reading a specific series of romance novels together that dived into that very concept. Essentially, we concluded that the whole idea of 'the one' was a manipulative PR move by men in an attempt to put pressure on women to commit and marry prematurely. If there was the fear that women could be missing their one opportunity for happiness, they were more likely to look past major red flags in their relationships and settle. Hard.

Discarding the archaic fairy tale of The One has only brought more success and happiness to both men and women because it made people feel safe enough to be as picky as they needed to be if they truly wanted to find a life partner.

"No, there isn't. But I do believe in 'the handful', and there is a possibility that Adam is part of *your* handful of possibilities for a successful and thriving partnership," Courtney explained, slipping her feet into her boots and bending down to tie them. I finished tying my laces up and thrummed my fingers on my knees, trying to channel her and be more thoughtful in my response.

She stood and nodded her head towards the door for us to head out and meet with the rest of our coworkers. As soon as we walked down the long hallway that led to the stairs towards the front door, I lifted my hands to continue our conversation in ASL in an attempt to keep it private in the presence of others.

I don't think I'm brave enough to handle his rejection, I admitted. Up ahead I caught a glimpse of the sexy red-head near the back of the group that was loading onto the bus, standing with Taylor and Eloise.

You might not be. But if he does reject you in any way, I will be here to supply the chocolate and tear-free pillowcases, Courtney smiled brightly at me and tugged on my ponytail. I snorted at her and tugged hers in return.

"Hey, girlies!" Eloise smiled and waved while standing on her tiptoes when she noticed us approaching. Sunshine incarnate.

"Hey…you!" Courtney was clearly caught off guard but leaned into it with a pair of finger guns. Eloise lifted her head back and laughed, clearly delighted by the interaction.

"You guys ready?" Taylor asked, leaning towards their shoulder to take a sip from one of those backpack water bottles people who have been on more than one hike in their lifetime tend to use.

"Nope, but I brought my Bluetooth speaker to make it bearable," Courtney reached into her backpack and pulled out a tiny speaker, then dabbed un-ironically.

"Oh, what a good idea! We can have a little party while we hike!" Eloise's bright blue eyes bounced between all of us, and after a moment of silence Courtney and I pasted smiles on our faces and replied with mumblings of, "Yeah, exactly."

When Adam forced himself into our group, it felt natural (except for the fact that I had wanted to jump his bones from day one), but for some reason when Eloise chimed in and forced herself into our circle, it felt uncomfortable.

"Alright, let's go," Adam broke the awkward silence by stepping forward, around Eloise's body and next to where Courtney and I were standing, herding us towards the bus doors.

I failed as a buffer again. In a panic of realizing I could sit close enough to Adam to touch thighs, I quickly plopped down next to Courtney, even though everyone was probably expecting Taylor to sit next to her again.

Thankfully, Taylor pulled through by piping up behind Eloise, who was eager to rush into the seat next to Adam's, "Oh, Adam, I wanted to ask you about one of our clients before I forgot—Eloise, do you mind if I sit there?"

She had been gripping the back of the seat in front of the one she was hovering over, before she pasted a pained smile on her face and nodded, surrendering the empty seat for Taylor.

Courtney elbowed me in the ribs, and I grunted and pretended to ignore her by pulling my phone out and connecting the Bluetooth with my own music to my hearing aids. I sighed and leaned back, listening to the angry feminist pop punk band I was slowly becoming obsessed with.

I felt an odd sensation on the side of my face, and without realizing I instinctively turned my head to see that Adam had been staring at me over Taylor's shoulder, turning to look away just as I turned to face him.

Was he upset with me?

That was ridiculous. There was no real reason for him to be upset. I just needed to chat with him as soon as we unloaded the bus and started the hike, and that would send the message that everything was totally fine and normal between us.

Once we unloaded the bus, Pat and Eloise ensured that everyone was accounted for, and we all started down the paved trail. As usual, our little group held up the rear of the party.

At first, the hike was beautiful (for inland California, which was normally known for being a hot, ugly brown desert), but that beauty was suddenly in the back of my mind as soon as my legs reminded me that we hadn't gone to the gym in months. After a while, everyone started to slow their pace, even though I felt like the only one with flushed cheeks and heavy breathing. Taylor and Courtney were occasionally breaking out in comical dances whenever a hit played through Courtney's Bluetooth speaker, which made me wheeze and laugh a couple of times.

I was finally physically exhausted enough that when Adam fell into step right next to me my reaction wasn't immediate panic. In fact, I wondered if he would be willing to support my weight because my legs were going to scream at me later tonight if I didn't stretch and drink a shit ton of water after this.

"How are you doing?" I heard his low voice ask when our friends were a few paces ahead of us. Courtney and Taylor started singing along with the music, while Eloise followed behind them and kept checking over her shoulder to keep an eye on Adam and me.

Probably to make sure I didn't pass out and die on the trail, I was confident I didn't look great.

"I'm...out of shape," I exhaled and gave Adam a weak grin.

"Want to take a break?" Adam asked, stepping closer to my space. I didn't want to look like a weakling, and I knew Taylor would roast me for this, but I nodded my head and started to come to a complete stop.

Adam immediately let out a whistle to get our friend's attention, but I didn't realize just how close he was standing to me until his shrill sound echoed directly into my hearing aid and made me see stars.

If that's what my hearing aids did when someone blew a whistle too close to my ears, it was definitely time to get new ones.

I felt myself stumble backwards away from the sound instinctively, blinking in an attempt to clear my vision. After a moment I decided the best thing to do was to remove the device from my ear completely so that it would stop recreating the whistle in my ear.

Man, these things were getting shittier and shittier by the day.

The ringing finally stopped and I blinked my vision clear, glancing over at Adam next to me in time to see his lips move, "Oh shit, I shouldn't have done that."

I shook my head and smiled up at him as I reached to put the device back in my ear. It was then that I realized he had one of his large freckled hands resting on my shoulder, his concerned expression scanning my face as if he might have blown my ear drum out.

I mean, that definitely felt like a possibility at the moment.

"You're fine, it was just unexpected," I smiled at him. I felt the heat from his hand seep into my body, and before I could let my treacherous heart mistake his concern for anything other than what it was, I shrugged out of his grip and stepped back, creating a little more distance between us.

At this, Adam made the smallest frown.

"Did Adam whistle too close to you?" Courtney asked, walking back towards where we stopped with Taylor and Eloise.

"It wasn't his fault; I think these devices are just getting worn. I need to replace them soon." Thank fuck California had started to distribute over-the-counter hearing aids. These things were four grand last I paid for them five years ago.

"You...wear hearing aids?" I heard Eloise ask, leaning towards me as if she could just now see them in my ears.

"Yup," I replied, not quite sure if she needed more elaboration.

"Oh!" Eloise snapped her fingers together and pointed at Adam and me, "*That's* what you meant that day when you said you were checking out her gear!"

I lifted an eyebrow as Adam pulled out a water bottle and took a chug from it.

"What? What day?" Taylor asked, shifting their weight on one hip and crossing their arms.

"A couple of weeks ago I thought I walked in on Adam and Beck in her office, like, on the verge of kissing or something," Eloise giggled and shook her head as if the idea was completely ridiculous, and I felt my cheeks burn with embarrassment, "And Adam said that he was just 'checking out her gear', which now makes *way* more sense as to why your faces were so close together. Man, my imagination was running wild for a bit."

The way she laughed and rolled her bright blue eyes made a rock start to form in my stomach. I was a couple of years shy of thirty years old, but I found myself standing in the middle of a paved trail, using both of my hands to grip the straps of my backpack out of comfort, shriveling in on myself like I would as a child. Hearing Eloise speak as if Adam and I almost kissing was something totally ridiculous made my insecurities I expressed to Courtney earlier resurface.

"Yeah. Crazy." I replied. I tried to add humor to my voice, but it didn't work at all. I could hear how flat and humorless I sounded.

Eloise's giggles subsided when she glanced around and realized that nobody else was laughing with her. Her delay was probably due to the music still playing on Courtney's speaker. Speaking of, Courtney was subtly glaring at Eloise, and Taylor's crossed arms pose looked way more defensive than it did at the beginning of our pause.

"Anyway, we should probably catch up," I glanced down at my feet, wanting to escape to a place where nobody would read into my tone of voice or look at my face, and quickly skirted around my friends to continue our trek.

It was a few moments later that I realized just how much information I had accidentally given Adam with that awkward interaction. Humiliation started to hum like electricity in my veins, and I wanted to hide in a hole. My reaction to

Eloise's jest was so obvious, I had practically screamed that I wanted Adam and I kissing to become a reality.

I wasn't brave enough to look behind and see if any of them were following, but based on the sound of hiking boots hitting the pavement I assumed that they were. I kept my head down the rest of the hike, even though everyone seemed to try to keep up a conversation that was light hearted the rest of the way. I decided it was best to just make occasional eye contact, what was done, was done.

I would glance up and smile at Courtney or Taylor when it was appropriate. I refused to acknowledge Adam or Eloise the rest of the hike though, which may be petty, but the reality was that I *was* petty. And embarrassed.

We ate our packed lunches at the hike's destination, and I pretty much disassociated the entire journey back to the bus.

I was spiraling with stress and anxiety.

How was Adam going to deal with this new revelation? Maybe he was clueless and hadn't picked up on the disappointment I had broadcasted to everyone with my voice and body language. It was doubtful, but a small shred of me still hoped. Maybe he was going to be a nice guy and pretend that whole awkward exchange about us potentially kissing never happened, and we would return to work on Monday and continue our friendly routine.

I felt a hand nudge mine on the hike back to the bus.

It took all the effort in my body to lift my head and acknowledge our newest coworker standing next to me, keeping my pace. His light brown eyes seemed to be searching for something, and softened with whatever he found, "Are you okay?" He asked, brushing the back of his hand against mine again.

I went with the tried-and-true millennial excuse for everything, "Yeah, I'm just tired."

He didn't seem convinced, his lips stayed flat as he studied me, but I couldn't take it anymore. I turned away from him which ended any potential for further conversation.

I sat next to Courtney again on the bus ride back to the cabin.

***

Everyone was given the afternoon to lounge around the outdoor seating or take naps before we all met up again for dinner. I rinsed off in one of the many bathrooms upstairs with the bunk rooms and tried to wash away my shame and embarrassment from that morning. It wasn't until I was in the shower that I realized Eloise had been unusually quiet on the way back to the bus and cabin as well.

I didn't care. I didn't want her to feel bad for embarrassing me, even if a small part of me thought she might have joked about us kissing out of some wild attempt to belittle me. Since Adam confirmed that she's still into him, it wouldn't surprise me if, in Eloise's world, she viewed other women as a threat to her instead of an ally.

When I got dressed in clean clothes and rejoined the group outside near some lounge chairs, I found myself feeling mildly better.

"Where did you find that?" I asked, pointing to the guitar in Taylor's hands. They were straddling a sun chair, plucking away at the strings.

"In our bedroom, actually, and I thought I could provide

some decent music that didn't screech at us like Courtney's shitty speaker." Taylor snickered when Courtney flipped them off.

"That's the last time I bring my Bluetooth on a hike," she threatened.

"That's the last time I go on a hike, period," I sighed and reclined in an empty sun chair next to my best friend.

"No way! Hiking is the best! Don't you feel so great now that you've done one?" Taylor asked, eagerness covering their features.

"If great means sore and lethargic, then yes, I feel just great," I nodded, resting my hands behind my head and closing my eyes.

I was wearing a black tank top with grey cotton shorts and flip flops. I usually used the shorts as pajamas, but I wanted to be in comfortable clothing after all the physical exertion earlier in the day. Plus, I applied my moisturizer that had SPF in it after my shower, and the feel of the sun on my skin was too comforting to pass up.

There was a very real chance that I would fall asleep reclined in the chair like this.

I must have because I didn't hear any of Taylor and Courtney's conversation afterwards. I vaguely recalled paying attention to the sound of the guitar strings being playfully plucked by Taylor, but I definitely had weird colorful dreams in and out of the music I was hearing.

Eventually, I heard Courtney mumble something along the lines of, "Yeah, do it."

"She looks so peaceful, leave her be," Eloise's voice chimed in.

I felt like I had a heavy, warm blanket over the entirety of my body. I could hear people talking, and I knew that I had fallen asleep, but I couldn't put in the effort to open my eyes and acknowledge them. I was trying, but I couldn't make it above the surface of consciousness.

"Quiet, nerd. Do it." Taylor added, their guitar playing paused.

I was struggling to make my body move, thinking I was just about to come out of the throes of unconsciousness when I felt something hard, cold, and wet against my neck.

It was icy to the touch, and it made my whole body jolt with shock. My eyelids flew open and were immediately blinded by the sunlight shining down on me.

"The *fuck?*" I gasped, rubbing the freezing spot on my neck. I rubbed my eyes in an attempt to adjust to the light and glanced around at my surroundings, eyes squinted. Courtney and Taylor were laughing at me, nothing unusual, but then I saw Eloise casually sitting cross legged in the patio chair, looking worried. I ignored that when I realized Adam was standing over me holding an ice-cold soda can in his hand, looking incredibly guilty.

I had never seen Adam look guilty before. He was biting his bottom lip while smirking at the same time, mischief glistening in his eyes. The sunlight glistening off of his dark red hair somehow adding to the effect. It was so endearing, my heart melted at the sight of it.

Adam had just pressed a cold soda to my neck, and innocently asked, "Oh, sorry, did I wake you?" I narrowed my eyes at him even more and shook my head, a playful smile teasing my lips.

Maybe this was his way of trying to make things not weird between us anymore. You know, because I made it super obvious that I wanted to make out with him earlier.

Or maybe it wasn't that obvious, and I was being paranoid.

It was hard to tell, having just been forced out of a peaceful slumber seconds ago.

"Nope, it was quite refreshing, actually," I tried to play it off as playful banter, and quickly turned my attention away from the man of my dreams and towards my friends. "Did you end up writing the next top hit yet, or have you just been dicking around this whole time?"

Taylor's jaw dropped, thoroughly insulted by my accusation. "First of all, you fell asleep on me. How could I possibly perform to a snoozing audience?" I laughed at how easily we played off of each other's theatrics, then gasped a little when I felt Adam's warm hands wrap around my ankles in order to lift my legs off of the lounge so that he could take a seat since all the other options were occupied.

That was…friendly of him.

I quickly tucked my legs and folded them towards my body, forcing him to release his grip on my ankles. He glanced at me, his gaze seeming suspicious, before leaning back on his hands and stretching his long legs out in front of him, crossing them at the ankles.

Even though he made it so that he was sitting directly in my line of sight, I still put in an effort not to let my gaze linger on him for too long. I could still feel his touch on my ankles minutes after he had stopped gripping them, and it took a lot of mental effort to stay focused on the conversation happening around me and not to picture other things.

Things like Adam playfully grabbing my ankles as I tried to teasingly crawl away from him, his laughter letting me know that he enjoyed the chase. Or things like Adam gripping my ankles and dragging me to the edge of my bed, where he could position me just right to...

Fuck, get a grip, Beck.

"Hey, you there?" I heard Courtney's voice before my vision registered the sight of her snapping her fingers in front of me.

I signed, *fuck off,* to her in return.

"...That's so cool that you guys speak sign language," Eloise chimed in, reminding everyone that she was also there.

"It is, until they have secret conversations about you behind your back," Taylor shook their head and lifted their brows at me. They knew a handful of signs because it was useful for their line of work with nonverbal kids. They definitely weren't fluent like Courtney and me.

"Do you guys have secret conversations often?" Eloise asked, looking worried that we possibly could do that to her in the future.

"Only when we want to talk about boys," Courtney smiled, barely looking up from her phone. I widened my eyes in shock, because that is quite literally what we did this morning, but then regained my composure.

"It's useful when I'm not wearing my hearing aids, mostly," I explained, trying to divert the conversation. Eloise nodded before leaning forward and resting her chin in her hand.

"It's really intriguing to watch," Adam spoke up in front of me, forcing me to look forward and acknowledge his beautiful fucking existence.

"What do you mean?" I asked, genuinely curious.

"I mean what I said," Adam replied with a shrug, making direct eye contact with me that for some reason felt like a dare, "That form of language is pleasing to the eye. Like a dance. It's beautiful." He held my eye contact so intently I started to feel myself start to sweat. What was he possibly trying to tell me with that intense gaze of his? Was I reading too much into the situation because of my history with anxiety and the men I'm sexually attracted to?

Possibly.

I gulped as I grinned and decided to jump ship.

"Alright, I'm going to go back up to the bedroom to check in on Gram," I announced to the group, startling Adam and forcing him to lean back so I could scoot off the sun chair.

"Tell her not to party too hard without us," Courtney reminded, eyeballing me suspiciously. I gave her a thumbs up and turned towards the cabin without another word.

I barely made it up the stairs when the main door to the cabin busted open and I jumped from the noise since most everybody else was outside somewhere. With one hand on the stair railing and the other over my racing heart, I turned around to see what the commotion was but felt a lump form in my throat at the sight of Adam power walking from the entryway toward the staircase where I was. His face was flat, but his movements told me he was upset.

"Hey," he greeted me with little to no friendliness in his voice. "We should chat."

"Um," I backed up a stair or two as he marched up them to meet me, "I was going to—"

"Avoid me again, I know," Adam interrupted me, storming past me on the railing and nodding his head towards the second story for me to follow him.

I shut my mouth and wordlessly followed after him as if I was a child marching towards my time out. It felt mildly demeaning, but I was curious to find out what had put him in such a mood.

He walked past the bedroom that he and Taylor were sharing, and stopped when he stood in front of mine and Courtneys. He turned around to face me and crossed his arms as he leaned against the doorframe, waiting for me to open it. When I made it to the doorway, I just stared at him and crossed my arms, my brow furrowed at his aggression.

His face wasn't hard, it seemed relaxed. Like it was a mask he was wearing, though his taut body language completely gave him away.

"What?" I asked, sounding snappier than I expected.

"It's up to you. We can chat in private or hash things out in the hallway here," he lifted a shoulder as if he didn't give a shit either way. He even glanced around the hallway once before meeting my stare head on again. I blew out an annoyed breath, gripped the doorknob, and tossed the bedroom door open. I was feeding off of the tension he was releasing in waves.

As soon as he entered the room, and I heard the door close I turned around and gave him an irritated look.

"What do you want?" I demanded, tapping my foot with impatience.

"What did I *do*?" Adam asked, stretching his arms out and dropping them, clearly at a loss. I blinked at him, my aggression wearing off at his abrupt question.

Nothing, you've literally done nothing.

"What do you mean?" I asked, leaning my hip against the footboard of Courtney's bed. It was against the same wall as the window and the farthest side of the room from Adam. It was already a small room without his large frame filling it.

"You've been avoiding me. Ever since yesterday. Was it because of my panic attack?" He seemed to drop his aggression act as well and morphed into the persona of loss and desperation.

"What? No." I shook my head.

Fuck. Courtney was right.

"So, why have you been avoiding me?" Adam demanded, looking behind his shoulder so he could adjust his position to match mine, leaning a hip against my footboard.

Deny it. No, don't deny it. Just tell him. This is already humiliating enough. Fuck, I think I need to come clean.

As if my thoughts were betraying me my cheeks started to fill with warmth. I stood there, silent. Trying to form words from my thoughts. My heart started beating faster due to a mixture of emotions, but mostly from my sudden rise of anxiety.

"I'm sorry, I should have told everyone about my fear of heights as soon as I saw the course," Adam started, clearly needing to fill the silence that I was set on creating. "It's just embarrassing. I don't like advertising it, so I usually try to tough it out. I'm sure there is some deep-rooted sexism behind that, but I thought I recovered reasonably—with your help of course," he paused his sentence and his light eyes widened. "Oh shit, it was when I tackled and hugged you, wasn't it? I didn't have your permission—" I felt my heart shattering into a million pieces. He was so desperate to resolve this riff in our friendship that he was spiraling because I wasn't brave enough to just tell him how I felt.

"No, no, that isn't—" I shook my head, but he wasn't listening. He ran both of his fingers through the sides of his hair and looked down at the ground. Anxiety coated his features.

"That was so inappropriate of me. I'm sorry! I just was panicking, and you were so kind and made me feel safe—" Adam was rambling now, and I wanted him to stop. He never rambled; in fact, he was usually so choice with his words. He was too sweet, setting incredibly high standards for men everywhere with every word that escaped his mouth.

"Adam," I tried again, stepping towards him.

"—but that doesn't mean that I had permission to hold you like that, I'm sorry—" Adam continued as if I wasn't speaking. I shook my head at him but worry just creased his brow.

"Adam, breathe," I stepped towards him, panic welling inside of me because of his stress. I felt like a shitty human.

"—I get it now, you really don't owe me anything. I crossed a boundary, and—" He wouldn't let me talk, because his anxiety made him incapable of listening to what I was trying to say. Blood was rushing in my ears. I clenched my teeth together and made a frustrated noise in the back of my throat before I crossed the distance between us and reached up to grab the side of his head, my fingertips digging into his hairline and gripping as gently as I could to get his attention.

He finally stopped talking and his anxious expression faded to surprise when I tugged his head down. The leverage my body needed for him to meet me halfway made it so that my breasts were crushed against his chest. I stood on my tiptoes, making me lose enough balance to lean my body into his for stability as I pulled his face to mine.

The moment my lips made crushing contact with his, I felt my whole body freeze as soon as the reality of what I did kicked in.

I was kissing Adam Hall.

21

Adam had literally just been rambling to me about his guilt for embracing me without my verbal consent, and I responded by shoving my mouth against his. Fuck.

I froze.

He froze.

I think time might have frozen, or maybe I was just in the throes of a panic attack. It was hard to tell.

We were both looking at each other, my vision incredibly blurry due to the lack of distance between us. His eyes were still wide, and right when I started to regain my senses and thought to release my grip on his hair, he closed his eyes and wrapped his arms around my body.

Holy fucking shit. Adam Hall was kissing me back.

Instinct took over, when I felt his large hands grip my shoulder and hip I leaned into him more, trying to absorb the feel of his warm lips against mine.

It was I who explored with my tongue first, tasting the smoothness of his lips. However, he was the one who breached my lips and caressed my tongue with his own. My pulse was thrumming in my veins for an entirely different reason than mere seconds ago. I wouldn't have been surprised if he could hear my heartbeat thumping away in my chest. The way Adam reached one of his hands up into the back of my head to tangle his fingers in my hair, in an attempt to angle the kiss for his benefit, told me that this was completely consensual.

Quickly I was lifted off of the floor and I felt my back come in contact with the wall of the bedroom, Adam's body taking up the entirety of my surroundings as he pressed himself into me.

"Holy shit," I breathed in between our kisses. He allowed me just to get those words out before kissing me again, nipping at my bottom lip and soothing the sting with his tongue. Our breathing was both labored and desperate. I lifted a leg and hooked it on his hip, using my calf to pull him snugly against me. Space between us had no purpose here.

Using the wall at my back as leverage, I felt one of his hands explore my waist, hesitantly sliding towards my backside before he pulled away a millimeter and breathed, "This okay?"

I responded by enthusiastically kissing his jaw while I took hold of his wandering hand to guide it toward my ass, encouraging him to grip it tight. He did, and it was glorious.

My other leg lifted and I wrapped myself around him, feeling myself searching for anything to create the sudden desperate need I had for friction.

As soon as I shifted my hips I was rewarded with the feel of a hard ridge. I ground against him enthusiastically, making him pause his devouring of my neck to exhale a grunt and meet my thrusts.

Since I was being supported by both the wall and the front of his body, he used his second hand to start exploring underneath my tank top, teasing my skin there with a gentle brush of his fingertips. His fingers slowly explored as he reached higher and higher, right below the cup of my bra.

"God, you're perfect," Adam grumbled against my skin as he continued to leave suctioning kisses along my neck.

Hearing his low voice as I was dry humping him made me pause, something he immediately responded to by pausing himself, having sensed the shift in me. Though he kept his face hidden in my shoulder and his hand seemed to tighten its grip on my ass.

"Wait," I breathed, even though he already was. I removed my own lips from his shoulder to catch my breath. I was gripping him tight, with my arms wrapped around his firm shoulders and my legs around his narrow waist.

Our breathing was heavy and labored as if we had just completed a sprint. Or the hike we did earlier in the morning. I leaned back, still holding his shoulders to encourage him to lean back and look at me as well. His usually light irises were engulfed by his black pupils, and his lips were red and swollen.

"I..." I gulped and squeezed my eyes closed to gather myself, embarrassment starting to creep into the moment. Adam seemed to be holding his breath, waiting. After hearing him speak as he kissed me, I realized I needed to speak up before anything continued between us. So I said, "I really like you."

"Oh—thank fuck!" Adam exhaled with a small smile and dropped his head on my shoulder again, a chuckle escaping his lips and tickling my skin.

"Yeah, I—wait, what?" I asked, smiling at his sudden relief. I mindlessly started rubbing his shoulders and neck muscles, unable to keep myself still when we were wrapped around each other like this. I was still pressed against the wall, but his hand on my ass released its grip and moved to my thigh, giving it a gentle squeeze.

Adam continued speaking into the safety of my skin, "I thought you were going to say something like, 'We shouldn't be doing this' or 'This was a mistake'. I would have died."

I scoffed in the back of my throat and laughed, delighted and shocked at his opinion on the situation that we happened to find ourselves in. His arms seemed to hold me tighter at the sound of my laughter.

"I mean, we probably shouldn't get too carried away..." I explained, unwrapping my legs from him and sliding down the front of his body until my feet hit the floor, "I just meant that I can't, like, hook up and have that be it." Insecurity was starting to creep in, and even though I was already pink and flushed from the thrilling experience of making out with Adam, I felt a new flush fill my neck. For some reason, it suddenly felt very important that I communicate this to him because if for some reason he was only interested in a quick fuck, I would have to be strong enough to call it quits. I simply couldn't handle that.

Adam's hands came around my waist and pulled me almost flush against him again, his face serious as he searched mine, "You mean, you don't want this to be a one-time thing?"

I licked my lips and resisted the urge to pull my top lip in between my teeth. It would probably be difficult to convince him to make this a regular thing between us if I pulled out Troll Face at the moment.

I shook my head in response.

"Oh. *Thank. Fuck!*" Adam groaned as he leaned his head down to capture my lips with his. His kisses seemed to be growing in intensity, making my mind spin and my heart rate increase in a way I still wasn't familiar enough with. I smiled against his lips and enthusiastically kissed him back before taking his face in my hands and separating us once again.

"Wait—wait," I giggled against him as he tried to move on to kissing my neck and jaw. He froze, his grip on my waist tight as he removed his mouth from me and tried to steady himself.

"Sorry, sorry," he mumbled against me before pulling back and using one hand to lean against the wall next to my head. He still surrounded me, and I didn't want him to stop. I pulled his waist close to mine again, wanting contact between us to never end. He was flushed as he stared down at me, making the freckles on his nose seem darker in contrast with his skin.

"I'm sorry. I keep pumping the breaks," I smiled brightly at him, a feeling of confidence taking over the more he struggled to keep himself from kissing me, "I just…there's more."

I truly hadn't been planning on telling him any of this right now (or ever, really) but I was realizing that it was a form of self-protection. I wanted to lay it all out there before things escalated between us and potentially got weird.

"What is it?" Adam kept one tatted forearm against the wall behind me while the other bare arm came up and started to play with the stray hairs that had come out of my ponytail, his fingertips twirling with the tips of the strands.

"I…I want to have sex with you." At this Adam's now dark gaze met mine, and a devilish smirk appeared on his lips.

"I'm glad we are on the same page," he joked, but lifted a dark eyebrow, letting me know that he was waiting for me to explain. I gulped again; my throat dry. My grip tightened on his t-shirt, nerves rising in me.

I squeezed my eyes closed again, using the fake shield as I forced myself to try to explain my concern, "I—I want to have sex with you. But I'm not good at having sex." I pressed my lips together, realizing that *that* was a fucking weird thing to say, and gave myself a few moments to hate myself for it.

I peeked one eye open to look at him, worried about what his reaction to that clusterfuck might be. His face was mostly relaxed as he studied me, but there was the tiniest pinch in his brow. He took a deep breath before speaking.

"So," he paused for a moment before he continued, "When you say, 'bad at having sex' does that mean…that sex hurts?" I opened both of my eyes to take him in, surprised that *that* was where his mind decided to take my confession. Then again, if the situation was reversed and a woman told me she was bad at having sex, I would have probably assumed that she meant that it was painful for her, too. Just like Adam did.

"Oh. Well, no," I took a steadying breath, his concern for me easing some of my nerves. "Sex doesn't hurt or any-thing, but…I don't have the easiest time…getting off." I lifted a shoulder. The pinch in Adam's brow smoothed at this.

"You mean reaching orgasm," he clarified, the words

sounding incredibly erotic with his low voice. I blushed at the forward term and nodded my head. He nodded his head once in return.

"…This might be inappropriate to ask, but," he lifted an eyebrow the tiniest bit before asking, "Can you orgasm when you're doing it by yourself?"

I felt my heart and gut both flutter at the question. I pressed my lips together in a tight smile and nodded my head, "That—that hasn't ever really been a problem," I clarified.

He studied me, his gaze bouncing between my eyes before saying, "So, it's just when a partner is involved, then."

"Um. Yes." I nodded. Adam's lips quirked to the side in thoughtful contemplation before he leaned forward to kiss my forehead, a gesture so unbearably sweet I didn't think my heart could handle it.

A small part of me truly expected Adam to respond with something like, *Sorry, that seems like a lot of work on my end. I don't think that this is worth it.*

But this was Adam, so that's not what he said.

When he spoke, he said, "Well, I'm willing to try. Do you *want* me to try to give you orgasms?" He smirked at me at the end of his question, immediately easing the tension that I hadn't realized was building inside of me since I started trying to explain my predicament to him.

A nervous laugh escaped from my lips for a second before I regained my nerves and replied, "Honestly, the idea of you trying to give me orgasms has been a constant, sometimes intrusive thought in my mind. It's been a problem, actually." I made a playful grimace at him before releasing his shirt from my grip and covering my face with my hands.

"God, this is so embarrassing to admit," I mumbled behind my palms. I heard Adam's low chuckle as his hands encircled my wrists to free my face. He leaned close to make eye contact with me, so close that I couldn't look away.

"This isn't embarrassing. I think that a lot of women deal with this, but are too nervous to talk about it with their partners. I'm glad you were brave enough to bring it up with me—seconds after our first kiss, I might add," he smiled encouragingly at me as he pulled my arms up around his neck, before wrapping his arms around my waist. "That being said, I want to explore this thing we have between us. So, I think that it's in my best interest to work with you on this." He leaned down to brush his warm lips against my temple, making my heart melt and my breathing become uneven again, "...Can I tell you a secret?"

My heart rate immediately picked up at the low and rough tone of his voice.

"Y-Yeah," I stammered. He brushed his lips lower, kissing my jaw as he replied.

"A horrible, shitty part of me is hoping that I can be the one to get you off. And that your past partners were just shitty in bed. It would do wonderful things for my ego." I snorted at that and tugged on his hair playfully.

"Well, in the spirit of being honest, I've never felt this type of...I guess I'll say 'crazy physical attraction'...towards any of my past partners. So, you at least have that going for you," I lifted a shoulder and kissed his cheek because I had permission to do that now. I could kiss Adam.

In the back of my mind, I worried that our friends were wondering where we were.

"Really?" Adam leaned back and smiled at me, his dark red hair ruffled from my hands running through it before. "God, I really am an asshole. I love that I'm that attractive to you."

"I still can't believe that my attraction to you seems to be reciprocated," I smirked, kissing his lips a few times before I gave him a chance to respond. He pulled away from me an inch or two and let his gaze wander all over my face and upper body.

"Reciprocated is putting it mildly," Adam explained before lowering his mouth and kissing me again. The kiss escalated, and our tongues seemed to be dueling with each other for dominance. My hands crawled back up into his luscious head of hair as if that's where they belonged. Things were heating up at a concerning rate, and I almost considered trying to dry hump his leg when I heard someone clear their throat to the side of us.

"Ahem." It sounded sarcastic and fake. Adam and I both froze, pulling away from each other and taking in the other person before slowly turning our heads toward the intrusion.

Courtney and Taylor were barely standing in the doorway of the bedroom, mere feet from Adam and I. Courtney was staring at us with wide eyes and an unrepentant grin. Taylor was leaning on one hip with their arms folded across their chest, a smirk on their face as their blue eyes danced between us. Neither Adam nor I had heard the door open.

"Oh, um..." I was embarrassed and shocked, still holding onto Adam but trying desperately to come up with an excuse that didn't give away the fact that we were just sucking faces like randy teenagers.

"First of all, let me just say that I am relieved that this is finally happening," Courtney said, holding up one finger, "But unfortunately I refuse to let the first time you guys bone be in a crusty cabin in the woods. So, you really should thank us for interrupting whatever this is."

Adam chuckled at that, stepping away from me for the first time since we started kissing, and looked down at me, nodding in Courtney's direction, "Did she know you were so hot for me this whole time?"

"What kind of question is that? Of course, I fucking knew. How dare you question our friendship like that," Courtney pretended to be offended and flipped her blonde hair over her shoulder in mock irritation.

"My bad, I was just checking," Adam smirked at my best friend, not looking nearly as embarrassed for getting cock blocked as I did.

"Hey, I think Eloise is looking for us," Taylor spoke in a low whisper. They leaned out of the doorframe at the sound of someone entering the main cabin, before turning back to look at all of us.

"Shit, she can't find us up here like this! She'll kill me!" I gently shoved Adam farther away from me and started to adjust my tank top and shorts, deciding that I probably needed to redo my ponytail so I didn't look freshly rumpled.

"Are you kidding? She'll finally get the hint that I'm into you," Adam tugged me back against his chest and wrapped his arms around me before planting a loud smack of a kiss on my neck.

"Okay, save the cute PDA shit for when I'm not around. Thanks." Taylor wrinkled their nose in mock jest as Adam and I embraced. I grinned and stepped out of his grip to face him. "She can totally know you're into me, but maybe when she doesn't know where I sleep." I joked but also was mostly serious. Women who viewed other women as threats had a tendency to be surprisingly hostile. Courtney explained that to me once.

Adam released an irritated sigh before nodding his head in defeat and saying, "Fine," right when Eloise's steps could be heard bounding up the stairs. We all turned to look at the doorway and I made quick work of pulling my hair back again as if we were all just hanging out casually in our bedroom.

"Oh, there you guys are! C'mon, we are starting some party games!" Her gaze lingered on both Adam and me before gesturing for us to follow her, disappearing down the steps again.

"I still can't tell if she's the sweetest thing alive, or if she's crazy," Taylor murmured before following after her. Courtney narrowed her eyes at us with a playful smirk before grabbing my hand and pulling me out of the room, separating me from Adam even more.

"Enjoy the crazy sexual tension for the rest of the trip, you two!" Courtney teased as she saluted Adam in our departure. Adam leaned his head back to let out an amused laugh, his light brown eyes glistening. I pulled against Courtney's grip for a couple of seconds so I could take in the beautiful sight of Adam laughing unapologetically before Courtney rolled her eyes and pulled me out of view.

***

"Fuck this shit," I grumbled as we finally ended team bonding games for the day. Courtney wasn't dicking around when she made fun of us for the guaranteed sexual tension the rest of the trip. It was as if making out with Adam had lit some flame of arousal inside of me. I couldn't focus. Everything he did the rest of the day somehow became twisted into the most erotic scenario my brain could come up with.

There was a tug-of-war challenge that went on between the PTs and the OTs, Adam being the only male PT employed. Watching his arms flex as he tugged on the rope made my mouth go dry. I was fanning myself and trying to think of my naked grandmother multiple times throughout the day to cool off.

Now the sun was setting, and because there were a few thin clouds, color was illuminating the sky in a beautiful combination of pinks and oranges. I leaned my head back to appreciate the sight and took a deep breath through my nose that I exhaled through my mouth. I couldn't wait to be home where Adam and I could plan on when the best time would be for us to get naked.

Because, and I still couldn't believe this, Adam actually wanted to get naked with me.

"God, you're grouchy when you are horny," Courtney grumbled back to me, leaning forward to stretch out her legs. We both had plopped ourselves on some sun chairs on the porch of the cabin.

"Ew. Please don't use that word," I cringed, the word made my skin crawl. It was a word only prepubescent boys used when they were running out of fun adult words to use.

Or a word that performers used in every porn video ever.

"Horny?" Courtney repeated like the asshole she was.

"Ugh. Gross." Taylor chimed in, wiping the sweat from their brow before slapping their baseball cap back on their head. They plopped themselves down on the ground and started stretching their legs as well. We had all just finished a potato sack race. It was embarrassing and juvenile, but thankfully our team made it fun and we got through it with minor scrapes and bruises.

"Use literally any other word," I growled again, stretching my arm across my chest to stretch my shoulders out.

"Yeah, something more like 'raging hormones'," Taylor nodded, folding one of their legs over the other and twisting their back.

"Or raging libby-doo," I slouched in my chair and closed my eyes. It only took a second for me to realize that the silence after my suggestion was mildly concerning. I reopened my eyes and looked up to see Courtney and Taylor both looking at me with concerned expressions.

"…Say that word again," Courtney asked, blinking once and looking suspiciously calm.

"Raging?" I clarified.

"No, the other one." Taylor encouraged, still frozen in their back stretch.

"Libby-doo?" I asked, surprised when Courtney made a snorting sound in the back of her throat and quickly slapped her hand over her mouth in an effort to contain it. Since when did she feel the need to contain laughter when directed at me?

"That's…not…how you say that…" Taylor was clearly

trying to keep it together too, holding in laughter at my expense.

I felt my blush rise in my cheeks, but I was too concerned about the proper pronunciation to worry about embarrassing myself at this point.

"Seriously? Libby-doo? How do *you* say it?" I asked, sitting up from my slouch and facing them directly. Courtney cackled when I said the word again, covering her face with her hands as her whole body shook with the silent laughter she was struggling to contain.

"Oh, honey. Oh, sweet baby child," Taylor cooed as they folded their legs towards themselves and wrapped their arms around tight, hiding their laughter in their knees.

"You mean, *libido?*" Courtney wheezed, keeping her voice low so she didn't shout it from the deck for all of our coworkers to hear.

"Oh my god," I couldn't stop the smile that spread across my face. Hearing her say it and hearing how I said it made me realize just how fucking hilarious that was. I started laughing, which gave Courtney and Taylor permission to finally laugh right along with me.

"I didn't know!" I cackled, holding my gut because I was laughing so hard.

"Clearly!" Taylor wheezed, coughing a little to catch their breath as they wiped a tear from their eye.

"I've only ever read that word before! This must have been the first time I've said it out loud," tears were trailing down my cheeks as I tried to get my words out, but my explanation only made Courtney throw her head back in her chair as she folded her arms over her face, her laughter uncontrollable at this point.

We gave each other time to release the laughter, and after a handful of minutes, we all finally calmed down and caught our breath.

"Holy fuck, I'll never recover from that," Taylor gasped as they rubbed a hand down the front of their face, still snickering on occasion.

"...Hey, guys," Courtney wasn't laughing anymore, and her whispered tone made us look up to see her nodding her head in the direction of the grass field we were sitting in front of. A few yards away, Adam and Eloise were standing next to each other and talking.

Though it didn't look like a fun conversation.

Eloise looked defeated, dropping her arms in exasperation as Adam stood tall with his arms crossed over his chest, his lips in a flat line as he listened to whatever she had to say.

"Yikes," Taylor whispered.

I immediately felt anxiety swell within me, *was he going to tell her about me? Here?*

"Poor thing," Courtney mumbled as Adam shook his head one final time before walking away from the conversation. He looked up to see the three of us sitting on the sun chairs, but instead of joining us, he nodded his head in acknowledgment before pulling his phone out of his pocket and heading inside the cabin.

Eloise watched him leave with a look of true disappointment, before sauntering over to where the three of us sat.

None of us were pretending we didn't all see whatever the fuck that was.

"...Hey..." Eloise spoke, sounding incredibly depressed in comparison to her usually chipper personality.

My phone buzzed in my pocket, and I pulled my phone out to see that I had a text from Adam.

Adam: Don't worry, she doesn't know about our kiss. But I'm worked up from turning her down again. I'm going to rinse off and collect myself before I join you guys.

It was sexy as hell that he texted with complete words and sentences, and not with any of that shorthand garbage that didn't need to be a thing anymore.

Plus, my heart made a little pitter-patter in my chest when I realized that he felt the need to let me know what his plans were, and that he wasn't trying to avoid me tonight. I would not have blamed him for not saying anything and cooling down first, it wasn't like he owed me an explanation. We only kissed a few hours ago, so I wasn't even sure if we were going to be considered exclusive at this point or not.

"Hey, how are you?" Taylor asked Eloise, scooting over to make room for the melancholy blonde. She slowly took a seat in a white plastic lawn chair next to Taylor.

"...Fine..." She was clearly not fine. Her voice was small, and she wouldn't make eye contact with any of us. Part of me felt bad that she came to us specifically when she was feeling down. It was both weird, but nice to know that she considered our little group her friends while we were all isolated in this cabin.

"...Want to talk about it?" Courtney asked, which was noteworthy to me. The fact that Courtney specifically asked her that question was interesting because she always talked about this curse of hers where people would just unload all their problems onto her. It didn't matter if it was a coworker or someone who happened to be waiting in the same line as her for morning coffee. Courtney was someone people felt comfortable talking to.

Exhibit A: Me.

So Courtney must have been picking up some significant vibes from Eloise for her to go out of her way to inquire about someone else's problems when she's constantly unloaded on against her will.

"Maybe. I—" Eloise finally looked up, her blue eyes making incredibly sad eye contact with the three of us, "Do you guys know that Adam and I used to date?"

For a moment we all stared at her, debating whether it was worth telling the truth or not. We all silently decided the same, because each of us nodded our head at her.

"Oh," Eloise's cheeks turned pink, like she was embarrassed, "So, I must look like a big joke to you guys, then." She sniffed, and the children's therapist in me started to emerge instinctively.

"Why would you say that?" Courtney asked, crossing one leg over the other and resting her chin in her palm.

Eloise closed her eyes and opened them again, keeping her gaze on the ground, "He's probably complained about me to you guys already. And here I was trying..." She stopped talking, sniffling again and wiping her eye with the back of her hand where a single tear had escaped.

"I thought maybe if—if I was able to fit myself in with this new life that he created," I mentally filled in the words, *without me*, that I was pretty sure she purposely omitted, "That maybe…I don't know, we could work something out again."

Bitch, don't you dare.

It took an incredible amount of mental work to shove the intrusive thought out of my head and focus on helping this woman. She was not a threat towards whatever Adam and I were starting, he had made that abundantly clear to me.

"…Why?" Taylor asked, still on the ground as they leaned back on their palms and crossed their ankles over each other.

Eloise sniffed before looking at Taylor directly, "W-what?"

"Why do you want to be with Adam again?" Taylor elaborated. Blunt as ever. I glanced back towards Eloise, obsessively curious as to what her answer was. It took her a couple of moments to think about it before answering.

"I…it makes sense to me, I guess," She lifted a shoulder as if she wasn't positive herself. "He's a wonderful guy," true, "And I feel bad for pushing him too hard before. I apologized, but he still…" She quirked her lips to the side before exhaling an exhausted breath and rubbing her palm against her cheek, "…It's obvious to me now, after talking to him directly on this trip, that we are over."

The three of us sat there, letting her wallow in the comfortable silence as she soaked in that revelation. Part of my brain was like, *you were over the moment my tongue entered his mouth.* Whereas another part of my brain just kept repeating the words, *poor girl* over and over again. I had never been this woman. I had never been the woman who was on the verge of getting the guy. It wasn't an incredibly victorious place to be, even though I preferred being in this position to Eloise's.

"...There are other options. Men, if that's what you're into," Courtney spoke after a minute or two of silence.

Eloise nodded her head once in acknowledgment.

"You're sweet, good looking, and have solid event planning skills," Taylor nudged her foot with theirs, making her smirk a little at the unsolicited compliments, "You'll find someone."

"Yeah..." Eloise didn't sound convinced at all, "But dating sucks."

"Preach," Courtney nodded.

"Absolutely," I agreed.

"...Can't relate, I love fucking around," Taylor added. Courtney snorted and shoved their baseball hat down over their eyes. They just snickered, with no remorse over their words.

"Don't you wish that you could find your person, though?" Eloise asked Taylor specifically, once they readjusted their hat.

"Hmm, not really." Taylor shrugged.

"You don't feel like your other half is out there somewhere?" Eloise pressed.

"Taylor is already whole," I chimed in, the words erupting out of me before I realized what I was saying. Eloise turned to look at me with question, whereas Courtney and Taylor gave me encouraging eyes.

I relaxed into my seat a little before continuing, "We are all complete, individual people. There isn't another half of us floating around out there, waiting to meet us, so that we can somehow become fulfilled. I am already fulfilled, all on my own. I don't need anyone else to complete me."

Eloise quirked her lips to the side at that, her expression contemplative, "...I get what you're saying, and I think I agree...but, that doesn't refute the fact that I feel like I have this gap. This space that needs to be filled by companionship...I hope I'm not the only one like that."

"No, you're not," I shook my head in agreement with her, looking down at my hands and picking at my nails as I explained, "Finding someone to love isn't a bad thing at all. It's beautiful, actually. What I'm trying to say is this; don't date or search for a partner because you think that that hypothetical person will complete some part of you, that you haven't been able to complete yourself. Find someone simply because you want to find someone. You are the only person who can find fulfillment. So...find someone who can elevate your life. Who can hold your hand along the way. Don't look for someone with the intent of putting pressure on them to complete some part of you, a part that you can't even complete yourself. It sets unrealistic expectations for the relationship from the start." I looked back up at the three of them, each of them staring intently. Eloise's gaze moved over my shoulder for a second before meeting my eyes again, everyone sat quietly with the faded voices of our coworkers laughing on the grass around the property surrounding us.

"Anyway," I cleared my throat and adjusted my seat, feeling uncomfortable with the silence, "I just think that the idea of *needing* someone is desperate and doomed to fail, whereas *wanting* someone is thoughtful and generally lasting."

"Wow," Courtney spoke up, looking up at the cabin behind us and leaning back in her chair to absorb my words, "I love that."

"…I feel like I have felt that way my entire life, but this was the first time I heard it put into words. So, thank you, Beck." Taylor saluted me before leaning back on the ground and resting their hands behind their head.

"…Thoughtful and lasting…" I heard Eloise mumble as she pulled her phone out of her pocket before leaning back in her chair and getting absorbed with the little screen. It was at that moment that I felt a presence behind me.

"I go to take a quick shower and come back to find you all actually having a serious conversation," I heard Adam's voice from behind me, startling me. "Which, for the record, I don't think has ever actually happened."

"It's a rarity," Courtney smiled at me when Adam walked around my chair and took the seat directly next to mine, his hair dark and wet, looking finger-combed fresh out of the shower, "Feel free to ask Beck how she says the word 'libido,' by the way." I groaned in my seat and tugged my t-shirt up over my face in mock embarrassment, tucking my legs in against my chest.

"Is there more than one way to say libido?" Adam asked, his tone teasing.

I lowered my collar to reveal my eyes and flipped Courtney off, trying not to giggle hysterically like we were before. Taylor snorted and rolled to their side, holding their gut as they said, "Libby-doo, fucking hell. That's a new core memory for me."

22

"Good news, because you and Adam made out for the first time this weekend, Logan owes me ten bucks!" Courtney smiled to herself as she rattled off a text on her phone before snuggling under the musty covers for the last time this trip.

"...Who?" I asked, lifting the covers to slide into bed as well. I had just finished changing into my pajamas and braiding my hair. My body was craving sleep after the long day.

"Logan," Courtney replied as if I should know who that was.

I blinked at her as she tried to get settled under her covers.

"Courtney," I spoke to get her attention and look at me, "Who the fuck is Logan?"

"Ugh, you know!" Courtney sighed, exasperated, "My new gym buddy, remember?"

I gave her a blank stare, not knowing a better way to convey to her that I had never heard of this person before.

"Have I really not told you?" She sat up and grabbed her phone, tapping away, "I met him at that new gym I'm trying out. The one you still refuse to come with me to."

"I'm taking a little break from working out," I shrugged.

"You haven't exercised in months," Courtney lifted an eyebrow at me.

"Not true, I went on a nice hike just this morning," I replied. Courtney rolled her eyes at me before leaning over her bed to show me her phone.

"Behold," she said as I grabbed the phone from her hands. On the screen was a man who clearly wasn't in the mood to have his picture taken. Either Courtney was sitting down, or he was just tall because he was looking down on her with dark eyes and a small frown on his face. He had dark curly brown hair, and could probably use a haircut. He was wearing one of those cutoff man-tank-top things that most gym guys wore.

Based on the size of his arms and chest muscles, I stereotyped him as your average gym bro. He probably lifted every day and guzzled protein shakes more than water.

"…Yeah, you've never told me about this guy," I concluded, finally noticing the rough light pink scarring on the side of his neck and face.

"Huh, my bad," Courtney took the phone back when I reached over to hand it to her. "He's pretty chill. I'm pretty sure he didn't want to be my gym buddy at first. Which is ridiculous, because I'm a delight to be around."

"Ridiculous, indeed," I agreed with her, only mildly sarcastically.

"But I wore him down. He doesn't speak, and with those scars on his neck, I don't think he really can. I suspect he had some type of injury, but TBD on that. Anyway, he tried to shake me off at first by throwing out ASL to me when I was rambling about my day—not that he asked—and I pulled a reverse Uno card on him and signed back. He seemed both shocked and resigned to his fate, and we've been best buds ever since."

I smiled at her. Of course she would bully a gym bro to be her friend so she wouldn't have to exercise alone. I knew my refusing to go wouldn't end up being that big of a deal.

"He's good looking," I lifted an eyebrow at her and gave her a knowing look, curious to know if she was interested in this guy. He didn't really seem like her type.

"He is, but the romantic vibe just isn't there between us," she shrugged as if she had thought about it for all of three seconds, "So we are going for platonic friendship. Plus, he shows me how to use the weights correctly. Just you wait, I'm going to be ripped."

"I'm looking forward to it," I smiled, noticing my phone vibrate on the nightstand and picking it up.

Another text from Adam.

Adam: I can't wait to be home.

Me: Me too, I feel stuck here.

Adam: We are. Anyways, I'll save you a seat on the bus.

Me: Can't wait.

We didn't say goodnight to each other, but that's what that exchange felt like. Did people still text each other good morning or goodnight? I think I tried that a little with my college boyfriend, but it felt more like an annoying task that I needed to check off for the day more than anything.

The thought of receiving cute unsolicited texts like that

from Adam, on the other hand, made my heart start to speed up with anticipation.

I had it bad.

Right when I removed my hearing aids and went to set my phone on the nightstand, it vibrated in my hand again.

Adam: You can say no, but is there any way I can take you out tomorrow evening?

I held my breath for a moment after reading that text. He was asking me out. He was actually asking me out on a proper date. Before I had a chance to wrap my brain around that fact, another text from him came in.

Adam: I just realized how pathetic it was for me to text you that right now instead of asking you in person. I'll just stare at the ceiling in shame for the rest of the night.

I immediately pictured him laying on top of his covers. His body stiff and staring wide-eyed at the ceiling in embarrassment. My heart hurt.

Me: Stop! I don't care. I'd love to go out tomorrow. Specifically in a place where we aren't surrounded by friends, coworkers, and exes.

Adam: Great. I have some questions that I would love to ask you about in private.

Me: ...Questions?

Adam: Yeah, just some casual questions about things.

Me: What kinds of things?

Adam: Intimate things.

I felt a prickle of anxiety start to race down my spine after reading his words. *Fuck, what could that possibly mean by that?*

Me: Any way you could be more specific? Or ask me a couple of questions now?

Adam: I think I'd rather discuss them in person because I think your answers might be elaborate.

My anxiety started to rise. What did he want to know? My brain was starting to hypothesize in a way that let me know that I would be the one staring at the ceiling all night, spiraling. I couldn't possibly handle being in limbo about this until almost twenty-four hours from now. How could I explain this to him in a way that he would understand?

Me: I think it's important for you to give me a little more detail because otherwise, I might throw up.

It was a little dramatic, but that was a part of myself that I figured he should know about sooner than later.

Adam: Please don't worry! I don't want to make you nervous. I've just been thinking a lot about what you told me earlier today, and I have some questions about that specifically.

Adam: Not in a bad way though.

Adam: More for research purposes.

Adam: Fuck. I'm not explaining this well.

Me: You should probably ask me one of your questions now.

My pulse was racing with anticipation. I could see the three dots appear at the bottom of our text thread, and every time they disappeared I thought I was going to die. It probably only lasted a couple of seconds, maybe a minute or two at most. Finally, after feeling like I was waiting for him to finish typing for an eternity, his question appeared.

Adam: I guess my first question is this, what has been the most successful for you in bed at this point?

That wasn't too terrible of a question, and his comment about research purposes suddenly made a lot more sense. Though, I felt a lump of guilt form in my stomach at the thought of him stressing about my orgasm predicament. I decided to use a little bit of humor to lighten the conversation.

Me: ...I'm confused. You mean what setting do I put it on?

Adam: Yikes. If you're serious, I'm grateful that you haven't given up on all men at this point.

Me: It's not necessarily the man's fault that I struggle so much.

Even though I felt silly texting this conversation as a late twenty-something in a cabin during a work retreat, I was almost grateful that Adam broached the subject. There is a security that came with communicating behind a screen, without the other person being able to read your body language and see you accidentally expose more of your insecurities.

Adam: Maybe not, though I'm eagerly anticipating the opportunity to try to rectify the situation.

Adam: Sorry, that was too forward.

My blush filled my cheeks and neck, and the chill of anxiety slowly faded away to warm excitement from reading the words that he intentionally typed out to me. It really had been a long time since I spoke with a man like this, in person or via text.

Me: Not too forward. I like forward. Be forward.

Which, was news to me.

Adam: Excellent. I feel like open communication is going to be key here. Which leads me to my next question: do you have any kinks that I might want to know about?

Me: Um, kinks? I don't think I'm into BDSM or stuff like that.

Adam: Okay, but are there other things that you like? Simple things like, do you like having more control and being on top? Do you like roleplaying? Do you like behind pressed down or anything?

Holy shit. My entire body was burning, even though he was asking these questions mostly in a way to communicate, just the thought of doing any of those things with him made my blood pulse with want. I must have waited too long to answer as I was absorbing the context that he was willing to try a variety of things with me in order to have a successful physical experience with him.

Adam: Maybe think about it a little before we get dinner tomorrow.

Me: I think that's ALL I'll be able to think about before we get dinner tomorrow.

Honesty, and all that.

Adam: I'm glad to hear that I won't be the only one. Goodnight, Beck.

Me: Goodnight, Adam.

Fuck, how was I supposed to fall asleep after *that?*

The next morning flew by. We all gathered together outside to eat a glorious pancake breakfast with eggs and bacon, our little group taking up the same set of sun chairs we had been occupying the entire trip. Eloise seemed like she was in a slightly better mood, and didn't seem to go out of her way to be near or gain the attention of Adam again. Instead, she was glued to Courtney's side, chatting about things that I quickly ignored as soon as Adam had come into my line of sight.

My dreams last night were about him, and they were absolutely filthy.

Based on the sheepish smile I gave him in the morning, and the knowing smirk he gave me in return, I suspected that he knew that. What really weirded me out, was that I wasn't as embarrassed for him to know how insanely attractive I thought he was. Before we kissed, I had anticipated the most crushing embarrassment if he ever discovered my dirty thoughts about him. It was a relief knowing that wasn't the case.

Everyone was tired and ready to go home, I could tell because the bus ride back to Orange County was significantly quieter than the bus ride to Big Bear. Courtney and Taylor had both situated themselves on their shared seat with jackets stuffed together as makeshift travel pillows so that they could each take a nap on the drive.

Adam and I seemed to be the only ones not sleeping or disassociating and looking out the bus windows. We chatted on and off about simple things, playing a two hour long version of twenty questions during the ride home.

We didn't talk about work once, which was exhilarating.

I learned that his favorite color was green.

He learned that I grew up incredibly religious and sheltered, which he admitted he was somewhat aware of thanks to Courtney during the week I was depressed from my mom's care package.

I learned that he enjoyed most sports, not just surfing and that he only pursued surfing in the Olympics because his mom seemed to make that decision for him at an early age.

He learned that after a long week, I occasionally get high with my grandma, someone he was now dying to meet in person.

I learned that he had been going to therapy for an unexpected bout of depression and social anxiety for the past year, a few weeks before he made the decision to quit surfing competitively.

He learned that I had been going to therapy off and on for almost a whole decade.

We learned a lot about each other; it was easy to do when we were stuck on a long bus ride like that, and I found myself less and less embarrassed. We both made our questions fairly blunt and to the point, something that I appreciated. I even told him that I still struggled with some social nuances and reading between the lines in a world where not everybody was on the edge of their seat, waiting for some white man's version of God to shoot across the sky and burn everything to the ground (except for the excessively religious, of course).

At that, Adam rested one of his large hands on my thigh

and gave me a comforting squeeze, letting empathy shine through his gaze.

When we all unloaded in the parking lot of our office building, Adam, being the wonderful person that he was, offered to take everybody home. Taylor declined because they were meeting up with someone they had been chatting with on Hinge, and only needed to walk a block or two to the coffee shop.

Courtney and I took him up on his offer though, and during the drive to our townhome, she chatted a lot about how she thought Adam and her new buddy Logan should be best friends, something Adam just nodded in response to. He was a grown man capable of making his own friends, after all.

Before I knew it we were pulling into the driveway of our cute little townhome. I reached for the door handle, but before I could open the door Adam reached over to still my movements with a hand on my thigh. He waited for Courtney to step out of the car before leaning forward to kiss me. It wasn't anything crazy or passionate, in fact, it was more like a lingering peck. Regardless, the feeling of his warm and soft lips against mine made my heart race and my skin temperature rise. Something he seemed to be aware of as he pulled back from me and scanned my face, smirking at me afterward.

Courtney teased me by attempting to grab my face and plant one on me soon as I stepped out of Adam's car, but thankfully I had quick reflexes and dodged her unsolicited advance.

Gram was waiting for us inside with a cute little charcuterie board she had thrown together, wanting to hear every detail about how our trip was as if she was our mother and we had just arrived from some youth camp.

"Did the condoms get used?" Gram asked after we covered the more vague parts of the trip; how fancy the cabin was, team building exercises, hiking, how the food was, etc.

"Courtney made sure that they didn't," I responded with a sly smirk in my best friend's direction.

"Yeah, you're welcome." Courtney had no remorse over her actions as she dipped a carrot into some hummus and crunched.

"Ah," Gram nodded absently as she returned to the living room with her mug of tea, before our words set in, "Wait— stopped you? As in, you were going to? What?" She rapidly blinked at the both of us, clutching her mug to herself as she grabbed a crochet throw blanket hanging on the back of the couch and threw it over her legs that she rested on the coffee table.

"I don't think I was," I shook my head and replied around a mouthful of grapes, "But there may have been some tonsil hockey at play."

"Tonsil hockey? The hell, are people still saying that?" Gram asked, lifting a pale eyebrow at my verbiage.

"No. No, they are not." Courtney shook her head, "But Beck and Adam finally made out! Passionately! You should have seen them, Susan. Beck was all like—" Courtney stood up from the chair and balanced on one leg, pretending to wrap herself around a large person as her tongue dangled from outside of her mouth in a comedic miming of kissing.

"You *saw* them kiss?" Gram grinned at the two of us, laughing mostly at Courtney's performance.

"I walked in on them like I was her parent," Courtney replied as she dropped her act. "I completely cockblocked them at a work event."

"Fascinating, that doesn't sound like Beck at all," Gram was smiling at me as if she was proud of me for making out with my coworker at a completely inappropriate time and place. "So, when will I get to meet him?"

"In a couple of hours," I replied, feeling nervous at the prospect of Adam meeting my grandmother. "He wants to take me out tonight." At that news Gram and Courtney both happily squealed and gave each other high fives, as if me going on a date was a team effort for them.

My phone started to vibrate in my pocket, and I was too distracted by my upcoming date with the gorgeous red-head to think that it would be anyone else trying to contact me. So when my mom's contact information showed up on the screen I had to blink a few times to register the sight of it.

"Who is it?" Gram asked, noticing how quiet I went as I stared at my phone. I turned it around to show my screen to both her and Courtney.

"Want me to answer it?" Courtney asked without missing a beat, quickly shoving another hummus-covered carrot into her mouth.

"No, it's okay," I exhaled a large sigh, liking the opportunity I had to answer a phone call from my mother with just Courtney and Gram in the room to be my silent support. I ignored the phone call and decided to call my mom back via

FaceTime, something she still refused to acknowledge was better for me for a number of reasons. Her argument was that I should just rely on the Bluetooth connection to my hearing aids, my argument was that sound wasn't perfect and it was easier for me to see her lips move during the conversation as well, so I didn't need to ask her to repeat herself as much.

Thankfully, she answered and didn't seem annoyed at the FaceTime call. Her big smile filled my screen, "Hey! There she is!"

It threw me off a little how aged my mother looked. I think a part of me would always remember her as a young mom like when I was a child, so seeing her have more grey in her light brown hair and a few more wrinkles made me realize how much time had passed since I saw her in person.

"Hey! How are you?" I asked, mimicking her positive and friendly demeanor as if we chatted all the time.

"Wonderful! I had a quick question for you." One nice thing about my mother was that she didn't dwell on small talk too much. "How would you and Gram feel if we wanted to visit you guys soon?"

I blinked and looked up at my grandmother, who just smiled and shrugged at me. She had an opportunity to see her son in person again, maybe even give him a big hug. Of course, she was fine with them visiting.

"Um, sure, when did you have in mind?" I glanced around our little townhome, realizing my parents had never been here since Gram and I moved in years ago. My brain immediately started wondering what we would have to do to prepare for my parents to visit because our house wasn't exactly conservative.

Would we have to hide our alcohol and cannabis oil?

"I'm not sure yet. But I wanted to run it by you first before we started planning in detail." *How oddly considerate of her.* "I also wanted to ask if Josh had been able to get in touch with you?"

I blinked at her, "Who?"

"Josh! Josh Patterson. I gave him your number and he said that he would reach out to you," my mother explained, reminding me about that random blast from the past. I tried not to roll my eyes at her while I responded.

"Oh, yeah, he called. But I don't really have any interest in speaking with him," I lifted a shoulder, considering the case closed. My mother responded by frowning the slightest bit as her brows lowered over her eyes.

"Rebecca, you guys aren't in high school anymore," she reminded me.

"I'm aware."

"He's really a sweet boy, I thought it would be nice if you guys were able to catch up and maybe—" I lifted a hand to cut her off, already knowing exactly where her brain was going. Get me to date Josh, I magically reignite my faith, move back home, and start popping out as many babies as possible. Gross.

"Mom, I know you're just trying to be helpful, but please don't." It was a line I had needed to say to her many times over the years. I was sure she was getting sick of it at this point. Based on how her lips flatted into a firm line, I suspected she was getting very annoyed at the constant boundaries I was blocking her goals with.

"We can talk about this later," my mother pretended the subject was still up for debate, looking off to the side when my father's low voice murmured in the background, "Anyway, your dad is hungry and wondering when dinner is going to be ready, so I should get started on that."

"Why doesn't *he* get started on that?" Courtney piped up from her spot on one of Gram's accent chairs. My mother narrowed her eyes at me, letting me know she heard before she decided to ignore Courtney's comment.

"...I'll talk to you about our visit later. I love you!" She smiled brightly again as if she wasn't upset with me for rejecting her attempt at manipulating my life again.

"I love you, too," I smiled and waved and hung up before she had a chance to say anything else. As soon as I ended the call and set the phone down, I released a heavy breath and noticed how fast my heart had been racing from the stress of speaking with my mother like that.

No child should ever feel that much anxiety from a simple FaceTime call from their parent.

"...When is Adam coming to pick you up? Do you need to shower and get ready?" Courtney chimed in, a part of me suspecting that she was trying to get my head back in the game.

Don't let your mother ruin the first date that you have actually looked forward to in years.

I smiled and nodded at Courtney, standing up off the couch to lean over and give Gram a quick kiss on the head before racing up the stairs to get ready.

***

The lights in my bedroom started flickering, letting me know that the doorbell downstairs was being pressed. Shit, he was here. A part of me was hoping he would just text or call me when he arrived instead of walking up to the door, but that was silly of me.

I was still trying to decide what to wear, having showered and styled my hair already. I only put on minimal foundation and a couple of layers of mascara, deciding to be more natural on the first date. I'd save my "extra" makeup face for when we got to spend more time together.

Because that was the plan. Adam and I both wanted to spend time together. It still seemed so unreal. Just the thought made butterflies go off in my stomach, and I quickly pulled on one of my more adult tops.

I wore blue high-rise jeans that complimented the shape of my butt and my narrow waist. There were no holes in them but they were still pretty casual. I rolled the hem of them up a little at the ankles. I threw on a form fitting tank top crop top to make up for the looser fit on the legs of my jeans. The top concealed most of my cleavage but was tight enough to still draw the eye there if I wanted to.

I did. Of course, I did.

I did my hair half up, and half down, and slid on some nicer flat sandals. I think Courtney would have called the look "elevated casual" and I found myself bouncing on the balls of my feet as I stared at my reflection in the mirror.

Shit, I realized Adam was probably stuck downstairs with Gram and Courtney.

I grabbed my purse and started to race downstairs and

made it halfway before I paused at the sight of the three of them gathered in the living room. Courtney was cleaning up the leftovers of the charcuterie board and Gram was sitting right next to Adam, who looked like he showered and changed into an elevated casual outfit, too. He wore dark blue jeans and a light grey Henley shirt, the sleeves rolled up to his elbows to show off his forearms.

I took in the sight of Adam in my living room before Gram glanced up to see me standing halfway down the staircase, her lips moving but no sound registering.

Oh, duh.

I had removed my hearing aids to take a shower.

Sorry, I signed, gaining Courtney and Adam's attention, *I forgot my aids, BRB.* I darted back up the stairs to retrieve them, shoving them in my ears as I made my way back downstairs. The sound immediately filled my ear canals with a moderately annoying squeal, and I could pick up the tail end of their conversation as I reentered the living room.

"...get tested?" Gram asked.

"Oh. Um. About a year ago. I haven't, uh..." Adam sounded nervous, and when I entered the room, he looked relieved to see me there. I could have sworn he mumbled, "Oh thank god."

"You haven't had sex in over a year?" Gram asked, raising her eyebrows in surprise as she let her gaze trail over him.

"Gram!" I almost shrieked as I scolded her, my cheeks were flaming at the realization of what they were talking about, "Mind your business!"

"Yeah, how *dare* I ensure my granddaughter practices safe

sex," Gram rolled her eyes and crossed her legs as if I were the ridiculous one.

"I'm with Susan on this one, don't be afraid to ask the embarrassing questions," Courtney chimed in. I did a double take when I realized that she was sitting upside down in one of Gram's ugly accent chairs, her hair brushing against the living room rug as she crossed her ankles to rest them on the back of the chair. She was staring at her phone, which meant the countdown was on for when she would inevitably drop it on her face.

"We're going, bye!" I grabbed Adam's hand and tugged him off of the couch, pulling him towards the door in a desperate attempt to rush out of there.

"It was nice to meet you!" Adam lifted his other hand to wave at my grandmother. I rolled my eyes and practically dragged him out of the townhouse, coming to an abrupt stop as we made it to his Tesla that was parked in our drive-way. I reached to open the passenger side door when one of his large hands came around from behind me and held the door shut.

"Hey," Adam's low voice was close to my ear, his breath grazing my neck in a way that I was starting to love. "Slow down." I froze and turned around to face him with a sheepish expression as he kept his hand on the passenger door.

"Sorry about my grandmother," I gestured vaguely towards the townhouse, "She wasn't trying to be rude, she's just... blunt. And likes making men uncomfortable." I lifted a shoulder. Adam smirked and nodded as if what I just said was clearly obvious.

"I'm not offended," Adam leaned forward to brush his lips

against my cheek, barely touching the skin there and sending my heart on a sprint, "You look beautiful."

"T-Thank you," I smiled, turning to capture his lips with mine. I relished in how confident I felt around him, and how he encouraged my confidence by kissing me back as enthusiastically as I kissed him. After I wrapped my hands around his neck and after he pushed my back and butt into the side of his car, he separated our lips to take a breath.

"Let's make a deal to always say hello like this," Adam suggested on an exhale.

"Deal," I grinned like the giddy woman I was, how could I not be when I was wrapped up in Adam's strong tattooed arms and knew what his lips tasted like? He leaned back to look at me. His eyes scanned different parts of my face, as low as my exposed shoulders and collarbones. Eventually, he shook his head once and gave me a smile as he took a step back from me and reached behind my butt to grab the door handle.

"We better get going, because I'd be happy to just stand in your driveway and make out all night," Adam rubbed a hand through his hair once, barely messing it up as it naturally fell back into place.

Ugh, to be a man with effortless man hair.

"For the record, I'm also okay making out," I shrugged as he opened the door and gestured for me to step inside, doing that thing that men did by pressing his hand on my lower back. That never actually helped guide women, but it showed me that he liked touching me. So I was here for it.

"Noted," Adam smiled as he shut my door, making his way around the front of the car to enter the driver's side. When he got into the driver's seat he shut the door behind him and buckled his seatbelt as he said, "Though, I do enjoy talking with you *almost* as much as I love sucking your tongue into my mouth."

I gasped at him, my mouth falling open in a moment of shock before laughter erupted out of me, earning a smile from him.

"I mean, it's very close. I really love sucking your tongue into my mouth," Adam's eyes seemed to light up as he took in my inability to control my laughter, placing my hands over my mouth as my shoulders shook from both embarrassment and his comedy.

"You're killing me," I finally gasped through some giggles, "C'mon, we better go so Courtney and Gram can stop spying on us through the curtains."

Adam blinked once at me before looking through the front windshield of his car towards the front of the town-house. I followed his gaze to see both Courtney and Gram standing in the front window, not even pretending to hide the fact that they had been staring at us for who knows how long. When they noticed our gaze, Gram waved politely as she sipped from her tea, and Courtney started to pretend to make out with the glass.

Adam met my gaze one last time before he chuckled and flicked his car into reverse, pulling out of the driveway to go on our date.

23

Adam ended up making the date pretty casual, which I greatly appreciated. For some reason, a tiny part of me was worried that he would take me to some high-end restaurant his parents were involved in and I would feel out of place, but instead, we drove to Balboa Pier in Newport Beach and walked around. We were able to pick up some hot dogs from a street vendor, which Adam paid for, and we found a spot on a cement wall to sit and watch the ocean while we ate and played twenty questions again.

"Do you like to read?" Adam asked after he finished his hot dog and balled up the wrapping paper.

"I do. And before you ask; yes, it's romance novels," I smirked as I took another bite of mine, not inhaling it like Adam seemed to do with all of his food.

"Ah," Adam grinned at me and pulled out one of the napkins we got from the hot dog cart to wipe off his hands, "So, you like reading porn?"

"Yup. Do you like watching porn?" Adam's eyebrows raised and his cheeks turned a little pink, darkening his nose freckles.

"…Touché." He stood to throw away his trash in a nearby waste bin before returning to his seat directly next to me, brushing his leg up against mine. A part of me wondered if he was as desperate to touch me as much as I was to touch him since he was always initiating contact between us.

"Do *you* like to read?" I asked before I took my last bite.

"I do believe it or not," Adam smirked at me as he handed me my own napkin, "I enjoy fantasy the most, I think."

"What?" I asked, my eyes widening in surprise.

"What?" He challenged as he took my garbage and balled it up. As he came back from the waste bin I explained my surprise.

"I totally had you pegged as someone who only read memoirs or sports books, maybe political books as well."

"Gotcha!" He gave me a sarcastic finger gun as he leaned back on the wall and stared out over the ocean, "I read The Hobbit in elementary school, and I think that's when I became a fantasy nerd."

"Huh, I always struggled with fantasy." I found myself staring at his profile as the sun started to set over the water, I loved how it lit up his warm features. "Excessive descriptions of world building tend to lose me."

"I'll read one to you some time." He leaned over and draped his arm around my waist, encouraging me to lean against his side and snuggle in. I was in heaven. He smelled so goddamn good, I decided to breathe him in without shame.

"Did…did you just smell me?" Playful accusation colored his tone.

"Of course. Whatever cologne or aftershave you use is

wonderful. Ten out of ten." I turned my face towards his neck and inhaled through my nose dramatically as he started chuckling.

"I actually don't wear cologne, sorry to disappoint," Adam's fingers started to play with the exposed skin at my waist.

"Well, it must be your body wash or something. I first smelled it on you weeks ago and I almost lost my mind." I wasn't planning on ever admitting that to him, but too late now.

"Really?" He seemed very pleased with that information. "You sure you aren't just into my natural musk?"

"Yuck," I leaned away from him and crinkled my nose, "Musk makes me think of a wet dog. You don't smell like a wet dog."

"What do I smell like, then?"

More like a wet dream. The intrusive thought made me pause, and I found myself hesitating a little too long as I struggled to come up with a clever response. A blush stained my cheeks as he waited patiently for me to come up with something.

"Like...something earthy. Yummy."

"I smell 'yummy'?"

"Yeah. It's better than a wet dog, that's for sure."

"I can't argue with that," He grinned before tugging me closer until my breasts were pressed against his side, one of his hands coming up to cradle my face as he leaned down, teasing me with his breath on my lips, "Now, what do I taste like?"

If I had to guess, probably like the hot dogs we just ate.

Before I had a chance to answer he pressed his lips to mine. It was a firm and sensual kiss. Usually, I never found myself that into the idea of PDA, because who knew who all would be watching? At this particular moment, however, I had no issue with PDA.

I could PDA all day.

He coaxed my mouth open with his and tasted my tongue, making me follow after him as he leaned back just enough to catch his breath, only to lean forward again and nip at my lips. Pretty soon the kiss escalated, and I found myself swinging one of my legs over his lap to straddle him on the cement wall we were on. It wasn't until I was settled onto his lap and my fingers were clutching his hair that I started to register the sounds of clapping and cheering coming from nearby.

I pulled back and looked around to see a group of teenagers with their E-bikes hanging out off to the side. They were clapping and fist pumping, teasing us.

I chuckled at the kids and looked down at Adam, who looked like he was struggling to control himself as he kept his gaze on my face.

"...Can I take a picture of you?" Adam asked, surprising me.

"Right now?" I was confused by his train of thought because our tongues were just down each other's throats.

"Yeah, just like this," Adam shifted until he could pull his phone out of his pocket, and instead of leaning in with me for a selfie he leaned back, keeping me in his lap, and held his phone up.

"I feel kind of put on the spot here." I glanced around at the few people who were spending their evening at Balboa Pier as well, embarrassment starting to trickle in.

"Trust me, just smile like you mean it."

"Like I mean it?" I furrowed my brows at him with a nervous smirk. His eyes locked with mine and his devilish grin appeared on his lips.

"Smile as if you just saw me naked."

My eyes widened and my mouth dropped open in surprise before laughter busted out of me at his prompt. It must have worked, because he took a couple of pictures and was smiling at his camera as he leaned forward again to loop one of his arms around my waist, keeping me in place. He turned his phone screen to show me the picture.

I looked photoshopped. The sun was setting behind me, but there was enough light reflecting off of my face as well that I wasn't some black silhouette. My lips were red from our kisses, and my hair was loose in the small breeze you get from being so close to the ocean. The smile on my face was genuine, even if it did make my eyes more squinty than I would have preferred.

I looked genuinely happy.

"See?" Adam asked as he pressed me against him. Then he turned to face me, splaying his fingers in front of his face before pinching them together, *beautiful*.

Adam just signed to me.

"You're learning ASL?" I asked, the thought simply making my heart race in my chest. It was galloping so hard it almost made it difficult to breathe.

"I only know some words at the moment, but I'll get there." He leaned down to kiss me before I could ask him some more.

I'll get there.

Those words seemed to mean a lot to me, and I hoped they meant just as much to him as well.

24

Adam drove me back to our townhome at a very reasonable hour, since we started our date before sunset. It was only 9:30pm by the time he walked me up to my door.

"Can I ask…" he seemed hesitant, even though I was currently leaning my back against my front door, fully hoping to kiss him some more and maybe grind a little, because my entire body was buzzing with unreleased energy almost the entirety of our date.

"Yes, you can," I nodded, gently grabbing the hem of his shirt and pulling him towards me. He smiled at how forward I was being and allowed me to take one of his hands and put it on the back of my neck, while the other stayed high on my rib cage.

"Have you thought about what we talked about last night?" Adam asked, quirking his lips in a way that made me suspect he was biting the inside of his cheek.

"Ah." I immediately felt embarrassed and tried to look down, but I had just pulled him flush against me and instead rested my forehead on his chest. A hard chest, that seemed to have a racing heartbeat as well. "I, um, kind of?" I released a nervous snicker as I wrapped my arms around his waist, keeping my face concealed. It was an odd sensation. I was embarrassed by this topic of conversation but also wanted to seek comfort by hiding in his arms. I hadn't felt these sorts of emotions before, and it was both exhilarating and nerve-racking.

"...Can you tell me your thoughts?" Adam pressed, wrapping his arms around me and gently swaying me from side to side, "Please don't be embarrassed, you don't have to talk about it if you don't want to. I just...God, I just want to be helpful, I guess..." I gripped him tighter to me as I breathed him in, enjoying the feeling of his hands rubbing my back and combing through my dark hair.

I took a moment or two to gather my thoughts, and process what his words made me feel. I felt my heartbeat start to level out, becoming more even. It was still something I was entirely focused on as he kept touching me, and I wondered if those feelings would ever fade with time. Though hearing Adam express his desire to accommodate me, with utter sincerity in his voice, made me feel less nervous and more... not nervous.

"Can we talk about this upstairs?" I asked, mostly against his chest. His hands stilled on my back for half a second before he squeezed me and said, "Yeah, sure."

I quietly unlocked the door and peeked inside, not surprised to find the living room empty. Gram was old as fuck, after all, and usually made it a habit to go to bed for the night early unless Courtney and I were watching TV with her. I took Adam's large hand in mine and we tiptoed upstairs, not for Gram's sake (she couldn't hear us without her aids, which she didn't sleep in), but so as not to alert Courtney to our presence. Courtney, who might take a second too long to read the room and realize Adam and I wanted to be alone.

When we made it upstairs, I noticed that her bedroom door was open and the lights were off, and I exhaled a breath of relief knowing she was out of the house.

Where she was, I had no idea, but I had Adam sneaking into my bedroom at the moment and that was all I could think about.

"Wow," Adam whispered as he quietly shut my bedroom door behind him. He took in my cluttered room. Organized, but cluttered thanks to the scattered plants and succulents that were stacked on shelves and my dresser.

"Yeah, I try to keep the living space more Gram's style, so I keep all my belongings in here," I lifted a shoulder, feeling a little insecure that I wasn't living on my own at this age.

"I like the plants." Adam walked over to one on my dresser and gently touched one of the dark green leaves before turning to look at me. "Are the walls thin?" he asked.

"Gram can't hear that well, like me," I pointed to my ears, a hint of nerves peeking through as the adrenaline pumped in my veins. "And Courtney seems to be gone somewhere, so, we're alone." I sheepishly grinned and bit my top lip for half a second before releasing it.

If I wanted to seduce Adam, Troll Face was absolutely not the way to go.

"Ah," Adam nodded before shoving his hands in his pockets and leaning against the dresser, "So... then what would you like to do while we are alone?"

"You."

Holy shit.

The word just came out without thought, and I covered my mouth instinctively out of mild embarrassment. Adam gave me a wide smile, but he stayed where he was, leaning against my dresser.

"...On the first date?" Adam lifted a skeptical eyebrow, "I normally don't."

"Would you be willing to make an exception?" I asked, attempting to sound seductive but probably failing. Seeing his large frame in my room, leaning against my little dresser was making my skin hum with all the dirty possibilities I could think of. I glanced at my bed, which was made, and my brain started to come up with ideas of how we could mess it up.

"That depends," Adam lifted a shoulder, acting not nearly as needy as I was feeling at the moment, "Do you want to sleep with me on the first date?"

"Yes. Absolutely," I nodded my head with emphasis, and took a step towards him, hoping for him to meet me in the middle, but he stayed rooted in his spot. *The fuck?*

Adam quirked his lips to the side, "Hmm, I don't know. You're fidgeting a lot. You seem a little... nervous."

"I am nervous," I lifted a shoulder, "But in a good way." His lips started to flatten a little at my words.

"I don't know if I want to sleep with a woman who is nervous about it. I would feel more comfortable if we waited and you were more...*enthusiastic* instead of nervous." At first, I thought he was teasing me, but when I locked eyes with him I saw that he was being absolutely serious. I was freaking him out, and Adam was genuinely a good guy. Meaning that he would never force me into something that I wasn't one hundred percent on board with. If I was feeling more like a maybe, he would respond with a hard no.

"Oh," I understood what he was saying now, so I glanced around my space to make sure I wouldn't knock anything over as I spun in a circle a couple of times and landed in front of him with jazz hands on display. "Let's have sex!" I cheered, complete with a full, real grin.

Adam lowered his head and pinched the bridge of his nose as he struggled to keep it together. It didn't work. He kept releasing small bursts of laughter, his shoulders shaking. After a few moments of failure, he finally lifted his gaze and wiped a stray tear from his eye as he collected himself.

"What the fuck was that?"

"You asked for enthusiasm. Honestly, I think I delivered," I grinned at him and closed the distance between us, "Adam, you can obviously say no if you're uncomfy—"

"—Not a word—"

"But if you're only saying no because you think there is a part of me that doesn't want to enthusiastically participate in activities of the naked variety—"

"—Of all the ways to say that—"

"—Hush!—Then you need to realize that if you say no, it's because *you* don't want to do this right now. Not me." I grabbed his hands to pull them out of the pockets of his jeans and guided them where they belonged; my ass.

Adam seemed content to stand there in my room, squeezing my backside as his gaze searched my face. Probably trying to make absolutely sure that I wanted to do this with him because he was ready to bail if I gave him any sort of signal. Finally, he nodded once and leaned his head down to kiss me. He released his grip on my ass and lifted his hands to cradle my head, his thumbs stroking my jaw in smooth motions.

I grabbed his hips and pulled them roughly against mine, desperately wanting to feel that friction I got a hint of at the beach. We kissed like that for a while, our tongues dancing against each other as my hands roamed all over his body, sneaking underneath his shirt to feel his hard stomach and back.

His hands stayed still on my face.

After a few minutes of kissing, I finally felt brave enough to reach in between us and start fumbling with the button of his jeans, to which he responded by pulling my face away from his just an inch or two.

"If we do this, I want to do this right," Adam breathed against my lips, his voice rough. I was struggling to form coherent thoughts, my fingertips frozen and barely breaching the edge of his pants.

"I have protection if you didn't bring any. But I haven't had actual sex with a partner in years, and after I did I tested and came back clean." Adam just nodded his head and kissed me some more, stepping forward and guiding me to the bed.

Oh, fuck yes!

"I'm clean too," Adam mumbled against my lips, "I brought protection because I was a fucking mess after our trip and couldn't help myself." He reached into his back pocket and pulled out three condoms on a strip before tossing them behind me on the bed. He grabbed my face to kiss me again, then mumbled, "I also had a vasectomy a few years ago."

I froze for a second before I gathered myself.

"You—what?"

Adam traced his tongue against my bottom lip before repeating himself. "I had a vasectomy a couple of years ago. So, if the condoms fail for whatever reason, keep that in mind." I blinked, hating the fact that this news was so surprising to me. When I asked my college boyfriend if he would ever consider getting a vasectomy, he scoffed and told me that he absolutely would not. That he was terrified of that twenty-minute surgery. Considering all the pain and drama women go through for their healthcare, I was a little annoyed.

He was equally annoyed when I told him I had no intention of taking birth control and messing up my hormones, and that we had to use condoms every time even though we were monogamous.

To hear that Adam took it upon himself to get a vasectomy, made my heart swell. He was a feminist after all. Of course, he wouldn't just assume the women he slept with would take care of the birth control part of sex. I took his face in my hands and made him pause to look at me so I could quickly tell him, "Thank you," before crushing his lips back to mine.

The more heated things became between Adam and me, the more confident and less nervous I became. I found myself aggressively trying to tug his shirt over his head so I could take in that glorious chest of his, tattoos and all. His hands were everywhere, and when they started to snake up my ribcage to find my breasts, I leaned back to rip off my own shirt and pull down my pants, kicking them off so that they flew across the room toward my laundry pile.

I stood up again to see Adam staring wide-eyed at me.

"Holy fuck," was all he said before he lunged at me, making me squeal with delight as he tackled me on top of my bed. I wasn't wearing anything incredibly sexy. It was a miracle that I even had a bra and cotton panties that were the same color. White. I figured if we did escalate to the seeing-each-other-in-our-underwear part of our relationship tonight, I wanted to be a little prepared for it.

"Beautiful," Adam murmured as he left suctioning kisses against my neck and collarbone. "Beautiful."

"If you leave a hickey, Courtney will never let me forget about it," I warned him at the same time that I gripped him tighter, my hips searching. I settled for rubbing against his jean clad thigh since his pants were still on for some stupid reason. He kept kissing me, his tongue teasing that sensitive spot between my neck and shoulder, and when I felt like I couldn't take it anymore I started work on his pants again.

This time I was able to undo both the button and the zipper and start to push them down off of his hips before he stopped kissing me and shifted to the side to grab my hands.

"I told you I wanted to do this right, Beck," Adam reminded me, shaking his head once as he started to crawl down my body.

I lifted up on my elbows, confused as to what he was doing. As soon as he settled between my thighs, I felt a wave of embarrassment wash over me.

"Adam, you don't have to—" My college boyfriend was

very open about the fact that he didn't enjoy giving oral to women, something I assumed most men felt the same about.

"—Yeah, I'm going to stop you right there." Adam rested one of his large hands right below my navel and pressed me into the bed as if he was worried about me running away. "I wouldn't do this if I didn't want to. If you think I'm going to be suffering through this, don't. Because I want to. God, I want to. I might die if I don't. So please...let me do this." I just stared at him, breathing heavily and only capable of a nod. He made eye contact with me a few moments longer as he kissed the inside of my thigh, a spot I didn't realize could be so sensitive until now.

"Tell me what you like and what you don't," Adam murmured against my skin, "I'm a quick learner, but you need to *tell* me, Beck. Don't just try to make it work if it doesn't. Tell me how to fix what I do wrong, got it?"

I was still leaning on my elbows, it probably wasn't a flattering angle of me where he was situated between my legs, with his mouth inches from my panties. He didn't seem to care at all though, so I simply nodded at him again. I swallowed once in anticipation even though my throat was dry.

"Got it," I saluted him, which made him chuckle once before he kissed the inside of my other thigh. He leaned forward and his nose brushed against the core of my panties, the groan he released made my entire body clench with anticipation.

"Holy shit, you're really in between my legs right now." As he pulled my panties to the side, his gaze on my center made me instinctively try to close my thighs, but his hands kept them open.

"Believe it or not, Beck," Adam murmured, his breath cool on my core, "I'm really going to enjoy this."

I widened my eyes as soon as his lips made contact, it was the most stimulating thing I had ever felt from another person. My college boyfriend had only tried this once before he told me he didn't enjoy it, and I had told him it tickled too much and that he needed to stop. It wasn't something I had ever thought to revisit.

Adam made the experience wildly different. He did his best to keep his eyes on me as his tongue dragged over my center, stopping to flick over my clit in a way that made my eyes roll to the back of my head. After a few minutes of Adam's mouth working over me, I had to flop down on my back and throw my hands over my eyes. I had no idea what sounds I was making, but I was sure they weren't feminine or sexy.

Adam then changed the pace of whatever it was he was doing down there, and I thought I was going to die. "Wait, wait," I gasped through my arms, "Keep doing what you were doing before, I think with your tongue."

"Got it," he paused to suck my entire clit into his mouth once, making me almost cry out with arousal, before continuing the same rhythm I requested from him. We were like that for a while, though time was completely lost on me as I felt my orgasm slowly rise.

Eventually, he did something different again. This time it was better, but he adjusted himself to continue licking as he was before. "Wait—do that again," I requested, completely breathless and shocked that I could make words come out of my mouth.

Adam hummed and repeated whatever motion that was.

"Yes! That!" I couldn't handle the sensation as he listened to my directions, the pressure building and building in me until I felt myself bucking under his hands that held me down. The heels of my palms were digging into my eyelids; I would worry about my smudged mascara later.

I was whimpering and a complete mess, but Adam had no mercy for me. He continued as if he could do this all day as if the possibility of his tongue or jaw being sore wasn't existent.

"I'm—almost—" I bit into the heel of one of my palms, giving up completely on words as he sucked on my clit once again before continuing whatever flicking pattern he seemed to master. After a couple of seconds of me panting Adam's hands adjusted themselves so that instead of holding my pelvis down and thighs open, they snuck underneath me to grip my ass and lift myself higher for him. His groan of approval from the new angle as he ravished me made me completely lose it.

It felt like I was a tightening string that had finally snapped. Waves of ecstasy pulsed through my center and created aftershocks of pleasure throughout my body. I felt every muscle in me lock as Adam continued to eat me out, riding out my orgasm to make it last an incredibly long time. My lips pulsed against his tongue.

After losing my vision and seeing a handful of stars in my peripherals, my orgasm finally started to fade. I felt myself floating back down to earth, my stiff muscles going lax as I lay there completely exposed to Adam.

I felt him kiss the inside of my thighs once more, realizing it was an opportunity for him to wipe his face clean. He crawled up my body, leaving a trail of kisses along his path. He kissed my pelvic bone, hips, my belly button, my ribs, and the swell of my breasts above the cup of my bra, and made his way to my collarbones before he reached a hand up and started to play with one of my nipples through my bra.

How he found them that quickly, I had no idea.

I finally opened my eyes to see him studying me, his eyes dark and a smirk on his lips as he trailed his gaze down the entirety of my body. "Incredible."

"That's one word for it," I replied, still breathless from that experience. Adam's dark eyes met mine.

"Was that okay?" he asked before leaning forward and kissing the sensitive spot underneath my jaw, his hand slipping under the cup of my bra.

"It was fucking amazing," I breathed as his tongue traced my skin. I slipped my arms out of the straps of my bra and arched my back to undo the clasp, throwing my bra across the room with my pants. Adam leaned forward, kissing my exposed breasts with a hunger I wasn't used to receiving.

"Adam," I groaned, my fingers finding their place in his hair, "I need you to do me a favor and take off your pants."

Adam chuckled against my skin, his breath tickling my nipple. "Do you a favor, huh?"

"Yes," I gasped as his teeth grazed my skin, "Because I've taken my underwear off and it's only fair that you're naked too."

"Ah, what's fair is fair," Adam murmured against my skin,

leaning away from me to slip his jeans down his hips, kicking them off like I did.

"Ahem," I leaned up on my elbows and tugged on the waistband of his boxers, getting distracted by the incredibly noticeable erection tenting them, "You forgot something."

"Whoops." Was his dry reply as he guided my hand to the inside of his boxers. I grabbed him and gave him a playful squeeze, loving the way his eyes seemed to roll back from my touch. I leaned over to kiss his neck as I sat up and continued to tug his boxers down his legs. His erection finally sprung free. I blinked at the size of it, realizing I hadn't had anything inside me besides my medium sized tampons and my fingers for years.

It was a little daunting, but seeing Adam laying on his back completely naked with his hands resting behind his head and a hooded gaze in his eyes, made warmth pool in my lower belly.

I thought he was beautiful.

"Ugh, finally!" I sat up on my knees and pretended to rub my hands together as if I was an evil villain. Adam cackled as he lay prone on his back, reaching out to grab my hips and pull me towards him.

"Wait—wait!" I giggled as he rolled us over and settled on top of me, his heavy erection resting against my lower stomach. I hadn't felt anything like that in such a long time, it was awaking instincts I had forgotten I had.

"What?" Adam asked, his forearms resting on either side of my head as he kissed my face all over.

"I thought it was my turn!" I giggled as he kissed the spot between my neck and shoulder again, sucking.

"Your turn?" Adam asked. He chuckled as he watched me struggle between wanting to hump the shit out of him or push him onto his back again.

"Yes!" I reached a hand down, grabbing his erection and stroking him once for emphasis. Feeling it pulse in my hand increased my confidence some more.

"Here's the thing," Adam reached forward and grabbed the sleeve of condoms I had completely forgotten about, ripping one off of the strip and then tearing the foil package open with his teeth, making my core clench at the sight, "I'd love for you to have a turn. I really would," he leaned off of me, resting on his knees, and rolled the condom onto himself so smoothly I almost missed it, "But it's been a while for me— you understand—and if I'm being honest," he leaned down onto his elbows again, his biceps flexing as he grabbed the side of my face with one of his hands to get my attention, "I'm not going to last much longer. So if you're okay with it, I'd like to finish inside of you."

"Oh," I grinned at his honesty, taking in this rumpled version of this crazy hot man, and nodded my head, "Of course. Proceed."

Adam laughed at me and kissed me hard, "'Proceed', you're so weird. I love it."

"Glad to hear it," I leaned forward to kiss him again, trapping his bottom lip gently between my teeth and tugging. The sound he made as he exhaled made me feel like the sexiest woman in the world, "I—um, did have one request. If you don't mind."

"I don't," was his immediate reply, "What is it?"

I caught his gaze for a moment before building up the

courage and found myself rushing to explain myself. "I'm not that experienced—obviously—but, I've thought about this a lot. You. Us. Anyway—"

"—Holy shit," Adam exhaled and lowered his head onto my shoulder as he mumbled into my skin. "You've thought about me while *masturbating?*"

...Well, when you put it like that.

"Um, yes," I nodded, even though his head was still hidden in my shoulder. I snuggled him closer and kissed his ear, nipping his lobe in between my teeth. He made a pained groan in response. "So, about that favor..." I squeezed my eyes closed and exhaled through my nose, struggling to gain courage.

"Anything, literally anything." Adam's voice was hoarse as he lifted his head to meet my gaze again. Seeing his freckled face so close to mine sent a thrill through me.

"...Would you maybe be willing to reach over and grab my vibrator from my nightstand drawer?" I reached an arm up to point to the correct one since I had two on either side of my bed. Adam didn't even blink, he immediately reached over and dug around in the drawer for half a second before pulling out my little pink bullet vibrator.

"This one?" he asked. It wouldn't be until later that I would realize that he rightfully assumed I had multiple.

"Yes, perfect—"

"Show me what you do," Adam grabbed my hand and placed the bullet in my palm, "So I know what to do next time." My breath whooshed out of me. Holy shit, he was already planning ahead for when we did this again, and he hadn't actually gotten off yet.

"Yes, sir," I saluted him again, a grin escaping me as he grabbed my hand that I saluted him with to quickly kiss my knuckles before rolling off of the bed, "What? Where are you going?" I whisper hissed at him. He responded by standing at the foot of my bed and grabbing my ankles to tug my body down towards the edge, a surprised yelp escaping my lips.

"This okay?" he asked, standing in between my spread legs and glancing between us where our centers were lined up. I was grateful that I had a bed frame that was tall enough for me not to need to stuff pillows under my butt or something. I could see his strong, tattooed body perfectly, and the thought of him doing this to me from that angle made heat flood my core again.

"Yup. Totally okay." I nodded as he reached over to me, taking the hand that I was holding my toy with and pressing the button to turn on the vibrator.

"Alright, proceed," Adam smirked at me as he nodded for me to start using it on myself.

I had never done this before.

My previous boyfriend was always slightly offended by the existence of my vibrators, which was where most of my nerves came from when I considered bringing this up with Adam. But he didn't seem offended in the slightest. He even seemed encouraging, the way his eyes darkened when they tracked my movements as I finally started working the bullet over myself made me relax into the moment.

"...Would you use this one?" Adam asked, lining himself up with my entrance, careful not to interfere with the toy.

"Huh?" I asked, surprised at how stimulated I already was after orgasming once already.

"When you thought about me," his dark eyes lifted and locked on me as he nudged my center, making my walls clench, "Would you use this one on yourself? What would you think about?"

"Y-yeah, this one," I nodded as he pushed himself in some more, my eyes rolling in the back of my head from the sensation, "This. I would literally think about this." I glanced down at where we were slowly becoming connected, my body happily adjusting to the stimulation from the toy and the intrusion from him.

"You would think about me fucking you? Like this?" He pushed the rest of the way in, to the hilt. I cried out. His eyes scanned my face, checking to make sure I wasn't hurt before he started to slowly pull back out again.

"Just like this," I rushed out the words on an exhale, struggling to form more, "You at the foot of my bed—but you were a little rougher."

"Rougher?" Adam asked, adding more emphasis to his thrusts, which were gaining in speed.

"Yes! Like that," I gave him a sloppy smile as I wrapped one of my legs around his waist, keeping him close. I could see a bead of sweat start to form on his brow, and I was stuck watching that when he grabbed both of my legs and stretched them flat against his chest and shoulders, gripping my calves as he thrust into me deeper.

"Holy shit, Beck," Adam grunted, his dark eyes locking on mine, "You feel too good." he shook his head once, his dark red hair was sticking out in random places, bobbing with his movements. "I'm not going to last much longer—"

That was all it took. I exploded. I'm pretty sure the

vibrations from my cry were strong enough to wake Gram up downstairs, but I didn't care. I had the decency to try to cover my mouth, but I couldn't control my voice. The way my orgasm felt around him was heavenly, way better than whatever I previously imagined.

I came back to earth much faster this time, blinking rapidly and taking in full breaths of air as my eyes found Adam again. He was pumping into me much faster now. His desperate grip on my legs against his chest was sure to leave bruises.

"That—" Adam gasped, "—Was the hottest thing I've ever seen."

I was positive that wasn't true, but if I didn't get to see what he looked like when he came I thought I might die. I turned off the toy and tossed it aside. I leaned on my elbows while I bent my legs and wrapped them around his waist again, tugging him towards me and encouraging Adam to lean over me as he chased his own orgasm. He quickly caught himself, gripping my waist and holding himself up on his elbows as he thrust into me. I laid back again and tangled my hands in his hair, gently raking my fingernails up his scalp, setting him off.

His eyes squeezed closed and his forehead dropped on my shoulder, his thrusts off beat as his fingers gripped my ribs with the same strength as he had held my legs. His back and shoulders tensed as he grunted his release into my skin, before shifting his body to put most of his weight on one arm as the rest of him lay limp on top of me.

We sat like that for a few moments, catching our breath while my fingernails continued to rake through his soft hair before he finally lifted his head to look at me. His usually light eyes were incredibly dark, and the tired grin he gave me made my heart melt.

Again. I was in huge trouble.

25

I originally wasn't expecting Adam to stay the night, but when he asked if I wanted him to leave after snuggling together in bed for an hour, I told him he should stay. After we cleaned up and I pulled on an old t-shirt and boy shorts for pajamas, I told him I didn't sleep with my hearing aids in. He nodded and said he didn't expect me to. So after I took them out I signed goodnight to him, which he did in return. Then I turned off the light and crawled into bed with him. He kissed my forehead and tucked me in his arms before we both quickly succumbed to sleep. Exhaustion from the long weekend and the fun naked activities we participated in took over our bodies.

Waking up to him kissing my shoulders and back was probably the best experience I had ever been blessed with. Adam signing, *hello beautiful,* made my heart skip a beat—even though a small part of me suspected that he only confidently knew the word "beautiful" in ASL.

The highlight of the morning was when Adam and I both made our way downstairs. We woke up early enough to give him time to go home and shower before work (the lucky jerk didn't have any clients until ten). Gram and Courtney were both at the kitchen table with their morning coffees when they turned to see us descending the staircase. Courtney's eyes widened and she gently set her coffee down to turn to face us in her chair, crossing her legs and resting her chin on her fist.

"So…was everyone safe?" Courtney asked with a wiggle of her eyebrows.

"Of course," Adam responded, his groggy morning voice sending a thrill down my spine. I smiled at him and squeezed his hand before asking if he wanted any coffee. He shook his head once and replied, "I'm good, I'll grab some on the way to work." He was dressed in the same clothes he wore yesterday. I noticed that there were some wrinkles in his shirt from being bundled on my bedroom floor all night.

"I thought I heard some excess noise last night." One of Gram's grey eyebrows lifted in suspicion as she smiled before taking another sip of her coffee.

"Is that what we are calling it now? Excess noise?" Courtney asked with genuine curiosity in her tone. Adam tugged on my hand, wrapping his free arm around my waist and turning me so that our chests were flush together.

"I'm going to head out, I'll see you soon." He bent down to kiss me. Not a peck, but a deep kiss that I probably read way too much into. He released me and planted a quick peck on my forehead before stepping back and waving at my family. "I'll see you all later, thanks for letting me crash here."

"It's not like we could have stopped you," Courtney shrugged and waved, as did Gram.

"Come back soon!" Gram grinned at the handsome redhead. Adam turned to give me one last smile as he let himself out of our front door. I stood in place for a while, watching him walk to our driveway through the living room window. When he got in his car and pulled out I finally released a breath I had been holding and turned to find Courtney and Gram staring at me.

They were both wearing twin expressions, both with their elbows resting on the kitchen table and their fists supporting their cheeks, staring at me with what could only be described as "big goo-goo eyes."

"Sorry about that," I brushed my hair out of my face as I walked to the kitchen to claim my own cup of coffee.

"Nothing to be sorry about," Gram replied, eyeballing me, "What happened to your neck?"

"And your legs?" Courtney added, pointing with her eyes toward my feet. I paused my coffee retrieval to lift a foot and see what she was talking about.

Holy shit, his fingertips actually left little bruises on my legs.

I bent and fit one of my hands on my calf, splaying my fingertips in alignment with the bruises, making Courtney squeal from the table, "Holy shit! That's from his hands? What position were you in?—oh," She figured it out in about three seconds before looking up at my face. "Is that a hickey on your neck?"

"What?" *Fuck, I knew he was sucking on my neck too hard!* I pulled my phone out of my pocket and used the selfie camera to scope out my neck. Sure enough, the faintest bruising was left in between my neck and shoulder, "…Shit."

"Really? A hickey? Is he a teenager?" Gram asked, making

Courtney laugh and raise her fist for my grandmother to bump it, celebrating the quick burn she delivered.

"Damn, I guess I have to wear extra foundation today," I frowned, not caring at all that I was being roasted for having a hickey at twenty-seven years old. I successfully got off last night, twice, and with a hot as hell partner. I was still running off of that high.

"Okay, but real talk," Courtney adjusted herself in her chair so she had both of her feet tucked onto the seat, reminding me a lot of Gollum. "How was it?" Her eyes widened at me, anticipation bursting in her expression.

"It was…wonderful." I couldn't stop the smile that spread on my face. "I had a lot of fun. The most fun I think I've ever had with sex, actually."

Gram took a bite of some toast that was sitting in front of her, so instead of speaking her question she tapped on the table for us to look at her as she signed, *How was it fun?*

"I don't know…We both laughed at each other a lot because we kept joking around," I lifted a shoulder as I retrieved my cup of coffee and joined them at the kitchen table, "He just made the whole thing feel…safe."

I looked up to see Gram and Courtney staring at me with small smiles on their faces, my words making their expressions warm with gratitude toward my latest sexual experience.

"Oh my god, I'm so happy for you!" Courtney jumped up from her chair and circled around the table to wrap her arms around my shoulder, almost making me spill coffee from my mug.

"Thanks," I smiled and hugged her back with my one free arm. Courtney kissed the crown of my head before she returned to her seat and leaned forward, seriousness covering her expression now.

"Alright, now for the fun details," She clapped her hands together before she slowly started to separate them. "Tell me when to stop…Really?…Still? That can't be true…*really?*" I reached over and slapped her hands down on the kitchen table.

"While I appreciate that joke as much as anyone," I made eye contact with her so she knew I was serious, "I am hoping to establish long-term relations with Adam if he's willing. So I don't think I'd want to make you suffer with the knowledge of his private anatomy if he's going to be around us much more often," Courtney's eyes widened before she smiled and nodded in understanding, "But I will say this…" Instead of speaking, I held up two fingers, loving how both Courtney and Gram's brows furrowed with confusion for a few moments before understanding dawned on their faces.

"*Multiple* orgasms?" Courtney blurted while my Gram just fist pumped around her sip of coffee.

"Two glorious, earth-shattering orgasms, yes," I nodded. I understood that to anyone else looking in, it was weird how much celebration was going on at the table over how many times I got off last night. However, that was our dynamic and I wouldn't have it any other way with these women.

Women celebrating women was something that the world absolutely needed more of, no matter how personal the matter seemed to be.

26

I had reached a point in my life where my days started to feel better than my dreams. It was a weird realization because I hadn't been self-aware enough to understand that a piece of my soul had been silently craving companionship as Eloise had expressed some time ago.

A familiar, fulfilling routine had taken place over the next month and a half. Courtney and I would ride the bus together to work every morning, her reading another smutty romance novel and me listening to music in my hearing aids and sending funny internet videos to Adam. We both appreciated a dry sense of humor, which made our social media algorithms sync up. After a few weeks of sharing content with each other, we started to send each other the same videos accidentally. It lit up my soul to realize how such a simple app could make us realize that we had similar thought processes and senses of humor.

While we were at work, we kept things absolutely professional. Courtney and Taylor were the only ones at work who knew that Adam and I were sleeping together. We never touched each other unnecessarily when our coworkers were around. Though if it was late and most of the employees had gone home for the day, Adam would sometimes surprise me by coming to my office while I worked on paperwork to passionately kiss me against my office door, where nobody could see us through my office window.

We didn't see each other every day, because we both had our lives to live (and because Adam made going to the gym multiple nights a week a priority, which sounded like a terrible time to me), but we were sure to text each other at some point every day. The simple ways we let each other know that the other person was on our minds made me realize that being in a relationship with someone was fun and brought additional encouragement for me to want to get out of bed in the mornings.

On the weekends, Adam would come over. Sometimes he would take me out on dates, other times he would stay with us when we were feeling lazy (or I was on my period and feeling gross and bloated). We introduced him to our unique taste in television, easily converting him to the comedic genius of *Ted Lasso*.

Another thing that developed over the last few weeks was Adam's determination to learn ASL. Apparently, he often scheduled time out in his evenings to watch YouTube tutorials on how to understand ASL vernacular, graduating from just using simple terms and phrases to get by. He had a genuine interest to learn a language that was so relevant in my life. Adam often would ask the three of us how to properly say something, since sentences were structured differently in ASL than they were in verbal English.

"So, for example," Gram was explaining one day, "Instead of saying, 'How are you', in ASL it can directly translate more accurately to, 'You-how-you'." She gestured towards Adam vaguely before flattening her hand to her chest and gesturing towards Adam again, demonstrating. Adam nodded, repeating the sign and mumbling, "You-how-you," to himself.

"Or sometimes verbal sentences are more accurately translated to one specific sign," Courtney chimed in, splaying her fingers while curling in her middle one, which touched her shoulders before turning her hands outward towards us, "Like, 'what's up?'"

"'What's up?'" Adam repeated the sign as he spoke, committing it to memory. He was sitting on the floor in front of me while I sat on the couch, working on an evaluation for one of the cute kiddos I met with for work. I reached forward to rub my fingers through the thick hair on the back of his head, a silent thank you as he made such an incredible and expeditious effort to communicate with me when my hearing aids weren't in.

"Something that helped me pick up ASL better as a kid was learning signs for the lyrics of the music that I listened to," I added, syncing my phone to our living room Bluetooth speaker and playing a popular Carbon Cut song. I had finally gotten Courtney to listen to a few of their hits, and she begrudgingly admitted that she could tolerate pop punk music if the lyrics weren't depressingly emo and actually lifted people up.

Even if they were still sung by men.

Adam taking an interest in ASL was incredibly helpful, especially when he told me that he wanted to take me surfing one day. I couldn't risk wearing my hearing aids and having the ocean water damage them, so it was our first date where we had to rely completely on my ability to lip read and Adam signing effectively enough for me.

There was a moment when we were both just sitting on our surfboards on the ocean (because standing up on one was an incredibly difficult feat for me), and Adam turned to look at me to verbally speak. Usually, I was a pretty decent lip reader once I got to know the person, but this time I couldn't understand anything he was saying.

"What?" It was difficult for me to respond verbally without hearing myself. Courtney had always teased me for how easily I transitioned to a deaf accent when my hearing aids weren't in.

Adam moved his lips again, but I swore they said something different than he said before.

"Say that again? I don't understand." I furrowed my brow before he broke his facade, grinned, and started laughing at me. I then realized that he wasn't actually saying anything at all. Just moving his lips randomly to confuse the shit out of me. I playfully glared at him before slapping water all over his handsome face, before he retaliated and splashed me back. Then he quickly leaned forward and paddled back to shore, escaping.

"Hey!" I was sputtering and laughing, struggling to paddle as efficiently as him since surfboards were fucking huge, and my arms and legs weren't as muscular as his. After finally making it back to shore we unclipped our anchors to our boards, seconds before Adam picked me up, threw me over his shoulder, and ran with me back into the ocean water.

"Hey! I'm getting cold!" I cried, laughing as he body slammed us into the water. We were both wearing wet suits, though that didn't stop the ocean chill I got from being force-fully submerged under the waves. I was only under the water a second or two before Adam's large grip pulled us back up and we were gasping for air. He held me with my front pressed to his.

I wiped the salt water out of my eyes before finally look-ing up at him and seeing pure joy on his face. Water droplets fell from his brow and nose, and his dark red hair was com-pletely disheveled from the ocean. His freckles were brightly on display, along with his grin. I forgot to pretend to be mad at him for wrestling me back into the ocean, and instead, I found myself smiling as I reached up to grab his ears and kiss him. He tasted like salt, and whatever mint gum he chewed before our date that day.

I wrapped my legs around his waist, my butt and legs still submerged in the water, and found myself getting carried away with our kisses. Something that happened frequently. I finally pulled back, not wanting to scar the kids and adults playing closer to shore, and got stuck on his light brown eyes shining against the sunset.

I love you.

The intrusive thought hit again. It surprised me, but I did an excellent job of keeping my playful smile on my face as I struggled to fight against the knowledge that hit me just as hard as the waves were crashing into our bodies.

I fucking knew *this would happen with him.*

Adam leaned forward to blow a raspberry on my neck, distracting me from my internal epiphany and bringing me back into one of the many beautiful moments life had created since his presence had been added to it.

***

As a person with horrible hearing, I never expected to be someone who spoke a lot during sex, and I especially never expected Adam to reciprocate that aspect, but we did. For some reason, it made the experience much more personal and fun. Sometimes it was a lot like the first time we slept together, with me being silly and Adam trying not to laugh and to keep the mood as sexy as possible.

Other times Adam took the lead, surprising me with the dirty talk I never realized I would love to hear. We were at his place one evening, even though he usually preferred to hang out at the townhome (because his sleek and modern apartment seemed so "colorless and empty" in comparison to Gram's house). That being said, we were able to be as loud as we wanted at his apartment, whereas we had to be careful to shush each other whenever we were intimate in my little bedroom.

Both situations were exciting for me because I was just grateful for the time I had when Adam was interested in being part of my life in this way. I was grateful to find a partner that I truly loved spending quality time with as much as I loved being intimate with. Adam always made sure that I was fulfilled as much as he was sexually, even on the days when I was down and it took more effort to ensure I got mine before he got his.

He was someone who got off knowing that *he* could get me off, when previously hardly anyone else could.

We were in his kitchen one day, which was monochromatic and spotless. As if he never used it. There was a large island meant for someone who enjoyed cooking large meals from scratch when we were both people who preferred to eat an insane amount of takeout. We were sitting at the island, waiting for our food to be delivered when Adam kissed my neck in that spot that filled my body with warmth, and then in a blink I found myself being bent over the kitchen island.

Adam's large hand was gripping my shoulder and my hip as he impaled me from behind, helping me stay in position while also supporting his weight. I could see our reflection in his truly stainless steel refrigerator, shocked that I was about to get off this way.

"To be honest," Adam spoke in between his thrusts, "I've pictured you—like this—a number of times—before I left for work—each morning."

"That—ah—must have been—ugh—torture for you." My palms were sweaty, my orgasm rising at a rapid rate, and I was struggling to hold myself on the island. I didn't want to stop staring at our reflection. It was crazy how erotic watching myself getting railed by Adam was. It felt like we had just gotten started and I was already trying to make it last.

"You—" Adam paused his movements to snake his hand that was holding my hip around my front to start drawing gentle circles around my clit, picking up his thrusts again, "Are *never*—a torture for me."

And just like that, I went off like a fucking bomb. I didn't hold back, Adam's neighbors be damned for all I cared. I dropped my head and cried into the cold marble of his kitchen island, allowing myself to be carried away in all the sensations I was feeling. My muscles loosened and I started to relax, and Adam followed soon after me, thrusting into me at an uneven rhythm before gripping my hips tightly and grunting out his own release.

After we both caught our breath he dragged me off of the island and guided me towards his black leather couch, draping one of his two throw blankets down on it first (because I had told him that I hated the feeling of my skin peeling off leather) before encouraging me to lay down. He snuck in behind me, wrapping his arms around me and resting his leg in between mine, and draped his second (because the psychopath only had two throw blankets) over us.

It wasn't a miraculous moment, it was a familiar routine we had established over the weeks of us being together, yet this feeling that had been growing in my chest finally burst open. Love. I was falling in deep, scary love with this man. The thought of whatever we identified our relationship as coming to an unexpected end made my heart start to break. At the thought of it, I felt a tear start to fall from my eye as we snuggled in and began to dose off, forgetting to have the mindset to catch it before it landed on Adam's arm. He realized what it was immediately.

"Are you okay?" Adam asked, adjusting to lay me flat on my back so that he could see my face. I gave him a wobbly smile before nodding and snuggling back into his chest, in a pathetic attempt to hide my face from him. I finally built the courage to mumble a response.

"I'm just...*so* happy," I breathed into his skin. Adam's large arms tightened around me, his cheek resting on top of my head.

"I'm happy too, Beck," Adam murmured into my dark hair, "Happier than I remember being in a long time." I exhaled a breath of relief, hopeful that we wouldn't end anytime soon. My crush had morphed into infatuation, and infatuation quickly formed into an addiction since the moment we first kissed in Big Bear.

"...I love that I get to fall asleep with you in my arms," Adam murmured after a long silence between us. My eyes were closed and my face was still hiding in his chest, unable to let myself face him in this unfamiliar moment of crisis I was in.

Finally, once my body was relaxing in his snug embrace, I replied to him through a long sigh, "I want you."

It was the last thing I vaguely remembered before dozing off that night.

27

The following morning we both washed in his fancy black tiled shower, falling into a routine we had established the nights we stayed at his apartment instead of the townhome, where we had to share a bathroom with Courtney.

We didn't say much, and I couldn't tell if that was because we were both still recovering from accidentally sleeping all night on the couch, or if it was because of the words we exchanged with each other. I didn't think saying, "I want you" was too forward at this point, but a prickle of doubt was running up my spine. I decided I wouldn't bring it up until he did, in case I was creating anxiety over nothing. A situation I found myself in often.

As we both brushed our teeth in the mirror Adam caught my gaze and winked at me once before spitting and rinsing in the sink.

"No noticeable marks left on you this time." He smirked at me as he reached into his bathroom drawer to pull out a comb. I loved watching him style his hair, a characteristic of his that I had become infatuated with since day one. He knew, so he usually put on a show for me by unnecessarily flexing his arm and chest muscles as he combed.

"At the moment, I don't mind it when you suck on my

skin," I reached over and pinched his ass which was covered with the towel he had tied around his waist. "It's the heckling I get from Courtney the morning after that grows old."

"To be fair, it is incredibly childish to do as a twenty-eight year old man," he returned his comb to the drawer and turned to face me, pulling on the towel tied around my front until we were pressed against each other, "But I can't help it. The noises you make when I do drive me insane."

I blushed and gently pushed on his chest, an embarrassed smirk tugging on my lips as I reminded him to get ready and escaped to his bedroom.

Today Taylor was coming over and we were all going to go on a mild hike at Crystal Cove. Taylor ensured that it was a family friendly hike, and wouldn't be as steep in some places as the one we did in Big Bear. My friend's constant effort to make me physically active was probably the only reason I wasn't morbidly overweight at this point. If I could get away with staying in bed or on the couch all day every day, I would. And everyone knew that.

Adam and I drove over to Gram's townhome early in the morning so that we could all eat breakfast together because Courtney was planning to make blueberry pancakes. They were famously delicious.

If Courtney saw Adam's fancy kitchen, and realized how little use it received, she would probably cry.

We entered through the front door, Adam hitting the doorbell just once so the lights in the house flickered and Gram would know that we arrived if her aids weren't in.

"Hello!" I called, kicking off my sandals and making my way toward our kitchen. I found Courtney at the stove, looking concerned as she managed to flip a blueberry pancake in the air before catching it in the frying pan.

"Beck," Gram was sitting at the kitchen table, but stood up when she saw me enter the room, her cell phone laying in front of her, "Is there any chance you can call Taylor and reschedule?"

I lifted an eyebrow, immediately picking up on the tense energy of the room. "Why?"

"Your parents just called…they will be here in about five minutes," Gram replied, wringing her wrinkled hands together nervously. My eyes widened at that.

"What?" I felt Adam's large hand engulf mine, squeezing once as he reached my side.

"They just called, I guess they decided to come to visit for the weekend…and your mom forgot to communicate to us that it was, in fact, *this* weekend that they wanted to come." Gram rolled her eyes a little, obviously irritated with my mother.

I had a sneaking suspicion that my mother went out of her way to not give us any real notice.

"Do I need to clean my room? Because if I'm being honest, I have a lot of stuff out and about that probably isn't appropriate for people like Beck's parents," Courtney asked from the stove.

"No, no," I rubbed my forehead, trying to process this information. A lump was forming in my stomach. I hadn't seen them in person in years, I was so unprepared.

"There is no reason for them to go into your room, Court," Gram shook her head at my friend before sitting down in her chair again. "And there is no reason to panic, Beck. They are staying at a hotel, knowing that we already have a full house here. It sounded like they just wanted to formally come visit for maybe an hour or two before they went to the beach or something."

I nodded my head, not realizing the death grip I had on Adam's hand until he pulled my arm to get me to turn to face him. "Do you want me to leave?" he asked. I widened my eyes and shook my head rapidly.

"No, please don't," I tugged him towards me so I could wrap my arms around his narrow waist. "I could really use some support at the moment."

"Done." Adam's large arms came around me and held me tight, the sounds of Courtney continuing to flip pancakes filling the room for a few minutes before Gram's phone buzzed on the table.

"Yes?" Gram asked, after tapping once on her phone to accept the call and Bluetooth it to her hearing aids, her hazel eyes glanced up to look out the front window, "Yes, I see you. It looks like you found it just fine."

I felt my heart start to beat rapidly and, miraculously, tightened my embrace around Adam. Over the last month and a half Adam and I had learned a lot about each other's families. He understood how intrusive my parents could be, considering his parents also tended to insert themselves into his life. He had quickly realized, however, just how toxic my parents' intrusion tended to be when layered with a thick religious aspect. I shared a few stories about my parents from my childhood that I considered to be funny because it was so chaotic and willfully ignorant that I had no choice but to laugh at the reality of it. In response, Adam had just stared wide-eyed at me in shock and said, "I'm so sorry you were told that at such a young age."

It made me feel embarrassed, but then he would continue to gas me up by saying how proud he was of me for deconstructing so much from such a young age, and how that proved how incredible I was for standing my ground.

I didn't want to be strong or praised for standing my ground.

I just wanted an understanding between my parents and me, so we could be part of each other's lives like we were supposed to.

"Hey," Adam's low voice mumbled into my hair as he held me tight, the sound of loud footsteps coming from the porch out front. "It'll be fine. You got this. Deep breaths." It sounded like Adam's Mom Friend Override was activated. I nodded against his chest and inhaled through my nose before exhaling through my mouth. The sound of knocking at the front door made me jump a little as I pulled myself away from Adam's warm embrace.

"Come in!" Gram called from the kitchen table, loud enough for anyone standing on the front porch to hear.

Nothing.

"Come in!" Courtney called as she set a place of blueberry pancakes on the center of the kitchen table. Not even an attempt at wiggling the doorknob.

Oh, right, my parents probably thought it was rude to yell "Come in" instead of just answering the door. With an annoyed sigh, I marched over to the front door and placed my hand on the knob, closing my eyes for a moment to compose myself before opening the door to reveal the two people who were once the center of my life.

<h1 style="text-align:center">28</h1>

"Hi!" my mother squealed, jumping forward to wrap me up in a tight embrace. I instinctively returned her hug, letting her rock us side to side on our feet before she pulled away and gripped my shoulders to give me a once over.

She smelled familiar, like my childhood. It was both comforting and nerve-wracking.

"Hi, guys!" I smiled, looking over at my dad who was cautiously stepping into the townhouse and looking around with a suspicious eye before meeting mine.

"Hello, sweetheart." My dad greeted me with a tight hug as well and patted my head twice before releasing me and taking in our audience.

"Hello, Ben!" Gram greeted, genuine warmth on her face at the sight of her distant son. She made her way over to the entryway much quicker than you would expect a seventy-four-year-old woman to be able to. As my parents and grandmother exchanged hugs, I took in their appearance for the first time.

They both looked much older and worn down. My mom's baggy fitting long-sleeved top and skirt were bland, sandy colors that mirrored my dad's button up and khakis. I knew they probably hated how short my shorts were. They stuck out like sore thumbs in comparison to the colorful living space we were in. My mother's grey hair was more noticeable in person than it was on FaceTime, as well as the wrinkles both had around their eyes and lips.

They were aging, reminding me that I had missed out on a large chunk of time with them.

"Come on in, Court was just making breakfast for everyone!" Gram grabbed my dad's arm and walked him into our little kitchen, where I turned to see Adam and Courtney working together to set the table for everyone to sit.

At the sight of Adam, my mother paused before taking her seat beside my father.

"I don't believe we've been introduced," my mother said, extending her hand toward Adam after he set a glass of orange juice down in front of her.

"Adam Hall." He smiled at her as he shook her hand once, and part of me made a note to remind him that he didn't smile once at me when he introduced himself to us at work but was apparently willing to turn up the charm for my mother.

I was coughing up a lung at the time, but still.

"Adam. What a great name. Are you Courtney's fella?" my dad asked, taking Adam's hand that he had extended to him in greeting.

"Oh, uh..." Adam looked at both of my parents before his light gaze landed on mine. Over all the time we had spent together, we had never once discussed *those* labels with each other. We had discussed the fact that we were monogamous and loved each other's company, but never referred to each other as boyfriend or girlfriend.

Courtney just snickered at my parents' assumption that she would have a partner and I wouldn't. Even though it was a fair assumption.

"No, he's mine," I replied, giving Adam a conspiratorial smirk behind my dad's back before I walked around the table to be seated across from my parents. Maybe it was rude of me to make Courtney and Gram literal buffers between my parents and me, but I wanted to be able to hold Adam's hand or squeeze his thigh under the table for support. All without the fear of my father eyeballing what he would consider "inappropriate" behavior.

"Oh," was all my mother said as her gaze tracked my movements by Adam's side, pulling a chair out for myself and grabbing his hand to pull him into the seat directly next to mine. Gram and Courtney took their seats on either side of us, successfully creating distance between my parents and me around the small circular table.

"Unfortunately, Beck snared this fine male specimen before I even had the chance to make a move." Courtney tsked once in fake disappointment as she took the spatula to start loading up everybody's plates.

"How did she manage that?" my dad asked, eyeballing Adam with obvious skepticism.

"She sack-tapped him at work."

Gram started giggling, and I caught myself fighting a smile as well. That whole scenario seemed so long ago; I had almost forgotten that it happened. Though the looming silence after Gram's snicker reminded me that my parents did not accept those crude words in their own home, so I wasn't surprised to meet their gazes and see them both looking uncomfortable at the table.

Well, we were off to a great start.

"So," my father cleared his throat as he waited for everyone's plates to be served with pancakes, "You work with Courtney and Rebecca?"

"Yes," Adam nodded, taking a drink from his orange juice. I noticed that his foot was tapping underneath the table, a nervous habit I hadn't seen from him in a while. I reached a hand under the table to rest it over his thigh and still the movement. "I'm a Physical Therapist at the clinic."

"Ah," My mother smiled at him, recovering from Courtney's crude remark, "How sweet. What made you pursue working with kids?"

"Ah, well," Adam cleared his throat, then continued telling my parents about himself. I lifted a fork and started cutting into my pancakes, taking the opportunity to eat while he couldn't. "I actually used to surf competitively. A little over a year ago I realized I wasn't happy doing that anymore, so I decided to put my degrees to good use. My parents are large donors to the non-profit Beck and Court work at, so they were able to put in a good word for me to get hired. I have only been working there a few months." I could tell the words were difficult for Adam to get out because he hated the fact that his parents were involved in any part of his career.

"Rebecca," my dad cut in, making me stiffen and pause mid bite, "Do you mind if we say grace?" I looked at my father who was eyeballing me in a way that let me know he was disappointed. I had a mouthful of food, and my parents hadn't touched theirs because they hadn't prayed over it yet. Did they address Courtney or Gram for eating their food already? No, because unlike them, my parents raised me to know better. My dad was reminding me of that with his penetrating gaze.

"I don't mind, you go ahead," I set my fork down and rested my hands on the table. It was a bit of a chess game, phrasing my words in a way to let them know that I did not mind if they wanted to pray, but that I would absolutely not be participating. My dad gave me a hard look before clearing his throat and taking my mother's hand. She lowered her head while my dad recited a prayer that lasted a little too long for a table where four out of the six people weren't religious. After he concluded grace, everyone reached for their silverware.

"So, Adam," My mom smiled brightly, in an effort to brush that awkward moment under the rug, "Did your parents name you after the first Adam?"

Adam. What a great name. Those were the words my dad used earlier.

"No," Adam shook his head once as he swallowed his first bite of pancakes, "I think I'm named after one of my great-grandfathers, actually. My family isn't religious."

My mother's smile faltered a little. I wanted to roll my eyes because her disappointment was willfully ignorant at this point. It had been literal years of me dropping her phone calls whenever she had a spiritual message to share with me.

"That's a shame," my dad added, frowning at his bite of pancakes as if the taste was now affected because of the realization that the man I was seeing was either an atheist or agnostic.

"Adam is wonderful," Gram chimed in, attempting to reset the mood my parents were set on destroying, "and he makes Beck so happy. I'm glad she's found someone like him."

I wasn't eating my pancakes anymore. I could feel the irritation my dad was releasing with his stiff body language as he quietly judged me, and the former child in me wanted to cave and lie to my parents, saying that Adam and I had both met at a church or something. Anything to get that pinched expression off of their faces.

The adult in me who had been going to therapy for years, however, knew that that was a terrible thing to do. I had worked too hard to create boundaries for my parents via digital communication, so now I needed to reinforce my boundaries with them when we were face to face.

I realized at that moment that I didn't enjoy their presence anymore. I didn't have this ache to be around them that most children who leave home had. Every time I felt melancholy about my parents in the last few years, it had been because I was mourning this unrealistic idea of a relationship we could have had. Not because I wanted to rebuild the same relationship that they were so desperate to shove in my face.

"I'm glad to hear that." My mother's smile toward Gram was one hundred percent fake before she met my gaze and continued leading the conversation at the table. "Has Josh gotten in touch with you yet?"

I froze, holding my mother's gaze with a hard look for a few seconds longer than necessary before slowly setting my fork down on the table and folding my hands in my lap.

"No." It was both a response to her question and a demand for her to drop the subject completely. My mother, however, chose willful ignorance once again and nodded her head before she continued on.

"That's a shame. He really is a kind man. I guess he's gone through a divorce recently; he has the sweetest little boy who—"

"—Stop it," My voice was louder than necessary, startling Adam and Courtney sitting on either side of me. Adam's hand had come to squeeze my thigh under the table. "I already told you I have no interest in speaking with him."

"Rebecca, be reasonable," my mother rolled her eyes at me, an action she had displayed for me repeatedly as a child. "You're acting like—" I raised a hand to halt her mid-sentence.

"—I'm acting like a twenty-seven-year-old woman who has to constantly reinforce boundaries with her parents."

"Rebecca Scott." My dad's voice held unquestionable authority, a voice he had also used throughout the entirety of my childhood in an attempt to keep me from countering him on anything. "You do not need to speak to your mother that way."

"I do, though." I squeezed my eyes shut and leaned back in my chair, exasperated. "I literally just introduced you both to my boyfriend and as soon as you realized he wasn't religious, she brought up some tool I went to high school with—for no other reason than that he's currently single and goes to church!" I shook my head at my parents, who were both open jawed and glaring at me.

"Don't put words in my mouth," My mother defended

herself, "I was bringing him up because I thought he needed a friend. He's going through a tough time right now, and—"

"So am I!" I threw my hands up before I groaned and rubbed them down my face. "I have parents who refuse to accept the fact that I am a single, non-religious, sexually active—" My dad scoffed and threw his fork on his plate as he rolled his eyes at that, "—Grown adult who is capable of making her own choices!"

"I am your father, Rebecca!" My dad raised his voice to match mine, leaning forward in his seat which made Courtney lean back in hers, "Until you are taken care of, I have a responsibility over you. I take my role as your father very seriously—"

"—Oh, cut the shit," I glared at him, enjoying the way he winced at my curse. "Don't give me that sexist-patriarchal, 'I care about you too much to let you make your own choice's bullshit. I have been doing just fine without your guys' influence for the entirety of my twenties. I sure as hell don't need you manipulating me now. You guys have been here for, what, five minutes? And you've already gone the holierthan-thou route. You just couldn't help yourselves."

My mother's glare transformed into a wounded look, complete with her chin wobbling. She was really putting on the act. My father reached over to rub her back as he fixed me with a look that was slowly starting to have no effect on me.

Gram knocked her knuckles on the table to get my attention, lifting her hands to sign to me, *Take a deep breath, you made your point, try to calm down.* I did as she instructed, closing my eyes for my inhale and reopening them during my exhale.

I'm sorry if I ruined breakfast with your son, but I'm not sorry for defending myself, I replied.

"What are you guys talking about?" my father asked, his eyes narrowing at the conversation between Gram and I. Adam's hand, which was still on my thigh, gripped tightly before he leaned forward towards my father.

"You don't sign?" Adam's tone was flat as he asked this question.

My dad just blinked at Adam before ignoring him and turning to me to say, "It's rude to have a conversation at the table that not everyone can understand, Rebecca."

"I think it's ruder to have a deaf mother and daughter and then to go out of your way to avoid learning a language that helps them communicate effectively," Courtney chimed in, grinning brightly at my parents after shoving an ungodly amount of pancakes into her mouth. How she kept her lips closed, I had no idea.

I rested my hand over Adam's, giving it a gentle squeeze as a realization hit with Courtney's words.

My parents could have learned ASL.

They could have learned ASL this whole time.

They could have learned ASL when I was a child, they could have learned it when I was a teenager and teaching myself. They could have learned it when I was at college, or when I graduated, or during the last couple of years when I expressed how FaceTime was easier for me to communicate because I could see their faces.

My parents *chose* not to.

My parents, who raised me, specifically went out of their way *not* to learn American Sign Language for their daughter with significant hearing loss. It was a choice they had made every day for the last twenty years.

It was at that moment, sitting at Gram's little kitchen table, feeling the heat of my dad's glare and ignoring the sniffles my mother was making, that I realized it.

My parents didn't care about *me*.

I was sure that they cared about me a little, I was their daughter after all. But instead of trying to get to know me, making an effort to learn my language, or understanding why I made the decisions that I had throughout my life, they chose to ignore it and pretend that they could still influence me in the way that was most important to them.

I take my role as your father very seriously.

My parents having their daughter live the lifestyle they deemed holy and respectable was *their* boundary. We were both creating our own boundaries, frustrated with the other for not budging. Which was why having any real or fruitful relationship with my parents was doomed to fail.

My heart was both racing and shattering with the realization.

"...I think you guys should go," I spoke after the long moments of silence following Courtney's words and the proverbial anvil they had dropped on my head.

My mom sniffled one last time before staring at me wide-eyed. "Rebecca, don't be overdramatic."

"...No, I think Beck is right," Gram said, standing up from

her chair. "I don't mean to be rude, but it's obvious that now is not the time to discuss these things."

"Mom, I'd like a moment of privacy with my daughter." My dad eyeballed Gram standing from her chair, refusing to get out of his. He considered himself the man of the house, after all.

"I have no interest in speaking with you right now," I replied, my tone flat. I grabbed onto Adam's hand with desperation, my eyeballs glued to the half-eaten pancakes on my plate.

"Rebecca," my father stood from his chair and crossed his arms, making me wince from the authoritative body language he had mastered over the years, "The least you could do is—"

"You heard her," Adam's low voice was hard, yielding no question. "It's time for you to go."

Suddenly the front door burst open, and an out of breath Taylor was running into the townhome and closing the door behind them. "Fuck—I'm *so* sorry I'm late! I hope you guys got my text—" They paused halfway into the living room, seeing the scene at the kitchen table: Gram and Dad standing, my mother sniffling, Adam holding my hand under the table and eyeing daggers in my father's direction. All while Courtney was helping herself to a second serving of pancakes as if nothing weird was happening at all.

"Who is this?" my father asked, glancing back at all of us for some sort of explanation he definitely didn't deserve.

"Oh, my bad. I'm Taylor," they walked forward and held a hand out to my father, "I didn't mean to interrupt."

"You didn't, my parents were just leaving." I stood from

my seat at the table and held tightly to Adam's hand, bringing him along with me as I started to walk around everyone towards the living room.

"Oh, you're Beck's parents?" Taylor's blue eyes brightened at the realization. They had heard many stories about their toxic and harmful beliefs.

"Yes," my dad eyeballed Taylor, who was wearing short blue running shorts that showed off the dark thick hair that coated their limbs. They had on a white tank top that read, "Mind your own uterus," paired with tan hiking boots. Their black baseball cap with the tiniest LGBTQ+ flag embroidered on it was backward on their head. Their septum piercing glistened in the natural morning light coming in from the living room windows.

My dad was trying to make sense of Taylor, and I immediately became defensive of them.

"They work with us, too," I explained, giving my parents an out by using their correct pronouns before they could possibly mess that up. "I'd love for you to get to know them some time, but again, it's time for you to go. We have a hike we promised T we'd do today before you two rudely sprung your visit upon us with five minutes' notice."

My parents both looked at me, surprise filling their faces for a second before they threw on a polite mask in the presence of the unexpected company.

"Yes, we will have to schedule a more appropriate time to get together," my mother nodded, pasting on a wobbly smile and lacing her arm through my dad's.

"I would wait for me to call you, going forward. There's no need to reach out to me first." My words made my parents pause, turning to look at me with a myriad of emotions running across their faces. After a few uncomfortable moments, acceptance seemed to flood my mother as bitter disapproval consumed my father's constant glare.

"If that's how you want things to be, then so be it," My father murmured in a pitiful attempt to take the blame off of himself.

"Rebecca," my mother tugged on my dad's arm once, halting his movements and looking almost remorseful as she caught my gaze, "We didn't mean…we just…we want you to be happy and blessed. We have been so worried about you. Alone, without us around—"

"I will take solitude and peace over toxicity and forced connections. Any day." My reply was immediate. I tugged Adam a hair closer to me, and he responded by wrapping an arm around my shoulders from behind and tugging me against his chest. Before all of this, the mild PDA would have made me uncomfortable in front of my parents. Circumstances being what they were, I was happy for the grounding Adam was providing as I expressed my feelings as concisely as I could for them.

Taylor clapped their hands together once, blowing out a low whistle as they walked back to the front door and opened it nice and wide, gesturing dramatically for my parents to make their exit through it.

My mom's chin wobbled one last time before she and my dad accepted the situation for what it was, and silently left without another word. Taylor waited until they made it to their car in the driveway before shutting the door and turning to look at us with their arms crossed.

I felt my own chin wobble, a few stray tears streaking down my face that I quickly tried to wipe away before they landed on Adam's arms.

"I'm sorry," I whispered to the room, embarrassment starting to wash over me.

"Don't be sorry!" Taylor rushed over to give me a hug, working around Adam's arms on my shoulders.

"You have nothing to apologize for, young lady," Gram scolded as she made her way to the living room to sit down in one of her accent chairs. "I am proud of you for standing up for yourself."

"Thank you," I let out a strangled sob into Taylor's shoulder, holding one of Adam's arms and wrapping one of mine around Taylor's waist. "It's just...they're my parents. They're *my parents*."

Taylor gave me one last comforting squeeze before leaning back and rubbing my arms with their hands. "Listen to me," Taylor lifted their eyebrows as they caught my gaze, "Don't let your empathy rob your parents of experiencing the consequences of their actions. You both made your decisions, now it's time to live with them."

I caught my top lip in between my teeth and nodded, a nervous smirk tugging my lips as Taylor took my face and smacked a kiss on my forehead.

"That's probably the smartest thing Taylor has ever said to any of us, for the record," Courtney piped up from her seat at the kitchen table, the only one still proceeding with the breakfast as if none of that drama happened.

"First of all, fuck you very much," Taylor leaned around

Adam and me to flip Courtney off, which made the room burst into laughter. After releasing the pent-up energy I had via laughter, I took a deep breath. I focused on the peaceful feeling I had experienced for years with my chosen family, quickly refilling the safe space I have created.

"Hey," Adam murmured, his lips near the crown of my head, "Are you okay?"

"Yeah," I nodded, turning to look up at him, "I think I need a few moments before we leave. Is that okay?"

"Of course," Adam kissed the side of my head and released his grip on me.

"We have all day, take your time," Taylor patted my shoulder before they hopped onto the living room couch near Gram's chair, and grabbed the remote to turn the TV on.

"...Can you come with me?" I asked, taking Adam's hand and tugging. He gave me a small smile as he nodded his head and allowed me to lead him upstairs to my bedroom. I started to feel a little lightheaded from the adrenaline rush that I was just now realizing took over my body during the entirety of that discussion with my parents. I wanted to go to my room, hug my favorite guy, and isolate for an unset amount of time.

29

My pulse was starting to slow back down with each passing second. The deep breaths I was inhaling through my nose and exhaling through my slightly parted lips were helping. Adam came and sat down next to me on the bed and swung one of his heavy arms around me, gripping my hip and tugging me in close to his side. His cheek rested on the top of my head, grounding me in ways I never knew were possible with the simple human touch.

He was comforting me without smothering me, still giving me space in the silence to process and grieve. Allowing my emotions and feelings to flow through me.

"I'm sorry," Adam murmured, not expecting a response from me, though I still gave him one after a few moments.

"It's okay." I felt him nod his head on top of mine. We could have sat like that for minutes or for an hour. A lot was going through my mind because what we just experienced was a lot to process. The fact that he was even there for that clusterfuck was a lot for me to deal with.

"It's okay for it to not be okay," Adam finally said, giving my hip a gentle squeeze. I smirked a little before responding, "I know, but it's also okay for it to be."

"Touché." He chuckled. I looked up at him and kissed him on the cheek, a thank you for being my support when I had both Gram and Courtney in the house, probably ready and willing to comfort me this weekend with junk food, weed, and TV.

"I will say, hearing about your parents and experiencing them are two very different things," Adam released my hip and pulled his arm back to grab one of my hands, his thumb gently tracing over the top of mine.

"That's true. I'm sorry you had to experience them like this. But, it looks like you and I will never have to experience them again if we don't want to. So, silver linings and all that." I shrugged my shoulders; I couldn't tell if I was feeling numb or shocked by what just happened. The more silence that settled, the more relief I felt. The relief started to slowly tap me, getting my attention. Over time it started to brush against me and suddenly I was consumed by waves of relief.

And how sad was that?

For all intents and purposes, I just permanently ended any chance of having any sort of relationship, distant or otherwise, with my parents. My entire immediate family unit will go on existing as if I didn't, and I would do the same. How many people in the world would truly feel relief after acknowledging that?

I released what felt like the biggest sigh known in existence, expelling the last of my guilt about my family dynamic into the world. I didn't need it anymore. Guilt would only harm me, poison me, and lead me to do something stupid like trying to apologize—even though there is no reality in which I should need to do that.

"When I was a young girl, I used to daydream about running away," I finally started speaking. Adam released my hand and started rubbing slow circles on my back. "But even in my dream, I always pictured a handsome prince of some sort blazing into town, falling hopelessly in love with me, and taking me away despite my parent's protests…even in my daydream, I knew I couldn't fall for any person that my parents would actually approve of." I paused, staring down at the grey fingernail polish chipping on my nails. I didn't pick at it, just traced my thumb over the rough edges of the paint.

"I'm glad you realized that from a young age," Adam murmured. I didn't look at him, I kept my gaze on my hands.

"Me too. I still imagine what my life would have been like if I did simply fall for someone they approved of, at the ripe age of eighteen or nineteen. Every time, I feel physically ill. I'm happy with my choices. I'm happy with where I am today." I felt his hand snake around and squeeze my hip again. I finally looked up at him and gave him a simple smile, "And I didn't even need a man to save me to do it as my little prepubescent brain thought."

"You don't ever *need* a man, Beck." Adam agreed with me, a true smile on his face. Adam, a man, was not offended in the slightest by my words. The whole time my parents were here he was at my side, ready to back me up if need be, but he still let me battle that out with my parents myself. He was silent support, but I knew if I gave him any hint that I needed him to step in, he would have.

That was an interesting realization to have.

"I know, thank you." I reached over and wrapped my arms around his neck, pulling him in for a tight hug that he happily reciprocated. He felt so good, like always. I closed my eyes and embraced the feel of him wrapped all around me. His scent, how he sounded when he exhaled through his nose and it brushed down my neck. How I knew that if I lifted my leg and straddled his lap right now that he would be happy to meet my physical needs as well.

I was the first to pull back, but not too far. We still had our hands wrapped around each other. I looked into his eyes, eyes that snared me in from day one and reveled in the fact that I had come to know them so personally. Even if we were just meeting each other's physical needs the past few weeks, I was so abundantly grateful to have had these experiences with him.

He didn't need to know that I was helplessly in love with him. He had already done so much for me. To put the burden of my emotions and attachment on him too soon just wasn't fair. I felt at peace with this decision. I would let him go when he was ready and done.

Adam's eyes started to sharpen the little longer we stared at each other. I never pictured myself to be someone who would just make longing eye contact with someone, but here I was. It didn't feel nearly as awkward as I imagined it to be. He slid his hands across my back and landed them on one of his many favorite places on my body, my hips. His fingers pressed snugly against my skin.

"But...do you *want* a man?" Adam asked, his facial features transforming in such a way to let me know he was being very serious. His voice was rough, as if it took a lot of energy for him to get those words out.

I blinked at him, surprised.

"What?"

He cleared his throat and blinked a couple of times, glancing at my shoulder, before flexing his grip on me and bringing his eyes back to mine. "You don't need a life partner, but, eventually, would you want one?"

I stared at him, letting my grip on his shoulders slide down past his biceps and settle onto his forearms.

"I...yes?" Was he asking what I thought he was asking? My heart rate, which had successfully slowed to a steady beat, was now climbing again. Anxious for a totally different reason. He slid his arms out from under my hands and gripped them tightly, his eye contact searing into mine. I couldn't look away if I wanted to.

"I...well, maybe this isn't appropriate to talk about right now..." Adam was blinking more, backpedaling. He leaned his body away from me a couple of inches to emphasize the backpedaling he was doing in his brain.

"No, you should probably talk about it right now," I disagreed with a head nod, gripping his hands.

"Beck, you just..." he nodded vaguely towards the door, towards where the clusterfuck of the day happened.

"Yeah, I did, but if you don't tell me what's on your mind and what's making you nervous, I'm going to throw up." Oh, god, was he trying to break up with me? Now? Seconds after I decided I was brave enough to let him go if he wanted me to. I was clearly an idiot seconds ago. I could already feel the heaviness in my gut, how the fuck was I supposed to find someone else after experiencing everything I had with him?

Adam's lips spread into one of his devastatingly handsome smiles and my breath caught in my throat, he chuckled before embracing me once again and pulling us down on the bed. We were on our sides facing each other. He brushed some hair that fell in front of my face back behind my ear.

What the fuck was happening?

"I'm sorry for making you nauseous," Adam was still grinning at me.

"You never make me nauseous. My anxiety makes me nauseous," I reached up to grip the sides of his head, my fingertips brushing his hair. "Now tell me what you are thinking."

"You are very demanding." Adam only raised an eyebrow at me, so I made a disgruntled noise in the back of my throat and released his head to roll onto my back. My forearms folded over my eyes. He just chuckled at me again.

I inhaled through my nose, out through my lips.

"...I do want a man. I love the idea of a partner. For my lifetime." I held my breath. It was an emotional rollercoaster. If there was a chance that he wanted to move on from whatever we were, I needed to be brave and get the conversation rolling.

For the record, covering my eyes with my arms so that I didn't have to look at his beautiful face as he shattered my heart was—in fact—bravery.

Thank you very much.

I felt his large hands grip my arms to pull them off my face, "Beck." His deep voice rumbled through my body.

"Adam," I repeated back at him in my deep mock Adam voice, struggling to keep my face covered. After a couple of seconds, he won, pulling my arms down and locking both of my wrists in one of his hands, and resting the cluster on my stomach. He held himself up on his other arm as he lay on his side and looked down at me on my back.

"I'm nervous, be patient," Adam murmured, leaning down to kiss my temple.

"I promise you, I'm more nervous," I replied.

"Just give me a warning first, so I can jump out of the splash zone." Such an ass. I made fake gagging sounds that made his eyes widen in alarm for half a second before he rolled them and realized I was teasing. I leaned towards him, giggling through my fake gags as he attempted to cover my mouth and pretended to be disgusted with me.

"Be prepared to see a bill from my doctor for the inevitable ulcer you're creating in my stomach," I narrowed my eyes at him playfully. Adam winked at me and went to tickle my sides, but I dodged the attack and rolled away from him. He caught me, which I loved. He wrestled both of my hands into his grip again and held my hands hostage over my head, laying his body over mine so I was pinned to my bed.

I loved when he held me like this. I loved giving control over to him in moments like this. His eyes were glittering with emotion, and his facial features relaxed as he leaned down and pressed his lips against mine. One of his hands holding my wrists, the other cradling my head as he kissed me deep, I almost forgot the anxiety his cryptic words caused moments earlier. After a few seconds, our lips nice and swollen, he pulled away a few inches to lock eyes with me again, his breathing heavy.

"I love you."

Air rushed out of my lungs. Maybe it was because we had just been kissing, maybe it was feeling half of his body weight pressed into me, but even though I had many daydreams featuring this exact set of words coming from him, directed at me, I was still unprepared.

"I am in love with you, Beck," he continued as I stared at him wordlessly, I swore my heart stopped completely before kickstarting again. "I think I have been in love with you, in some form, since the beginning."

I narrowed my eyes at that, "That can't be true." That made worry appear on his facial features again, but I continued, "The first time we met, I had a coughing fit and wouldn't let you shake my hand." The nerves stayed on his face, and after a few moments, I realized he was working up the courage to say something else.

What else could possibly be scarier than admitting your love for someone?

"…That wasn't exactly the first time we met." Adam held his breath after he choked the words out, his eyes never leaving my face.

What the fuck?

"Yes, it was, when Pat introduced you to Courtney and me in my office."

"Okay, maybe that was the first time we *met*. But the first time I saw you was in the parking lot outside the clinic."

I didn't know what my face was showing him, but I could

see insecurity starting to rise in his. He released his grip on my wrists and started to pull away, sitting up. I stayed laying down for a second, trying to process what he was saying.

But I also didn't want space from him.

I quickly sat up and grabbed his biceps and shoved him back on the bed. Surprise colored his expression. It was time for me to turn the tables here. I straddled his lap and pinned him down by the shoulders, confidently meeting his eyes.

"Explain," I demanded. My heart rate was making it difficult to breathe.

"I'm trying, but," he squeezed his eyes shut a few seconds before opening them, "I feel like I should have told you from day one."

"Well, you can't go back in time. So, you can tell me now." I leaned down and kissed his forehead, trying to ease away the creases there. "Please." I needed to know what the fuck he was talking about. He exhaled, expanding his chest and meeting mine. I slid my hands up his arms and rested them on the sides of his head, using my fingers to gently massage his scalp. An attempt to relax him, so he could finish a fucking thought. His hands came and rested on my thighs, gripping.

With a dramatic exhale from his lips and his eyes drifting closed, he finally started talking. "...We kind of met a little over a month before my first day at work," he started. It took everything in me to control my breathing so I wouldn't spook him. "After Eloise and I broke up, I felt a ton of emotions for a while. Closure, grief, relief, loss of purpose...I was in therapy, which helped, but I also became incredibly antisocial. My therapist encouraged me to find work, and not just live off my trust fund alone in my apartment. I already had my

PT license and some work experience, so I started investigat-ing what I could do with that. I applied to a few facilities," he leaned into one of my hands, wanting more pressure, so I provided, "Then at dinner with my parents one night, my mother mentioned our clinic."

I paused my massaging, and he slowly opened his eyes to look at me, so I encouraged him, "Keep going." I was wrack-ing my brain trying to remember seeing him in the parking lot outside of work, and I was coming up with nothing.

"I toured the facility near the end of the workday, my mother basically holding my hand throughout the process. After seeing the building and having her ask a ton of ques-tions to Pat on my behalf, I was ready to decline the job. I had already left one profession that my mother manipulated into my life; I wasn't exactly trying to get involved with her again. Then, as we were leaving the building, I heard you snort." I blinked once at him and groaned. I lowered my head to his chest, embarrassment washing over me because he specifically remembered my *snort*.

I only vaguely remembered laughing so hard in the park-ing lot at work that I snorted.

"I hate that you noticed my snort of all things," I mumbled into his chest.

"I don't," Adam murmured against my hair, rubbing his hands on my thighs, still pinned under me. "I saw you and Courtney laughing together as you guys were leaving the building." I raised my head to look at him.

"Did we speak to each other at all?" I asked, not sure if

I should be surprised or embarrassed that I had almost no memory of this.

"No, I don't think so," Adam lifted a shoulder underneath me, "You and Courtney didn't even realize my mother and I were there talking to Pat. I'm pretty sure you bumped into my mom. She was very annoyed at you two causing such a ruckus."

"Sure," I chimed in, nodding once as if I had any recollection of this. At least that's a possible reason as to why his mother was so irritated with me when we met in the waiting room that one day. Adam couldn't stop the quick smirk that came over his lips for a second before he continued.

"Courtney stopped you both and announced she had to run to the bathroom, saluting you before she quickly ducked back inside. You said you'd wait for her as you scrolled on your phone, pulled out a bag of pretzels, and shoved a solid handful in your mouth." He chuckled after that sentence, his eyes flicking all over my face, "You were so pretty but so unladylike. I loved it."

I gently tugged on one of his strands of hair.

"No, it's true, I loved it," Adam explained, sliding his hands up and playing with the waistband of my leggings. "That level of confidence is always sexy."

"Especially when I'm confidently stuffing my face with pretzels that Gram packed me that day," I remembered the pretzels.

"I never understood why women are expected to take delicate little toddler bites of food without dropping a single crumb, but men are allowed to thump our chests and chug beers with loud slurps. Society is stupid."

"Agreed, but what happened next?"

He sighed, less nervous but still reluctant, "Not much. My mother and Pat continued with their conversation, talking about the details of my potential job without including me in the conversation at all. While that was happening, I just watched you eat pretzels. Like a creep. We were only about ten feet away from each other, but you hadn't noticed me."

I nodded once, trying to remember any sort of situation where I felt like I was being watched by Adam. Nothing. How disappointing.

"Courtney came stumbling back outside, laughing at some-thing she had pulled up on her phone and shoved in your face for you to observe." I snickered because that sounded like her.

"Was it funny?" I asked.

"I have no idea. You both were in your own little world, oblivious to my mother's glares and my longing looks." He stopped and took a few breaths here, staring at me. Probably trying to gauge my reaction to all of this.

"Longing looks?" I asked, wondering if the question sounded stupid.

"Yes. I don't know if you know this, but I think you are an incredibly attractive woman," Adam replied with more confidence than I expected. Okay, so maybe it wasn't a stupid question. "Having my Physical Therapist license already put me in a niche field, but I liked the idea of working with young kids. I also may have thought about you for a while after that night, wondering how two grown women could be so happy and content with their life when I felt so lost in mine. Granted, I only witnessed a couple of minutes of you two laughing outside of the building, but I was so desperate to feel desire or connection or pride in any aspect of my life that...I decided it was worth looking into," He rolled his eyes and leaned his head back farther on the bed, "And then I let my fucking mother get involved."

"How?"

"When you both started walking off towards the bus stop, Pat called out to you and waved goodbye. You both turned to finally look at us and waved goodbye, too. I could have sworn our eyes met, but you barely glanced at me for half a second. I was suddenly desperate that I wouldn't get a chance to talk to you. On the drive home, I mentioned my complete interest in working at the facility my mother was so involved in. Two days after, I had my own interview with Pat," I crinkled my nose, knowing how much he must have loathed having to go out of his way to get an interview without his mother there, "There were two locations, one in Irvine and one in Laguna Beach, and I didn't think the universe was kind enough to assign me to your location. But apparently, it was." He gave me a small smile, and I smiled back.

Thank goodness it did.

"So, when Pat introduced you to us in my office..."

"I thought you started coughing because you remembered me from the parking lot, and I was worried that you thought I was stalking you."

"Well, to be fair..." I shrugged and he pinched my side, making me twitch but keeping me in place.

"Yeah, I guess I was. But I wasn't trying to seduce you or lead you into a dark alley. Something about you, I guess, just spoke to something deep inside me. It felt natural to want to be around your orbit. Also, you were beautiful. So, that made things weirder for me."

"Oh, poor *you*." I mocked him. We were at the part of our story where I had to deal with my insane attraction towards him, so for him to describe how liking the way I looked was "weird" felt comical.

"Yeah, I know. I had no idea you were coughing because I was just too sexy for you to handle." He winked at me and I laughed, because of how silly this whole conversation was. He watched me laugh for a few seconds and waited for me to catch my breath and focus on him and proceed. "It took a few days for me to realize that you and Courtney didn't recognize me. I quickly understood that there was no way you two would have remembered me and not said anything about it." That was true. "I thought I was being annoying at first, inserting myself into your guys' lunch breaks. I couldn't help it. You all accepted me so easily into your circle, and I felt like I had a group of friends at work for the first time in years. I even started to open up to you about my personal life. At the retreat, when you suddenly started avoiding me, I thought you may have remembered me then. I was worried I made you guys uncomfortable because I started to get to know you better, Beck. You held me through a panic attack when I was too embarrassed to admit that I have a stupid fear of heights. It wasn't until the retreat that I realized myself that I wasn't hovering around you because I wanted to siphon some of your joy for life, but because I wanted to be around *you*. You, specifically." His breath was getting shakier and shakier, "And then you kissed me…"

"Without securing your consent first," I folded my hands over his chest and rested my chin on top of them.

"Oh trust me, it was consensual," he smiled, and then it faded, he started to trace shapes on my cheek with his fingertip. "I was in shock for a bit, because it wasn't like the physical feelings weren't mutual. And after you explained your side of things, I felt like I had a chance." A nervous smile teasing his lips again, "What a gift from whatever deity to not only provide me with employment that brought fulfillment, a circle of friends who for some reason accepted me without question, and *you*. This beautiful woman I could spend the entirety of my day with. At home, and at work…Then I overheard you speaking to Eloise. Your ability to describe how important *want* was in a relationship really settled in me. I knew that I wanted you. All of you. I had only been in your life for a few weeks, maybe a couple of months, and I could already picture you being an endgame for me. I could visualize it *so* easily." I immediately remembered how Adam kept saying "Thank fuck" every time I explained that I wanted to sleep with him, but not have it be a one-time hookup.

Now I really understood his relief.

He continued to stroke my cheek, and my jaw, and just looked at me. I looked back at him with lots of questions spiraling around in my mind, but I couldn't pick a single one to ask. I got so absorbed in his admission that I needed to take time to process it. This was something Adam was used to from me. Taking a few moments to think before I spoke.

He had been so patient with me, since day one. I thought he was being so patient with me when we were learning how to be intimate with each other. It had been like he had been waiting for me to catch up to where he was. Which I guess was true, but I hadn't realized how far he was waiting for me to catch up.

"So, in conclusion," Adam exhaled with his nervous smile back on display, "In the beginning, I think that I was in love with the idea of you. But now...now I know that I am in love with the reality of you."

I felt tears start to prick at the corners of my eyes, *please don't let me cry again.* Crying was so inconvenient right now. I wanted to bask in this moment, of Adam laying it all out there for me. This man, who was usually so picky with his words, was brave enough to use all the scariest ones. With me. Reaching that point in our relationship where frankly, we both needed to cut the shit with each other.

"Adam, I—" I reached a hand up to wipe a tear building up in my eye before it had a chance to fall, "I... it feels like I have loved you since the moment I assaulted you in the break room."

Adam coughed out a laugh that was filled with relief as he grabbed me and rolled me back underneath him, smothering my face in kisses. Cheeks, jaw, nose, eyebrows, temples, and eventually lips. A couple of tears managed to fall during, and he kissed those up as well. He pulled back from me, cradling my face in his warm hands.

"Be honest, you really fell in love with me when I gave you your first orgasm in under fifteen minutes."

"Actually, it was when I saw your naked chest in the parking lot. Holy hell, your body is incredible," I rolled my eyes and playfully smacked his arm. He caught it with his opposite hand and brought it to his lips to receive more gentle kisses.

"I love you," I said again, wanting him to understand how serious I was. He paused with his lips pressed to my knuckles and locked those eyes of his on mine. Those eyes caught my attention on day one. At least, the first day I remembered seeing him.

"I love you. I want you," he replied against my knuckles.

"I want you, too…We're endgame." He grinned at that and lowered his head to mine. The kiss was aggressive, with a heaviness to it that hadn't ever been there before. A finality to it.

"I'm all in, Beck," Adam mumbled against my lips. He didn't give me a chance to respond, instead, I focused on how his tongue felt stroking against mine, and how we both seemed to have this near desperate urge to be as physically close to each other as possible. Our friends downstairs could wait, because I needed to let my entire being soak up this beautiful moment we found ourselves in. Expressing our love for each other in the best ways we knew how in the peace of my little bedroom.

I wanted this man, as much as he wanted me. We were intentionally choosing each other, and just the thought of how we got here to this point made my soul soar.

30

Epilogue

Six months later Adam, Courtney, Gram, and I were all sitting in our living room. We had just ordered Chinese take-out and the TV was playing some sports game in the background. Adam was sitting on one end of the couch, his arm spread over the back of it behind my shoulders. One of his legs was propped up on the coffee table. I was filling out some paperwork for a new client I had just taken on, with music playing in my hearing aids while I was snuggled into Adam's side. He scrolled mindlessly on his phone, probably looking at new recipes to try out with Courtney this weekend.

Gram and Courtney were on the living room floor trying something called a pigeon pose. Gram had accomplished this during her younger years and was trying to help Courtney execute it as well. I paused my music to watch Courtney and Gram's conversation, curious.

"I think that Logan has been dropping the ball on my

flexibility training," Courtney panted as she winced with the stretch of her muscles.

"I think flexibility falls more on you, not the body builder," Gram encouraged. "Now lift your feet off the ground."

"No," Courtney wheezed in protest.

"You got this, young lady," Gram encouraged by tapping her fingers on Courtney's feet.

"The fact that my body can bend like this is an accomplishment in itself, Susan."

I giggled at their antics before tuning back into the music I was listening to. Adam reached a large hand over my laptop to disconnect the Bluetooth from my hearing aids, letting the music play from my computer speakers.

"Of course," he shook his head at me in jest as he muted the TV and settled back onto his phone.

"Ah, feminist emo punk!" Courtney smiled, unfolding herself and jumping off the floor to head towards the kitchen. Gram clicked her tongue at Courtney's easy surrender. I watched as Courtney wiggled her hips to the music and pretended to sing into a whisk she snatched out of the utensil holder.

"I've converted her," I nudged Adam as I watched my best friend jam to Carbon Cut.

"You have," Adam smiled, and it still made my heart jump. I kissed his bicep since that was the closest part to me as I turned my neck to watch Courtney. Adam had also listened to a lot of their music because the three of us have been helping Adam learn different phrases of ASL by translating the band's lyrics into signs. It was a fun way to practice.

"Do these guys go on tour?" Courtney asked, mumbling the lyrics as she opened the fridge in search of food.

"I don't know, but I can check." I turned back around and opened up a browser.

The band Carbon Cut was a great looking group of guys, each with their own smattering of tattoos and unique hair styles of different colors. The drummer had purple hair that was long enough to curl at the ends. The bassist was the most vanilla looking, with his plain brown hair cut close to his scalp, and usually wore a simple t-shirt and jeans. The lead singer recently dyed his hair blonde, which wasn't a terrible look for him. He was covered in tattoos (very on brand for any pop punk band member) and had a lip ring.

I asked Adam one time if he would be interested in getting a lip ring, and he said he would if I was willing to get one too. The thought of both of our lip piercings getting stuck on each other as we made out made me cringe and I never brought it up again.

There was an incredible amount of news coverage of this band when I searched them online. It looked like they had been on a number of late night talk shows, as well as SNL as both the musical guest and a couple of guest appearances in skits. They were also covered at a number of charity events, making me happier to support their artistry.

I saw one interview with the band that was posted about a week ago, and I was curious, so I played the video but muted it with closed captions so I wouldn't interrupt the music already playing for everyone else.

"...And where did you grow up, Josh?" The interviewer, an attractive brunette in a wrap dress, asked. Ugh, I hated that the lead singer had the same name as the tool from my home-town my mother had desperately tried to set me up with.

"Oregon." He replied proudly, I glanced back at Courtney, who was always excited about fellow Oregonians.

Even though that word sounded wrong to me every time she said it.

"Do your friends and family still live there?"

"My family does, yes."

"...No friends?" The interviewer asked without shame. Lead Singer Josh blushed as he looked down at his lap, his band mates teasing him with 'Ohhh burn' and brotherly shoves, almost knocking him off the chair he was sitting in.

"Believe it or not, Josh was a bit of a loner before we accepted him into the fold in college," the second lead guitarist teased, tussling Josh's bleached hair. Josh smacked his hand away with a stern look, but he looked like he was taking the teasing well.

If they were making the money I assumed that they were, they were probably okay with teasing.

Sorry, I can't hear you over the size of my paycheck!

"Yeah, I wasn't the most popular growing up," Josh shrugged good naturedly, crossing one ankle over his knee.

"Really?" The interviewer asked, leaning on her crossed legs as if this story was engrossing, "No girlfriends? No crazy prom stories?"

"Sorry to disappoint," Josh chuckled good naturally before pinching his brows and thinking about something. "There was this one girl I was friends with my senior year." His band mates all shifted in their seats to give him their full attention, staring wide eyed at this piece of information. Josh rolled his eyes at their theatrics. They seemed like a fun group of guys, but that could just be because they were being recorded for this interview.

"Oh, how sweet! A high school sweetheart!" the interviewer exclaimed. She gave me the suspicion that she was part of a gossip magazine and not any reputable outlet.

"Well, not exactly," Josh rubbed the back of his neck, a movement that reminded me a lot of Adam. I glanced at my boyfriend, who glanced back at me and kissed my head before focusing back on his phone.

"…She kind of took me under her wing, invited me out to parties and stuff like that. She didn't care that I was shy and had the social skills of a hermit. She was truly the most genuine person I had ever met. It was impossible not to form a huge crush on her." Josh's eyes looked like he was picturing this girl, and my heart melted. Even though there was a good chance this was all bullshit he made up for the sake of this interview.

But oh my god, was he the sweetest?

"Where is she now?" The interviewer pressed.

"I'm not sure. We didn't keep in touch after graduation. But I still think about her sometimes," Josh brushed his thumb over the top of his hand. "She had this unique birthmark on her right hand, in the shape of a semi-colon."

The fuck?

I paused the video, rereading the captions that appeared at the bottom of the screen. Yup. The captions still showed the words "birthmark on her right hand in the shape of a semi-colon."

I resumed the video.

"Oh, do you think she would recognize you now? With all your fame?" the interviewer continued, clearly grasping for straws.

"Absolutely not," Josh chuckled, "I look and act like a completely different person now than I did at seventeen years old. I've changed, hopefully for the better." The interviewer seemed to get bored with this information before asking the other band members questions about their personal lives.

I rewound the interview, looking for key words.

"Oregon." The lead singer had clearly said.

I opened a different tab and started to super sleuth this situation, wondering if my suspicion was right. When you were famous, you lost a lot of aspects of your privacy. Something Adam got a taste of while he was training for the Olympics. I'm sure these guys had even less privacy than Adam, so I wasn't surprised to find a Wikipedia page about each of the band members specifically. I quickly found the lead singer's page.

Joshua Madey, born in Tigard, Oregon...

I wasn't particularly curious about his parent's names or siblings, but within two clicks I found what I was looking for.

Hometown, Lake Oswego, Oregon.

Education, Lakeridge High School.

No. Way.

"Hey, Court?" I called, eyes not leaving my computer. "What was the name of your town in Oregon, again?"

"L.O." Courtney replied, making me turn around to see her stirring pasta at the stove.

"What does that stand for?" I pressed, wanting to be absolutely sure.

"...Lake Oswego, why?" she asked, lifting an eyebrow at me.

I tried to play it cool. "That's a smaller town, right? So, was your high school just named after the city?" Courtney always talked about how weird California public schools were, such as the hallways and lockers being outdoors, and how there were so many high schools that it was tough to remember all their different names. As well as how large the student body each high school had.

"It is, but we actually had two high schools. One was Lake Oswego High School, and the other was Lakeridge." My heart jumped up into my throat.

"Which did you go to?"

"Lakeridge."

Holy fucking shit.

I found myself staring directly at Courtney's right hand as she held the wooden spoon, her semi-colon birthmark on display. I turned back around to my browser and looked up the birth date of Joshua Madey, lead singer of Carbon Cut. Sure enough, it was the same birth year as Courtney.

No. Way.

Was my best friend really the huge crush he had in high school? It wasn't like semi-colon shaped birthmarks were common. I doubted multiple people in their graduating class had them. Plus, the way he described how she took him under her wing reminded me of the beginning of my friendship with her.

"...Did you see if they have any shows near us?" Courtney asked, ignoring my random interrogation of her public education.

"One sec, I got distracted," I quickly searched for their show schedule and found that the band was doing a fundraising event in a few months, so tickets were probably already sold out. I decided to try anyway and was immediately shocked to see ticket availability, as well as all the different ticket options. One of them was for guests who needed specific accommodations for the show.

...Such as guests who were deaf or hard of hearing.

Purchasing these tickets assured that you would be close to the stage and given equipment to allow you to hear the band more efficiently, and though the ticket prices were a little more than I'd like to pay, I couldn't pass up this golden opportunity.

"It looks like they're playing at FivePoint Amphitheater in Irvine in a few months, I'm going to buy us tickets," I replied, reading the fine print on these specialized tickets to ensure I could bring hearing friends with me. I shrugged, realizing that Courtney and Adam could pretend to be deaf if they had to. It was worth it, and the fact that the special needs section of the audience looked like it was as close to the stage as possible made me feel like the universe was trying to make this happen as much as I was.

"Cool deal," Courtney continued to hum along to Carbon Cut's music, in complete ignorance of the plan I was forming in my mind.

I looked at Adam, knowing I wouldn't have the chance to sit with him like this, relaxed on my couch, if it wasn't for Courtney pushing me outside my comfort zone since the moment I met her. Without her, I wouldn't have this overwhelming happiness and joy I feel from being with Adam. From finding love with Adam.

Maybe, just maybe, I could return the favor for her.

I grinned mischievously as I confirmed my ticket purchase.

THE END

Courtney's story,
WHAT IT MEANS TO BE BRAVE
is coming 2023.

Acknowledgements

I'd like to thank my husband and partner, Clayton, for holding my hand throughout this entire process. You were a safe space for me to open up to about my writing and you encouraged me to take the next steps whenever I spoke about potentially self-publishing my girly love story. You did a lot of the heavy lifting when it came to website design and researching ISBNs for me. Having a supportive partner helped me be more confident in pursuing this little dream of mine. You and I have been through a wild amount of growth and chaos in our marriage, but I am grateful that we still love each other—even though we seem to be entirely different people now than when we first met.

Next, I'd like to thank my therapist. She is also a safe space for me to process my own religious deconstruction. When I was in the deepest, darkest parts of PPD and PPA, my therapist was there for me to hold my hand and patiently guide me out of my funk. If I hadn't been seeing her for two years prior, I wouldn't have built up the courage to tell my friends and husband that I have always enjoyed writing, and that I wanted to seriously pursue writing romance novels when the time was available.

I'd also like to thank Jayden and Genna for being true homies, and for taking the time to encourage me to become the best version of myself. We are "trauma bonded in a really cool way", and our friendship has helped pull me out of poor mindsets and vernacular. Your friendships constantly inspire me to learn and improve on myself, and I am grateful that my daughter will have you two in her life as she grows and learns more about the world around her.

I'd also like to thank my wonderful friend and artist, McKenzie, for being super nice and designing the cover art for this novel incredibly last minute. I could not have been more unclear on what I wanted for the cover, and that must have been wildly annoying to deal with. Your patience as I tried to put what I was imagining into words was very appreciated.

I'd also like to thank my child, Madeline. You are young and won't remember this adventure I took by the time you are reading this for yourself, but your beautiful existence has encouraged your mother. Whether or not I go on to publish more books or if the journey ends here, thank you. You have reminded me to stay calm and breathe. To not sweat the little things, and to take the time to enjoy the moments we are in now. The patience and calm you have as a three-year-old blows everyone's mind, and I cannot wait to see what kind of beautiful soul you grow into.

I'd also like to thank my parents, Monte and Lorrie, for allowing me the opportunity to explore creative writing as a preteen on mom's lime green Dell laptop. Thank you for respecting my space and not reading anything I wrote (and deleted), because I didn't want you to realize how much I liked boys, and for some reason thought I would get in trouble for what I wrote. Sorry for being dramatic, but to be fair, I was twelve.

Andrea Andersen is an author living with her little family in Southern California. Using her maladaptive daydreaming to her advantage, she likes to write love stories filled with kisses, laughter, and happily ever afters. When she isn't writing, she can be found rewatching her favorite TV shows or taking too many naps.

Socials:
Tiktok: @andreaandersenauthor
Instagram: @andreaandersenauthor